SCARS

BY

LAURA ROSSI

Beware of the monster

Copyright © Laura Rossi 2018

Editing and Proofreading by Gem Louise Evans and Monja De Jager

Cover art by Talia's Book Covers

Self publishing

laurarossiauthor@gmail.com

ALL RIGHTS RESERVED. This book contains material protected under International and Federal Copyright Laws and Treaties. Any unauthorized reprint or use of this material is prohibited. No part of this book may be reproduced or transmitted in any form or by any means, electronic or mechanical, including photocopying, recording, or by any information storage and retrieval system without express written permission from the author/publisher.

This is a work of fiction. Names, characters, businesses, places, events and incidents are either the product of the author's imagination or used in a fictitious manner. Any resemblance to actual persons, living or dead, or actual events is purely coincidental.

To love, the one that saves you from hell.

INTRODUCTION TO SCARS

Dear Reader,

As you read in the blurb and description of the book, Scars is the sequel to Skins. Although you can read this book as a standalone, I highly recommend reading Skins first. It would help better understand the characters, their love story and their actions in Scars.

While Skins is a gritty, romantic suspense novel, Scars is darker. You'll find themes like Mafia, prostitution, violence and abuse in this book.

Please do not read this story if you are not comfortable with these themes. I will not be offended and you have my complete understanding.

It wasn't an easy story to write, I can tell you. All the characters involved go through hell in their own way, not just physically but emotionally.

For months I hung out in the mind of a sick, twisted man. I had to take breaks from writing, breaks from the story but I couldn't write it in any other way. I didn't want to set a limit, I didn't think it was fair to the characters, to my readers.

Anyway, if you do decide to read the story, I want you to think of this.

It wasn't me, it's the characters' fault. They made me do it!

Jokes aside, I'm sure we've all been through bad times in our lives but we are still here, no matter how much it hurt at the time. We made it. Read Scars with an open mind, let the emotions flow and enjoy.

Thank you so much for reading, I really appreciate it. It means the world to me, I know every author says this and it is true. It means more than anything else, I'm happy just knowing you are spending time with my words and characters. That is all.

    Con amore,
    Laura

PART 1

OUT OF HELL

We are each our own devil and we make this world our hell.
Oscar Wilde

PROLOGUE

SAINT CATHERINE INSTITUTE, NAPLES

ALEJANDRO DE LA CRUX

Rage, I was blinded by rage.

My hands were burning, fire consumed my insides. I breathed out hatred and let that lead the way.

I'd slapped her. I'd touched her the way I never wanted to, but it was done. I saw Andrea move on the floor, trying to crawl out of the shed and get away from me.

You can't get away from me, I wanted to shout at her but I grabbed her arm and pulled her up instead, ignoring her screams.

She wasn't crying, despite what I had done to her. Her cold blue eyes looked at me, not with fear, but with disgust, I wanted to throw her back on the ground and shout at her to look away, to stop looking at me like that.

Fear was something I was used to, something I knew how to deal with. I always wanted to be feared.

It's what makes you stand out amongst the rest in the sick world I live in. When you're feared, nobody dares to cross you, nobody dares to stop you. But Andrea wasn't scared of me, I realized that then. She never truly was. I had no control, no hold over her despite everything I'd tried.

Control is power and I made sure I had plenty on the things I cared about. I wanted Andrea on a damn leash and I wanted to pull it as I pleased. I'd never wanted anything more than to keep her in my hold and keep her by my side, but looking at her then, seeing how she still had the strength to taunt me, after what I had done to her, I realized she was never mine to control. I had no power over her, none.

"Get up," I grunted, watching her scramble up from the floor.

She straightened a little and I grabbed her arm again, pulling her out of the shed.

Andrea tried to fight back, to dig her feet into the ground but I easily pulled her up and took a good look at her face, at the blood dripping from her mouth.

My face hardened.

Sorrow? There was no room for sorrow. This wasn't the woman I'd married, that I thought I could have by my side. There was no sign of that angel-faced goddess I had fallen so hard for in Budapest. My eyes only saw the whore in the shed, being fucked by a worthless piece of shit, a human waste.

The Killer, I spat on the floor and dragged her out, into the daylight, recalling what I had learned from my father, from being the leader of my clan.

Nothing can get in the way of revenge and pride, nothing. Not even Andrea, not even feelings I'd had for her. She had disgraced me, my name and my family again and again. I'd warned her, I'd told her this day would come.

The moment she'd left my house with our son, Andrea had set a timer, a countdown to her death sentence. One day I'd be back for her and her life would've been my pleasure to take. She had betrayed me, dared to cross me; making a joke of my honour.

Her life, for my honour.

She fell again on the grass. Her voice came out shaky and weak. I yanked her up again and she let out a cry, as I whispered in her ear the words I knew would crush her.

"I don't want Eddy to see me killing you," her eyes darted to the car up the driveway and she broke into sobs.

Whatever she said after that, I didn't even pay attention to it. I took her around the shed and slammed her against the wall.

I cursed under my breath, cursed at her, at myself. Nothing made sense as I stared at her. I was disgusted, I hated the sight of her, but I just couldn't stop myself from wanting her. Andrea was mine, still mine. I could do to her whatever I pleased.

Once you take a vow, once you stand by my side, you can never walk away from me, not until I say so. I decide when it's over.

"You are mine, I can do whatever I want with you," I told her, my lips pressing hard onto hers, my hand sliding down to her waist.

Her scream came out muffled against my mouth, but I heard it. Loud and clear, it ripped my insides.

Shut the fuck up!

I slammed my fist into her stomach and then hit the wall beside her as she bent forward, desperate for air.

The air is gone, you can't breathe, I don't want you to fucking breathe anymore.

The darkest thoughts crossed my mind then.

Andrea was still bent forward, gasping when I took her by the neck and pushed her against the wall again. That was all that was left for me to do. I couldn't look at her like I used to. I couldn't kiss her, touch her, fuck her. I hated the sight of her, even though a part of me still wanted desperately to love her, feel her, possess each and every inch of that body.

The body that someone else had touched, fucked, violated.

My grip tightened, her neck changed colour as I held her in place.

Those were her last breathes, her last moments with me and she didn't look away, her eyes never looked down.

Even facing her defeat, Andrea stared at me with the same ardour and hardness, as if her fight wasn't over. She wasn't pleading like I'd wanted, wasn't begging me to stop, begging me to take her back and the thought almost drove me insane there and then.

I wondered what it would feel like to look at her lifeless body, knowing I had taken that life away from her, the woman I'd once loved. That I still loved.

She took my pride, my honour and almost my sanity away, a voice whispered in my mind.

Her bones, I wanted to break each and every one of them. I wanted to tear her apart, break her soul. No, more than that, I wanted Andrea to disappear, I didn't want her to exist. She didn't deserve to, not anymore, but she was staring at me, murmuring a curse in her last breathes, I found myself doubting my own intentions. I was killing the mother of my son, the woman I'd wanted so badly by my side.

No, she betrayed me. She deserves to die.

I told myself I could have washed that blood off my hands, like any other time, and sleep soundly, as if nothing had ever happened. This was Andrea's life I was taking, that same life I once wanted her to share with me.

That I still want.

Her neck had turned purple, when three words took that decision for me.

"Let her go!" I released the pressure against her neck almost instantly, when I heard his voice.

It wasn't the gun to my head that made me do it, it was the sight of him.

"The Killer," I murmured, almost laughing in his face.

I let Andrea slip to the floor and out the corner of my eye I saw her roll on the ground, her hands tight around her throat.

He was talking to her, he was making sure she was alright and good to move. All doubts were suddenly gone and the rage was back. Full on. I wanted to kill them, kill them both.

I spat, disgusted at how caring they were to each other, how protective he was of her.

She wasn't his to protect or take care of.

She's mine, forever, my mind screamed.

"Worthless piece of shit. You rat," I growled and watched him flinch, his gun pointing straight at my head.

Sebastian eyed Andrea quickly, as she ran to the car where Eddy was, his stare always on me.

He knew better than to look away from someone like me. I would have snapped his neck.

"I want you to turn around, hands over your head," he told me and I laughed to his face.

What sick, fucking joke was that? What did he want me to do?

"You fucking heard me, now fucking turn around!" he said through gritted teeth.

I shot him the deadliest look I could pull off and slowly turned. My back was almost to him when my elbow jammed into his side and I saw the gun fly to the ground.

I was on him in a second, my fist flying through the air. I hit him somewhere, but before I could even strike back,

Sebastian had rolled on top of me, slamming me to the ground, pinning me to the wet grass.

One punch, two punches, he hit me ferociously, I couldn't stop him or break from his hold.

"You fucking touched her, you son of a bitch!" he screamed at me and then to Andrea "GO!"

That moment there, that was the moment I realized- as he held me down in place, his worried eyes on my ex-wife running to the car- that Andrea was both our weakness, our flaw in the sick twisted world we lived in.

Hit him now.

I reached for the gun but Sebastian was quick, he grabbed my wrist and held my arm up, the barrel far from his face. We rolled downhill a little more, until my finger found the trigger and pulled it.

One shot, we rolled again, breathing and spitting in each other's faces, neither one of us ready to surrender.

She's mine, mine. How dare you even touch her? I wanted to growl in his face.

Another shot, my eyes snapped open and I let out a cry.

Nothing, I suddenly felt nothing- no more rage, no anger, resentment nor hatred. It was all gone, I felt nothing but the flames of hell burning inside me. They swallowed me up, spreading across my chest.

I gasped for air and counted my last breaths.

One, pain shot up my stomach.

Two, my throat burned.

I kept staring at the sky, as I lost any will to move.

Before my eyes closed, my last thoughts were of Andrea.

In the end, she'd managed to get away. In the end I was the one that had gotten the bullet. As memories of how it all began, came back to me, I realized that my obsession for Andrea Szerov had earned me a one-way ticket to hell.

CHAPTER 1
THE GIRL IN THE CAFÉ

BUDAPEST, SEVEN YEARS BEFORE

My fall began when I first saw her.

One look, one and I was hooked. I was doomed.

It was sometime in the middle of the day, I was walking down a busy street in the city of Budapest with two of my men. I turned around and I saw her, my eyes met hers.

The girl in the café.

Blonde hair, skin as white as snow, perfect small features, her blue eyes innocent and pure.

What a waste, I thought. Someone so beautiful cleaning tables like a servant, a common waitress.

I rubbed my lips as I stared at her, unable to walk away. I fell for her suddenly and all at once, no hesitation or overthinking. I knew I had to have her, I had to make her mine.

She looked up at me, while wiping one of the tables near the window, and I smiled. She didn't. Her cold, unimpressed stare cut through me like a thousand shards of ice and then it was off me, back to cleaning the tables, back to her duties. The girl in the café moved around with grace and elegance, she glided from one task to another like a dancer.

She certainly has the body of one, my eyes stayed on her toned legs for a moment and then moved up to her small waist and slender arms.

She'd look my way from time to time, but never long enough to really notice me.

I was just a man outside of the café, walking by like any other. Or so she thought. I was anything but just another man. I was a rich man, I'd just closed the deal on a good business in town, I was going to make millions.

Budapest wasn't so bad, too cold for my tastes but the city was full of young people, so many university students, tourists and young professionals.

So many potential customers, my cocaine was the best in Europe, pure clean batches directly from Columbia. From the producer to the consumer.

I wasn't just any man. I was a king, I ruled every fucking goddam place I set my eyes and heart upon. Nobody could stop me and I wanted her to know, just how on top of the world I was. I was Alejandro De la Crux, no woman could resist me.

I'd never gotten a 'no' out of a lady's mouth. I was so used to having them around me, I fucked and slept with whoever I wanted. They couldn't say no to me; I'd convince them one way or another.

Everyone had a price, I wondered what hers was.

Three days later I was supposed to fly back to Rome, but I didn't leave. It took me that amount of time to find out her name and who she was. A training nurse, university student, dancer and musician, no siblings, from the countryside, no husband or boyfriend, a rose tattooed on her back.

The girl in the café.

The goddess in the café.

Andrea Szerov. My obsession had a name and two long sexy as hell legs, no matter how good she tried hiding them behind her black little apron. I had dreams about them, dreams of me squeezing those smooth, toned legs while I fucked her. I wondered how good she'd taste, if that pretty little mouth of hers would take all of me. That was how desperate I was to make her mine.

All mine.

I had her followed until I was sure I knew how to get her, seduce her.

Half measures weren't my thing. I gave women everything, immediately. When you hold the right cards, you bet everything you've got and play like a winner. That's how you take it all. That's how a winner like me plays out his little games- some call it arrogance, I like to think of it as determination.

The first time I went in, I introduced myself, ordered a coffee and tipped her, tipped her well. I still remember Andrea's stunned face, as I winked at her and walked out of the café casually, like I hadn't planned it all out like that.

I went back the following day and the day after that. The third time I brought a rose, velvet red, long stem, beautiful like her. Like the tattoo on her back.

"It made me think of you, so beautiful, precious...intense," I smiled and looked into that blue, cold sea that were her eyes.

Mine were dark, but they were alive and passionate, I made sure she saw the fire, the flames that danced inside mine.

You want to get burned, angel? My eyes dared her, I never took them off her, as a sly smile danced on my lips.

"Thank you, I don't know what to say," she looked me up and down, then back to my eyes again and smiled. Her first smile. *"Aren't you scared of my thorns?"* she teased, her warm, raspy voice scratched something deep down inside of me. My

stomach tightened, I began to wonder about that sensual voice and the sounds she made in bed.

Andrea Szerov, the goddess in the café.

I rubbed my lips and went in for the kill. *"Something tells me your thorns are worth getting stung for."*

"My ex-boyfriends would disagree with you on that," she laughed a little and took the rose from me, leaning down to smell the petals.

Ex-boyfriends, my pulse quickened, jealousy pounded in my chest.

I know what you are thinking, it was just her past but I'll have to disagree with that. Her past was my present, I cared. I hated that she had a past, hated that she'd had boyfriends, that another man had dared touch her, that white soft skin was mine. The idea of someone else kissing those red lips, drove me crazy.

I don't care if you think it's absurd, whatever. It isn't, not to me. Andrea was already mine, she was made for me. Why? Because I fucking decided she was mine and she had no choice, even if I'd let her think she had. I had made up my mind already.

No more boyfriends, no more men in her life. She was mine.

Andrea Szerov, the goddess in the café.
My woman, my obsession, my fall.

She wasn't going to be just another one of my whores, another woman in my bed. I was going to make her my wife, the mother of my child. She had no choice, the decision was made. Either that or her life wasn't worth living anymore. I'd make sure she'd pay the price of refusing to be mine.

Luckily it never came to that. Andrea was impressed by my good manners, the way I made her feel.

"Like a woman," she told me after our first date.

No half measures, just as I said. Dinner in the finest restaurant, tour of the Danube on a boat at night, the city lights were the perfect scenery for our first kiss.

It was gentle but passionate, just as I imagined a woman like her would be. She wasn't easy to impress, someone so beautiful must have had many suitors, but I wasn't any ordinary guy either. I was a De la Crux, rich and powerful, women usually liked that in a man. I was up for the challenge. Nothing made me hard like a challenge.

Especially a sinful, beautiful one like Andrea.

My arms wrapped around her body, I pulled her in, close to my chest and ran my hand through her hair. I made sure she got a good feel of me, of my hot-blooded Columbian nature.

My exotic looks lured her in, just as much as her delicate beauty drew me closer. When her tongue circled mine I almost lost all my senses, I nearly ruined my plan and fucked her against the wall on that boat.

Fuck.

"You taste like sugar, senorita," I broke the kiss and whispered against her mouth, while we sailed through the night.

"You taste like fire," her words stunned me, so deadly accurate. I was trouble, devastating like fire.

"What does fire taste like?" I asked, keeping her body against mine, as the boat passed under the white lit Elizabeth Bridge.

"Hot, good, until it burns you," Andrea mumbled.

That's when I knew I had her. She was falling for me, falling for everything I'd shown her I was. A powerful man, a passionate, caring and respectful one. That's all I needed to take her with me, her innocence would do the rest, it would work in my favour.

Andrea was mine.

Until it all fell apart. I hated all the attention she received, I hated she stood out in any room, any place I took her with me.

Once we got to Rome, she moved in with me, we were married in just a few months. The things I found so appealing in her, her skin, her eyes, her features, others found appealing, too.

Mine wasn't just an obsession anymore, it was pure, insane, jealousy.

I kept seeing my whores, kept hooking up during my 'business' deals. That's how things worked in my world. You strike a deal with someone, taste the drug, drink the finest champagne and fuck one of their whores or get head. I was a man, that's what men like me did. Real men. You have a fine woman ready to go down on you, you let it happen and enjoy it to the fullest.

I made sure Andrea knew nothing of what I did, who I saw. I kept my part of the bargain. She was my future wife, I wanted her to be happy. I gave her everything; the finest jewellery, the best clothes money could buy, trips, holidays and sex.

I could never get enough of her, no matter how much sex I was getting. She was mine, only mine and so it had a different feel, a different taste.

My woman.

Nobody could look at her, if I caught anyone staring too much at Andrea, I'd make sure to give them one admonishment, before getting rid of them.

That's what happened to my best man, my partner in crime. He'd fooled around with her, I remember her laughing at one of his jokes during our wedding, my hands turned into fists. That was it, he had to go.

As soon as we left for our honeymoon, I took care of him. A wedding bonus for ruining my day. My soldiers gave him a bullet straight between his eyes, in the basement of my house. He was gone, no more fucking around with my wife.

His punishment gave me pleasure like a good fuck, he'd taken it too far, stepped over the line. It set a good example for all of my soldiers, nobody dared to speak to her unless I said so.

The jealousy was uncontrollable by then and that's when Andrea noticed.

"You're a monster," she yelled in my face.

She'd heard me give the order, her eyes searched mine in horror. Disgust, hatred, no fear. She looked straight at me, told me I was sick, I'd just given the order to kill my best man, my friend.

"What did you do?" Andrea shook her head and covered her mouth, just before she threw herself against me and started hitting me.

One fist slammed against my chest, but I took hold of her before she could touch me again. My hands held hers, even though she tried to push me away.

"Don't touch me," she yelled, I stiffened and shook her a little, holding her firmly right in front of me. We were face-to-face, my eyes dark, cold.

"You did this. It's all your fault," I told her and she shook her head, screamed, kicked and screamed some more. I shook her again and she looked back at me. *"You fooled around with him, didn't you? Did you let him touch you? Did you want him to fuck you?"*

"*You are crazy! Let me go, don't touch me. You are a monster,*" she screamed again but I didn't give a shit.

I held her in place and pushed my forehead against hers hard, she began to shake.

"*Alejandro,*" she shrieked. "*You are hurting me.*"

I glared at her, my true nature out in the open. I wanted her to see me, know it wasn't a fucking joke around there. She'd do as I said, she was my wife, mine. *Mine.*

"*You listen to me,*" I shook her again and she let out a cry. "*You listen to me good. Don't you fucking talk to me like that ever again, do you understand me Andrea? Keep that mouth shut and do as I say. Stop fucking with me. You are mine, do you hear me? Don't you ever forget that. Don't fucking mess with me, Andrea. You are mine. Mine.*"

CHAPTER 2

THE DARKNESS INSIDE

IN THE PRISON OF ST VITTORE, NAPLES

The bullet crossed my chest, two inches from the heart. I'd been lucky, the doctors said after three hours of surgery. Instincts had made me move in the right direction at the right time or it would have centred the heart.

Instincts, luck… whatever, I made the right move and defied death. I was alive.

The Killer's aim had been deadly, he'd ran off and disappeared somewhere with my wife and kid. Flawless job, I could have clapped my fucking hands at him, though he made the terrible mistake of leaving me there, on the grass, without making sure I was dead. A terrible mistake.

It wasn't easy to kill me, so many had tried over the years, but I'd always gotten back up, stronger than ever. It seemed as if God had granted me more than one life to live and I always learned something new from every single one of them.

No mistakes, not this time. I wasn't going to give The Killer a second chance to fool me, I wasn't going to let Andrea run from her fate again. I was going to plan my revenge to the slightest detail.

The doctors' words after surgery still make me smile.

Lucky, I had been lucky, indeed.

Not so lucky for you Andrea. I will find you.

Silence, pitch dark, nothingness.

When you are in isolation, night and day both feel the same. I was all alone, in my cell. I was left to myself, to my own thoughts, away from anyone and anything. They thought prison would change me, that isolation would make me weaker, maybe break me. But I wasn't alone, I always had the darkness with me.

Some people are scared of the darkness. Behind my closed door, I heard their muffled wails after lights-out, I knew it wasn't loneliness or the night that they feared. The darkness inside them, that was scarier, the scariest voice of them all. You carry it with you and you can't run away from it. When you are left alone, you have nothing else to do but search and tear down the world inside you.

I wasn't afraid of the dark, I embraced it. I was the darkness; I ruled it with a fucking grin on my face. It whispered things in my ears, dragged me down into oblivion.

Darkness helped me reason, kept me sane. It helped me understand what I had to do, what needed to be done.

Every night, I laid down on my bed staring at the ceiling, embracing the silence, but my head was restless, drowning in thoughts, dark, twisted thoughts.

Twenty-seven, the ways I came up with to kill them. All very different and very gratifying at the same time. Hatred kept my heart beating, my mind at peace.

I was going to find her someday, I was going to find them both, the darkness reassured me. If they still breathed and walked on these grounds, I would find them. No matter how long it would take me, The Killer was going to pay the price of taking away what wasn't his to take.

I could already see it in Andrea's eyes, the pain I was going to impart. That same pain I'd felt years back, watching her being fucked in the shed.

It happened once, but so many times in my head. I kept seeing her against that wall, her beautiful body naked in the dim light, as that piece of shit filled her up from behind. Every now and then the memory would pay me a visit and I would hit the wall one, two, three times, harder, faster but without letting out a sound.

I hated them in silence, feeling revenge pulse in my body, in my bloody fists.

I cursed their names under my breath a few times, wishing I could turn back time and kill them in that shed, while he was still inside her.

But no, I wanted to do it slowly, wanted to take one thing at a time from them; Eddy, then kill Andrea and leave The Killer to find her there, behind that shed, knowing he would have suffered and maybe looked for me. I would have been ready, waiting for him to come for me, ready to take his life too, but only once he'd suffered the pain of crossing me, Alejandro De la Crux.

Patience, I wrote the word down every single day. I told myself it would have been worth the wait, my revenge. I was a De la Crux, I told myself, touching my chest where I'd always kept the family emblem. They'd taken it away from me, the guards of course, but it was just a symbol. They couldn't have taken away what that emblem represented, not even if they'd tried. The De la Crux blood couldn't be tamed. We knew too well that revenge, the real thing, came with time.

Patience, revenge takes time, it will come, my time will come and with it the joy to hear you scream, Andrea, you will plea, scream, beg me to stop. You will never be yourself again, once I am done with you.

My thirst for revenge kept me sane.

Time runs differently once you are inside, it has a different meaning, you tend to lose perception of it and start living according to the rules you are obliged to follow. I never lost track of time, I kept counting the days and the hours, never changing my habits.

Push-ups, eating, walking. I created my own routine. I was alone most of the time, kept away from the other prisoners- too influential, too dangerous to be trusted.

Damn right, I knew some of my men were in there, I knew my lawyer was trying to get me out of isolation but I had no hopes. I just didn't care. I wanted to be free, that's the only thing that mattered to me.

Footsteps sounded in the corridor, my eyes jarred open immediately. Not that I was sleeping, I was awake. I never really slept at night, my mind never stopped thinking. Still I didn't move from my bed, I waited in silence, in the dark until the lights were turned on. That was my wakeup call, when my surviving started. They told me when to sleep, wake-up, eat, shit.

"De la Crux, get up," a voice rumbled behind the door, as the guard turned the lock.

Slowly, the door crept open and I sat up, shirtless taking a good look at the man before me.

He wasn't one of mine, one of the poor fuckers I'd helped get a job in prison. Half of the guards in St Vittore were people I'd placed there, to talk to my men that were inside. They informed me of what happened to them, brought in information and drugs- my drugs- to sell.

I smiled, even though it wasn't one of my guards. I smiled because I was fucking everywhere, I had my hands on everything, even his future, but he didn't know, that stupid idiot had no idea.

Even though I was in isolation, the guards smuggled stacks of clean clothes, food and cocaine in for me. I wanted to tell him that, wipe that smug look off his face. If I wanted to, I could have made a phone call and sent him home, get some of the men I knew inside. I was everywhere.

Corruption is my favourite sin. Such a wonderful opportunity for me to get things right, the way I want them to be. I still haven't met a person without a price.

"Take your stuff, clean up. You have visitors," he grunted and I decided I wanted to piss him off so badly that day.

I took my sweet time, collected my soap, my clothes and walked out of my cell at a slow pace, smiling every time he told me to hurry up.

The scar on my chest itched under the warm water in the shower, I touched it immediately. It was a constant reminder of why I had to get out of there, why it was so worth not losing it. I needed to keep quiet and wait for the appeal.

"Hurry up, come on," the guard roared from outside the shower door.

I rubbed the soap off my skin and smirked.

"Did you hear me, De la Crux?" his voice threatening this time.

"I did," I assured him and rubbed my hair, turning off the water, walking out of the shower.

As I took my time putting on the robe, I stared down at the man. He wasn't new to me, I'd only seen him a couple of times. He was in his fifties, had a small tattoo on his wrist. Dark lines circled his eyes. He represented the average guard-frustrated, underpaid and tired. Sick and tired of all the crap he had to take from inmates like me. *Powerful, untouchable and dangerous.*

"What is your name?" I asked and smiled, my dick still in sight, water dripping down my body.

"I am not here to chat, De la Crux. Come on out," he grunted and pointed to my clothes.

Slowly, I walked to the chair and started dressing again, rubbing my short hair with a towel.

They had cut it off as soon as I'd set foot into that fucking prison, my long ponytail. My head had been completely shaved, like the rest of the prisoners. We were all the same to them. Well, fuck that shit!

The hell we were. I was Alejandro and no matter how some guards pretended I wasn't important, deep down I knew they all feared me a little.

"I just asked for your name," I said, my tone snarky.

"I am the guard that's going to kick your ass, if you don't follow my orders," he hissed.

I kept doing what I was doing, kept my face blank and slid on my shirt, but before we walked out of there, I made sure to set things straight with the guy. With the newbie.

"It's not important who we are inside here," I said and something changed in the way he was looking at me.

Understanding, he was starting to understand where this conversation was going. "This isn't real, it's a temporary thing. What matters is who we are outside. Do you know who I am?"

I moved a little closer, as I set foot out the bathroom door. "I'm sure you have family outside, a wife? A couple of kids?" I smiled a little, seeing him squint at me but he didn't dare say anything back.

My words, his reaction to them told me we had an understanding, the newbie and I. Immediately, he knew it was best for everyone that he watched his mouth.

With a smug smile on my face, I crossed the corridors all the way to the front of the prison, passing by the canteen.

Breakfast was being set up, I could smell that moulding, creamy shit they fed us. A few inmates eyed me, surprised; their stares followed me down to the meeting room.

"Hands," the guard told me and I turned, my eyes cold as he handcuffed me again, before letting me inside.

My lawyer stood up immediately, like he wanted to shake my hand as a sign of respect but couldn't. There was a glass wall that separated us, my wrists were tied together.

I slumped into my chair and watched him spread all his papers across the small wooden table in front of him, rambling something about the accusations and how the appeal was getting closer. Everything was set, he reassured me. He'd ask for a sentence reduction.

"I managed to get you out of isolation. From today, you'll be with the other inmates of the prison."

"I want to get out of here. I don't care about isolation, I don't care about a sentence reduction," I leaned a little closer and clenched my teeth. "Get me out of here."

"I understand, Mr. De la Crux but it's not that easy. I've advised you already on wanting to plead not guilty again. It cannot work, you were found guilty, people pressed charges against you. We have testimonies, depositions for your crimes."

"How many?" I wanted to know, how many people had had the courage to cross me.

And who??

"I've managed to convince the judge to discard a few, as their testimonies weren't relevant, but there are a few people that used to work for you on this list…" the man was saying but I cut in again.

"Settle it. Speak to my family," I said and the man nodded, his small eyes darkened a little once they met mine. He knew what I was talking about, exactly how I wanted to 'settle' it.

Let my family find the motherfuckers that dared say a single word against me, they will know exactly how to shut their mouths. Forever.

"I have been," he said and I nodded.

Then he showed me all the things he was going to present to court and told me the first good news in years. Two potential testimonies were out of our way already.

My wife was nowhere to be found, Sebastian Esposito had disappeared into thin air, after he'd been let out of prison.

They are together, fucking behind my back somewhere, that son of a bitch and that whore…

"They will be called into court but they can't testify against you. We have two people less to worry about," my lawyer reassured me.

He had the case in hand, he'd eventually get me out of there, but justice and bureaucracy in Italy were slow. Patience and faith were necessary, he'd do everything in his power to make me a free man again.

"I have both, patience and faith, but you better fucking get me out of here," I lowered my head and glared at the man, my face menacing as I watched him swallow hard.

Or else… he didn't need to hear the words, my lawyer knew who he was dealing with. I'd hired one of the best ones in Rome, my family was making him a rich man, but it all came at a price. It all depended on the outcome of the trial. *Or else.*

That day I was let out of isolation as promised, my things transferred to a four bunk-bed cell. Two of the inmates there had worked for me, they had been drug smugglers from the South of Italy to Rome.

They respected me, everyone knew who I was and lowered their stare as a sign of respect, when I crossed the room or the yard outside.

Corruption, clans and hierarchies work the same way, inside and outside of prison. I was a god inside and out, nobody crossed me, everyone asked what they could do for me, they knew there would come a time when I'd be out again and their help would not go unnoticed, unpaid. The De la Crux family always had a special place and gratitude for those who were faithful to them.

The day I took my things and moved out of the silence of isolation and into the rowdiness of the prison of St Vittore, I was told everything I had missed. Updated on the trafficking inside the place.

It was suddenly loud, I hadn't been around so many people in a long time.

I sat there in my cell and listened, observed, studied everything and everyone with a wicked grin on my face- content, like I had one foot out of there already. Isolation had toughened me, strengthened my mind.

I wasn't alone anymore, but still, I took that darkness with me and listened to its promises. It was louder, it reached deep down inside like nothing else around me could.

Patience, Alejandro. You'll find them, you'll destroy them. Slowly. You'll make them suffer until their last breathes.

CHAPTER 3
THE APPEAL

My family was given permission to visit me. I sat there in front of them- my mother, my brother Ramirez and my right-hand Cristiano- asking the same question I asked every single time someone came to see me.

"What about the 'Rats'?" that was all I wanted to know.

Business, money, I didn't give a fuck, but the 'Rats', Sebastian and Andrea. I wanted to know about them.

"No news," my friend Cristiano answered every time.

"Find them," I hissed through gritted teeth.

I was running out of patience. I needed answers, something to hold on to. Almost three fucking years in that shithole and no sign of them, no new trail to follow, not even in Hungary. Her parents were gone.

"Fucking find them," I snapped.

"We have been looking for them, everywhere. We asked our friends, no sign of them," my brother Ramirez cut in one day.

"What about their 'friends'?" I asked, referring to anyone that knew that motherfucker. *The Killer.*

I had my men dig up every little bit of information they could find on him; where he was born, lived, what he ate, who he fucked and the names of the people that knew him. Sebastian Esposito and the worthless, disgusting life he lived in Rome were no secret to me.

The search had been thorough, I knew my brother and my right-hand Cristiano had done their best, following Sebastian all over Europe until he'd vanished, just like that, leaving no trace behind. Not even one.

Shit, fucking shit, I'd cursed the name of that son of a bitch again and again.

He couldn't have disappeared, nobody could. I was missing something, but what?

There was only one thing we could do at that point. We were at a dead end and needed to go back, back to the start and this time we needed to keep our fucking eyes open, wide open and head back to Rome. Start the search all over again from there. From the fight club, his little friend, his manager Joe and beat the shit out of that motherfucker until he'd vomit something new, something that could lead us to Sebastian Esposito and my wife.

Tear the place down, rip the city apart.

I was a waking human rage, a caged lion, pacing my cell day and night, restless and eager to run out and burn the world down, until I'd find them.

"No new information," my brother told me.

I took in a deep breath, my hands curled into fists. It took all my will power not to hit the glass wall in front of me.

Fuck the wall, fuck the guards, I wanted to let that anger out, but my mother was looking at me, like I was killing her by being on the other side, by being in that goddam place.

I stared at her a moment longer before speaking again, thinking it through.

"Squeeze 'the lemon," I used our code.

The lemon, in this case Joe or whatever the fuck his name was.

"See if something new comes out," I said and my eyes went back to Cristiano.

He nodded and I knew he would follow my orders.

Something is missing, something isn't right, I kept thinking about it over and over.

Two people can't disappear like that, without leaving a trace, a small, tiny trace.

"Everything is ready for the appeal," my brother tried to calm my nerves.

He nodded as he said the words and I saw a twinkle in his eyes. That's how I knew, he'd paid off and settled anyone that wanted to testify against me.

My family kept telling me I had to focus on getting out of there, but I already was out of there. I was thinking ahead, keeping the flame alive, planning my revenge.

Nobody could cross me and walk away like that, vanish and live happily ever after.

When the day of the appeal finally arrived, I sat there behind the bars, wearing a clean white shirt and my best smile, listening to every single witness being questioned.

"Did you accuse the here present Mr. Alejandro De la Crux of the following crimes?" the prosecutor asked every time.

"No, I never said those words," *One.*

"I made a mistake," *Two*

"That is not my deposition," *Three.*

"I was under the influence of drugs," *Four.*

Not guilty.

The appeal commission had to dismiss the trial earlier than intended; they had nothing substantial to work with. All charges were dropped and I walked out of court a free man.

It took me years, almost three years but I was free again. I felt high, like I'd just done a line of cocaine, like I'd fucked the most gorgeous woman in the room.

My skin prickled, I kept looking at my hands – no handcuffs, no guards around me.

As I slid inside the car- my car- I cleaned my sunglasses slowly and waited for the driver to pull out of the parking lot, before telling my brother what needed to be done.

"Call a meeting, I want all the guys that control our streets there," I looked up at Ramirez, before putting my sunglasses back on.

My hand went to the family emblem, it was finally back where it should have been, over my chest, over my heart.

The cross, the snake and the roses, I held it tight and thought about those snakes, the ones that crawled all around me.

The traitors, the men that had tried to destroy me and tried to build a case against me.

Some I'd suspected all along, some I'd never seen coming, never noticed the lies, fake smiles, plotting behind my back.

Like my wife Andrea.

"I want you to call up every single guy that testified against me at the trial, I want them there too. Tonight, at our house."

"Mr. De la Crux, I must advise you not to. Keep a low profile…" my lawyer cut in immediately but one look at me and he stopped talking- my silent glare didn't need words.

My wish was others to command, the king was back. I snapped my fingers and shit happened.

Three hours after I was made a free man, I sat in my living room, my brother quiet and wary beside me, surrounded by my men, the ones that did the dirty work for me- the ones that kept the business running on the streets. They needed to see what was to come, how things were going to change around there. How I'd changed.

No mercy, no forgiveness, no exceptions.

They all kissed me and shook my hand, commenting on the huge success of my release – a blessing, a new beginning- I heard them mumble with pride and honour.

I looked every single one of them in the eye, smiling to myself and searching their faces.

Who's going to be the next traitor? Who's going to be punished and set an example for them all?

I needed an example, I wanted to give my men something they'd never forget. An execution.

As my eyes wandered around the room, I smiled, content, my brother had done exactly what I'd asked. The four men that had testified against me in the trial were standing right in front of me, trying to avoid my stare as much as they could. One in particular caught my attention.

Sergio, a sixty-something-year-old sleaze bag. Two scars crossed his face, I knew he'd been shot a couple of times, he'd served my father before me and never really liked my ways, how I'd directed the family business.

There he was, the only one looking me in the eye, that kept his face hard, tense, like he was angry. *Or scared.*

That was it, he was scared. I would have bet a thousand dollars that he was shitting in his pants. Sergio seemed the only smart one, the only one that knew why I'd called them up there. Maybe the others were just faking, pretending they were relaxed and okay about being summoned up to the house of the lord, the king, their leader, the one they'd betrayed and then helped get out of jail.

True, they'd taken back their word and helped my lawyers get me out of that shithole of St Vittore. My family had showed their appreciation by paying them off and paying them well. I was anything but ungrateful, I always paid off my debts but forgiveness? Forgiveness was another matter, there could be none in my heart, for those snakes had tried to destroy me.

Forgiveness isn't for men like me; I'm going to leave that to God. I'm all about retribution.

Eye for an eye.

"Sergio," I said, rolling up my sleeves. I stood, one of my soldiers walked by my side with me, as I approached that two-faced scum.

He looked up at me and nodded but didn't say a word.

"Aren't you happy to see me?" I asked him, spreading my arms, opening them to a hug. "Are you not going to kiss me, your leader, wish me well and compliment me on my release?"

Sergio eyed me in silence, we were so close, face-to-face but he knew better than to answer my questions. He knew I wasn't looking for answers, we were beyond words by then. Beyond excuses and redemption. Too late, we'd crossed that line. He'd been sentenced already and I was his executioner.

I moved closer, hugged him, patted his back, his body went rigid until I released him and took a step back, grabbing my soldiers' gun.

"Serpe, traditore," *Snake, traitor.* I said and hit him in the face with the barrel of the gun, as hard as I could.

Sergio's yell bounced off the walls and shocked the entire room, his body rocked backwards and hit the chair behind him, but I didn't stop. No stopping, I'd just begun.

"Son of a bitch," another blow.

"This is how you repay me, huh?" I snarled and hit him again, his hands went up to shield his face, muttering something. Was it a plea? Was he begging? Too fucking late for that.

Traitor!

"I made you a rich man, you piece of shit," I gritted my teeth and hit him again, the gun hit his cheek, his nose, my hands were covered in blood but I didn't stop. I didn't care.

Traitors deserve to die, the darkness whispered in my ears. *No forgiveness, he asked for it. Kill him, kill him now.*

Sergio's face was swollen and unrecognisable when I finally stopped and let go of his shirt, letting him drop to the floor. That's when I cursed his name, loaded the gun and shot him right between the eyes.

The whole room seemed to hold its breath, some jumped back and looked at each other concerned, but those that had done me no harm knew I wasn't coming for them. They knew this was just a warning, a message.

I was back, the king, the fucking ruler was back. No more messing around, no more sneaking behind my back or my family business. I wasn't going to let things go like it was all good, no fucking way. My hands rewarded those that were worthy and punished the unworthy.

I ran a hand through my short hair, sniffed and spat over Sergio's lifeless body.

Scum, traitor.

"Kill every single one of these filthy, motherfuckers that testified against me," I told Ramirez. "Take them somewhere, out of my fucking house."

My brother turned to look at me but I was too busy lighting my cigarette, enjoying my first one outside that shithole they called prison.

Smoke and blood, it felt good to be home.

"They all took the money, they all agreed to change their testimonies," Ramirez tried to make me see reason.

"They backstabbed me and dumped shit on our 'famiglia'. They can't be trusted, they don't deserve forgiveness. Kill them all," I eyed him, the tone of my voice cold and determined.

We weren't discussing it, I was giving an order. I was back at giving orders.

Then I turned to the other three- yes those three fuckers that dared say my name to the authorities, they were still standing. I took joy in watching them shake, as my soldiers quickly circled them and started dragging them out.

"I'll keep your wives and children alive. I'll keep sending them money. Show them the greatness of our family, how we take care of our people and keep our end of the deal," I went on, looking them straight in the eyes.

That and they'll think twice before rebelling against me, I thought taking another drag of my cigarette.

God, that burnt, itchy taste of tobacco felt amazing on my tongue, it made me lightheaded like I was high.

I was high- high on freedom, on life and death.

On revenge.

"May this be an example to you all," my eyes scanned the room, making sure everyone was getting the message. "I want everyone to know that crossing me is never a good idea," I said, watching my brother nod out the corner of my eye.

Alejandro De la Crux was home.

No, not just that. I was back where I belonged, ready to set things right, free to go out there and look for them. *Yes, them.*

Now that the balance in my family was restored, I could carry out my plan, my revenge. This was only the beginning. I was just sharpening my knives.

I am coming, Andrea.

CHAPTER 4
THE HAPPILY EVER AFTER ON THE ISLAND OF FOLEGANDROS

ANDREA

It was the little things that we did that made our love great. Small steps, we took them hand in hand. We were cautious, careful not to draw attention, but we were us. Sebastian, Eddy and I, no one else, nothing more. That was all we needed.

On the highest hill of the town centre we got married one day at sunset. Sebastian held my hand tight and kissed my knuckles, one by one, slowly, looking me straight in the eyes.

Those lips, that mouth. They were mine. And I was his, all his.

My stomach clenched, as shivers travelled up my arm. I smiled at him, my finger rubbing against his, not listening to a single word the priest was saying.

Not that I understood anything, he spoke Greek during most of the ritual.

We didn't even need a ritual, a formal union but we wanted Eddy to see it, how in love we were, how much it meant for us to be a family.

I just kept my eyes on Sebastian, stunned at how handsome he looked in a white button-up shirt. It suited his golden, tanned skin, it brought out his dark eyes, his chiselled arms and black tattoos.

As the priest went on, I smiled not afraid to do so anymore. I was finally free to be happy, my eyes staring up at the man I loved.

I loved. I never thought I could love again, that I could trust someone after Alejandro, that I could give my heart to anyone after all that I'd been through.

That was all before Sebastian, before our souls touched.

Minutes later we were both wearing our rings. Forehead to forehead, we whispered words, promises and hopes.

"In the darkness I saw you," I whispered.

"And I saw you," he whispered back.

"You'll never be alone again," I promised.

"You'll never be alone again," Sebastian repeated after me. "I'll always be here, by your side," he said and kissed my lips gently, holding my chin up.

The sun was fading in the distance, the fire between us brighter than ever.

Katerina Kochenov had just married Antonio Russo. Our names were different, but I didn't care. I didn't feel like the Andrea I was years ago and I didn't want to go back to how I'd felt, to who I'd been.

Sad and alone, I'd been trapped and afraid of my ex-husband or that one of his enemies could hurt me and my son. I'd been caged, no matter how much I'd tried to put distance between myself and Alejandro, I'd still been a prisoner, forced to walk around with soldiers all the time.

Until Sebastian came into my life and showed me the way out. He'd been my light then and I wanted to be his now, forever.

Up that hill, Katerina and Antonio promised each other all of that and more. Those were names, just names. We were still us, after all we had been through. We were both damaged goods, Sebastian and I; life had hardened us, made our skin thicker but our souls were the same.

We needed nothing but each other.

Eddy ran towards the little altar under the white, wooden gazebo, and hugged us tight. Everything was perfect, so perfect I was sometimes scared to let it show.

Our life together had just begun and I willed the sad, bad memories to disappear. Whatever had been, it was over, I told myself. Sometimes the past can haunt you, it tries to bring you down. The darkness tries to claim you, but it can't touch you if you have someone by your side ready to fight with you.

I had Sebastian and he had me. I couldn't stop looking at him, I couldn't stop smiling. Life had given us another chance, we could run free and feel whole again.

We took Eddy in our arms and watched the sun shine over the blue infinity that was the sea. We could call each other whatever we wanted, it didn't matter. We knew who we were. We knew we had everything.

Our new life in Folegandros was very quiet, ordinary and I loved every single moment of it. Eddy went to school, while I gave piano lessons and taught English. I did everything I could, kept busy and helped the villagers there, paying them back for the kindness they'd showed me since the very first day on the island.

I would always be grateful and in debt to them, for making me feel at home and giving me the will to carry on, before I knew that Sebastian was alive and well. Before he came for us.

Sebastian was home during the day. After dinner we kissed goodnight under the moonlight on the terrace of our house, just before he headed down to the docks.

He was at sea every night on large fishing boats and was back only minutes before sunrise, his face tired but happy, the fishing nets full, ready for the early morning market.

We had created a new life for us, I knew how much Sebastian had given up to be with me and Eddy- his career in the police, his home country, his freedom. We could never go back, we had to stay away from Italy.

Sometimes I wondered if he missed his previous life, the one he had before he met me. Then his smile, his touch would wipe away all my doubts and thoughts.

Sebastian came back one day before sunrise, holding four small, fuchsia flowers.

"They are called 'Lights of the night' in Greek," Sebastian told me.

He had found them on a nearby island, where they had stopped to sell some of the fish in the early hours of the morning.

"They made me think of you. I think of you on that boat," he said, his hand running through my hair, all the way behind my neck.

I tilted my head and grabbed his shirt, pulling him towards me. My back against the dinner table, the lights were out and the sun was still nowhere to be seen. We still had the night, we still had time.

"I think of you all night, too," I bit my lip. "Very naughty thoughts," I murmured and watched his eyes widen with desire.

His hands slipped under my top then, his fingers tracing every inch of my skin and all the way up to my bra.

Yes, I closed my eyes as his big, rough hand cupped my breast tight and I squealed with pleasure.

"How naughty?" my stomach clenched at the sound of his deep voice.

That voice, those hands, I could never get enough, never.

Oh god, I arched my back and my breathing picked up.

I wanted him so much, I waited for those hours we had with each other like one craves a drug. An addiction, Sebastian was mine. Nothing made me feel the way I felt when I was with him.

Nobody had ever looked at me that way, like I was the most amazing, the most precious thing that walked the earth. Like I was special.

"Look at you," he said then, one hand pulled at my hair gently and we both turned to the window of our living room.

I saw our reflection, how our bodies were wrapped around one another, how his chest caved to take in my small body, our arms so entwined we didn't know where he ended and where I began; a haze, a beautiful reflection, a union of our souls.

"You're perfect," he moaned into my ear, as one hand dropped to my waist, then slowly to my thigh, and I shivered all over.

Perfect, I wasn't, far from it and I felt guilty for an instant, for deceiving him like that.

I was anything but flawless, but it felt so good to be loved that way, I didn't have the courage to tell him how messed up and fragile I was. How I felt insecure and broken inside. But I wanted so desperately to be perfect, I told myself I wouldn't let him down.

"I'm perfect when I'm with you," I panted, slipping my hands down to his trousers.

He looked at me, studied me, like it was the first time he really saw me, like it was the first time he saw what his hands did to me.

"Aren't you tired?" I moaned, closing my eyes a little, smiling to myself.

When I opened them, his lips were on mine, hard, demanding.

He shook his head.

"Tired? I couldn't wait to get home for this," and pulled off the last bit of clothes I was still wearing.

"I want you in the shower," Sebastian's voice came out husky and greedy.

One arm around my back, he lifted me up, my body pressed against his, I felt the waistband of his worn-out jeans between my thighs.

His shirt was already on the floor, my breasts against his naked chest.

I tasted his lips again and mumbled a soft plea.

"Hold me tight," I panted, losing myself in him, feeling that need to be held, like I belonged to him, in his arms.

Sebastian never questioned my needs, I never had to ask him twice. His muscles twitched and I felt his grip tighten, pulling my body closer to his.

"Don't go to work today, baby," he tempted me as we walked into the shower. "Call in sick. I want to make love to you all day, while Eddy's in school."

Oh god yes, my body tensed and shivered, just thinking about him inside me all day.

"All day?" I bit my lip again and watched him nod, a hint of a smile playing on his lips.

"All day," Sebastian nodded, turning the shower on, his eyes never leaving mine.

Under running water, I moaned, calling out his name, holding on to him, thrust after thrust, losing myself under his touch.

"You taste amazing, I can't wait to get home to you," he groaned against my mouth and kissed me hard, harder, our tongues hungry for each other.

More, deeper, he tasted amazing, warm and intense, I suddenly felt lightheaded.

I broke the kiss and turned, pressing my hands against the wall, welcoming his body against mine and the thrusts became more intense, deeper.

"Don't stop," I moaned, his fingers reaching for my lips.

I kissed them and eyed him out of the corner of my eye, leaning my head back against his shoulder as I let out a cry. Both his hands snaked over my neck and Sebastian pressed his mouth on mine, gently muffling any sound.

"Ti amo," *"I love you"* he moaned against my lips, our bodies rocking together like we were one.

My legs gave in a little as Sebastian went on. "I love you. It feels so fucking good, I don't want to let go, Sad Eyes."

"Don't let me go," I moaned again. "I love you, so much," my voice broke a little as I told him the words I vowed to never say again, to any man.

But Sebastian wasn't just any man. He was my rock, the 'light of my night', the one and only, brave enough to lead me out of the dark.

That day I called in sick, locked the doors and windows of the house, while Sebastian took Eddy to school and I waited for him at home. We stayed in bed all day, we needed nothing but each other.

It was the little things that made our love great.

SEBASTIAN

My mornings were everyone else's evenings, but I still called it my morning ritual- the series of things I did as I woke up every day.

I always made sure to tell Andrea exactly how beautiful she was. I kissed her slowly, I took my time, like nothing around us mattered.

Coming out of the hell we had been through, changed me completely. I gave her and Eddy everything I could, my full attention.

I made sure to spend some time with Eddy every day, before my training, before I went down to the boat again and he went to bed. He looked like his mother, but as time went by he reminded me of myself when I was a kid.

Eddy was still the happy child I met the first time, in that golden prison he'd been living in with Andrea back in Rome, although at times he seemed lost in thought and stared at nothing, his face glum.

That stare worried me but I didn't say a word to Andrea. The last thing I wanted was to see her sad. She didn't deserve to be sad, not anymore, never again.

I caught Eddy staring at me a few times, before it happened. Before what Andrea and I had dreaded over the last couple of years happened.

The questions. I knew that look, I knew that seriousness in his eyes. Eddy had questions and he wanted answers.

"Why did we leave Italy?" he asked me one day, while we were fishing on the beach together before work.

I eyed him in silence and thought about what to say next. What could I say? How could I explain our story to a six-year-old? My son?

As I looked down at my hands, I considered lying, I considered telling him anything but the truth, though I knew there would come a day when he would ask that same question again and I would have to tell the truth.

"It wasn't a choice. We were in danger. We had to leave. Your mom and I had to take you away, make sure you were safe," I said, watching him closely.

Eddy seemed satisfied, grateful I hadn't dismissed him, avoided his question like his mother and I had done a few times already.

His thirst for truth, wasn't entirely satisfied

"Who was after us?" Eddy wanted to know.

He kept his face blank, solemn but I wondered if he was hiding something, keeping his feelings from me. He had become so good at that, just like me.

"Bad people, people that wanted to hurt you and your father," I nearly choked on the last word.

It made me sick, referring to that piece of shit as his father. I was his father, not Alejandro.

I didn't want Eddy to think that a sick son of a bitch was his father, but it wasn't easy to explain to him what happened. Andrea and I had agreed to tell him the truth, the whole truth when he was older. Now was not the time to tell him who I really was.

"Did my father want to hurt me?" it killed me, his words, his shaky voice.

Eddy kept his face hard, unemotional, but I knew he'd been afraid to ask, I knew he feared my answer. The truth about his father, about who he really was.

I turned and stared at the sea, at how calm the water was that day. For the time being at least, but things could change quickly out there, at sea. Just like in life.

One word, a thousand lies and when the moment of truth comes, everything changes and there's no going back.

We never see the storm coming, we are never really ready to face the truth, the changes.

Eddy wasn't ready.

"Your father would never hurt you, not intentionally," I said and saw him nod a little relieved. "Sometimes bad things happen even if you don't want them to happen. Your father wasn't well, he wasn't capable of taking care of you and your mom," it killed me to lie.

It killed me not to tell him the truth, but I had to lie. I just couldn't hurt him like that, like I'd been hurt as a kid. The truth about my mother- how she earned a living selling her body on the streets- had almost killed me, I didn't want that for Eddy, I didn't want to break him.

I could break, I could wait for the truth. Eddy needed to feel good about who he was, about who he thought his father was. It was easier that way, until we he was old enough to brace the truth.

"Thank you," Eddy said to me. Nobody ever answered his questions, he was glad I had. "I am happy you are here. You are like a father to me."

I nearly told him then, but he smiled at me so sweetly I wrapped an arm around him, swallowed down my truth and stared ahead at the sea again.

It was so calm, soundless, no waves ahead. I willed myself to be that sea, to give Eddy that serenity and peace.

We weren't ready for the storm, my heart had to be patient and wait.

CHAPTER 5
OBSESSION
ALEJANDRO

Prisons aren't just made of walls. I was a free man but I felt trapped, tied down.

The darkness, the one that had kept me company for over three years, was aching to run free.

Find her.

Seek revenge.

Kill her, kill them both. No, better yet: make them suffer.

I was a prisoner of my own thoughts, caged by my obsession.

Every day I asked my men the same questions, demanding to know about Andrea and Sebastian.

"You are not looking hard enough," I shouted to their faces. "Scrape every little corner of this fucking country, squeeze every little shit that knew them and come back with news. Find them," I ordered.

Rome had been turned upside down, street corner after street corner, but still no sign of 'The Rats'. Nobody knew where they were or if they'd been back at all in the last few years.

My vengeance had become an obsession.

I saw the worry in my mother's eyes, she knew it was consuming me, devouring me from the inside.

My mother followed me around the house in silence, shooting me hard, serious glances. She filled me in on the things that had happened since I was gone. Three years is a long time, but nothing seemed different to me. Nothing.

The family still owned the same neighbourhoods, we were still doing good in the drug trade, my brother working hard on the prostitution racket, too.

Nothing seemed different, not one word they said was of any interest to me. Until my brother told me he'd found the fuckers that had wanted me dead to begin with, the gang from that neighbourhood, The Ruins, and had them killed, all of them.

"The Ruins are a mess right now. We broke their alliances, there is a war going on between the smaller gangs," Ramirez told me during my welcome home party.

We were in one of his nightclubs in The Market, we had just moved out of the main room and into the VIP area.

He chuckled, rubbing his nose a little, tilting his head back, waiting for the cocaine to kick in.

I bent forward and snorted some too, the burning, itchy feeling travelled all the way up my nose and to the back of my throat. For a moment everything felt numb and then I saw it. My chance.

"It's fun to watch them kill each other," Ramirez said but I cut in immediately.

"Give one of the smaller gangs weapons. Let them kill each other. Then we take over," I growled and felt my brother's eyes on me instantly.

He couldn't believe what I was saying.

"You want in on the war?"

I shook my head.

"No. Let them fight. We step in at the very end. We takeover and those that don't work with us… we get rid of them," I took a shot of whiskey and added, "I want The Ruins.

Those fuckers there fucked with me first. It's time to fuck them."

It all started with The Ruins, I thought.

It was their fault I had gone into hiding. Their fault I had to put an army in place to protect my family. Their fault I had gone looking for Sebastian The Killer to protect my ex-wife and son.

I spat on the floor, the thought of him fucking Andrea- and betraying me- was driving me insane.

"Welcome back bro," Ramirez smiled and handed me a drink.

We needed to celebrate my return and our new projects. Now that I was back, he told me, we could finally extend our trade to the city centre, like we always wanted to. Take them all down, takeover Rome.

Ramirez was still talking, I took another shot of whiskey. I hadn't had a drink in years, hadn't seen a woman in a long time and all of a sudden I was sitting on a leather couch, tossing alcohol down my throat, whores walking all around us, wiggling their asses, serving us on their hands and knees, like we ruled that goddam city.

I should have felt on top of the fucking world, but there was something missing, something was off. Maybe I was king, but not the king I wanted to be. The Market, The Ruins, the whole fucking city of Rome weren't enough for me. Maybe for the old Alejandro De la Crux, the one before prison, before Andrea.

Before The Killer, I cursed his name under my breath.

I imagined him fucking Andrea somewhere, happy and in love.

With my son, I spat on the floor.

As we sat there in Ramirez's private suite, behind a glass window where no one could see us, I listened to my brother in silence and kept my eyes on the girls stripping on stage, at the men drooling at the mouth.

The mind plays funny tricks sometimes, but it never lies. Never. We call them illusions, but they are half-truths, dreams and hopes we keep inside.

That night I thought I saw Andrea strip on that stage. I remembered her dancing in that upper-class strippers' club years back and felt it again, the rage, the venom running through my veins.

How could I have allowed that? How many times had I let her cross me? My family had been right all along. I had signed my death sentence, losing my head for a woman like Andrea. She wasn't a woman you could tame, she wasn't a woman that kept quiet, that did what she was told.

All of that is going to change, once I find you, Andrea.

I was going to rip that audacity from her, destroy her emotionally until she was mine again, until I had complete control over her.

"You are not listening to me, are you?" my brother gave me a funny look and then turned his attention to the naked waitress serving him another drink.

She wasn't wearing a single thing, she was butt naked, tall, dark hair and dark eyes.

Ramirez took her hand and pulled her down, licking her lips, grabbing her behind. I stared at them and my brother eyed me again.

"You need a woman," he said, not asking me a question but stating a fact.

I hadn't fucked one in ages.

"You want to fuck this one?" he took her by the wrist and spun her a little, the woman smiled and titled her head to the side, staring at me.

She was fucking hot, I got hard from her staring at me like that.

But no, she wasn't who I wanted.

I turned my head, back to that stage and pointed to a stripper, not just any stripper but one in particular. Blonde, long hair, fair skin, thin and sinuous like a dancer.

Like Andrea.

"That one," I said, glancing at my brother again and finishing my whiskey.

She was too skinny, no curves, my brother was saying in the background.

Her, I wanted her.

Ten minutes later, the brunette that had been fucking around with my brother came back with her little blonde whore friend, the one I'd seen on stage.

Blue eyes, I knew she would have had blue eyes. She was perfect for me, I licked my lips ready to unleash my rage on her.

The blonde whore stared at me, no smile, and said nothing, not a single word- Ramirez told me she hardly knew any Italian, she had just been brought into the country from Poland.

She was Eastern European, just like my Andrea, but her name was Ana. That was all she said, her name.

"You guys have fun, take your time. I'll see you upstairs when you are done," my brother said and walked out of the room with his whore.

I was left alone with mine. *Ana, Andrea.* My mind kept playing with their names, the alcohol was fucking up my brain.

"Sit," I ordered and she walked towards me, smiling a little.

I took a good look at her, as she sat on the black leather couch beside me and gave her my glass, my drink. She didn't question me, she didn't ask what was inside. Ana just gulped it down, all of it, closing her eyes a little as she did. She didn't dare ask, doubt or speak at all. Exactly what I wanted, what I needed. *Obedience.*

Her blue eyes were on me again, I could tell she knew what was going to come. She knew I was going to do to her whatever the fuck crossed my mind and she needed the drink, to take it. To take me, so she wouldn't care.

YOU WILL CARE, you will feel the pain, I squinted at her, my fingers digging between her thighs, slipping inside her, until she gasped.

I was a devil, my looks didn't lie, not anymore, not after what I had been through.

My eyes were black, small and evil. And Ana could see exactly what I was, she obeyed my every word.

"You are not Ana," I said, as my other arm went around her back. I grabbed her hair and she gasped again. Then I moved closer, my mouth inches from her lips. "Your name is Andrea and you will say 'Yes, Alejandro' to every single thing I tell you to do."

"Yes, Alejandro," she said and her soft voice came out a little shaky, her accent so strong, it reminded me of Andrea's when she'd just moved to Italy with me.

My eyes darkened.

"You are my whore, Andrea," I grunted as I undid my trousers fast.

I wanted her to shake, I wanted her to fear me. I wanted to see her succumb, beg, plea for me not to break her.

Even though I was going to break her for life. Everything I touched, I destroyed and corrupted. I wanted to poison her skin, change her forever, like I never could with Andrea.

My hand gripped her hair tighter and I pushed her down on me.

"Suck it," I groaned.

Wet and smooth, her mouth was so hot. I kept her in place and made her work, work for me. She was my whore.

Andrea, I thought. *My obsession, my curse.*

I gulped down some more whiskey, as my whore moved between my legs and closed my eyes shut tight for a moment.

My head was foggy, my perception distorted. For a moment, it was just a moment, but it happened. I saw Andrea, fucking in the shed with that rat, letting him pound on her, touch her, possess her beautiful body and my eyes flew open again.

"Fuck," I grunted, pulling the whore's hair again.

She looked up at me, crying out a little, her face shattered, the red lipstick smeared on her cheeks.

Good, I wanted to shatter her, I wanted to destroy her. *My Andrea, my whore.*

"Turn," I said and seeing her a little lost I shouted. "Now, you fucking whore. Now Andrea."

She got up, her legs trembling like she was cold- she wasn't, she feared me, my darkness, the one that ran through me, that possessed my soul.

One hand on her back, I pushed my whore down on the couch, while the other one pulled her panties to the side.

Fucking wasn't the only thing I needed, I wanted to torture her. I wanted to get hard on her tears, I wanted to hear her beg. Fuck her so hard, I wanted to hear her call me the devil.

My Andrea, my obsession.

"Cry, beg me to stop," I roared into her hair as I pounded harder inside her.

And my whore cried, more than I'd ever thought she would. She whimpered in Polish as I pounded into her, making me thirsty for more.

Cry, cry.

"Puttana," *Whore,* I grunted. "I love how you beg," I said and made sure she would remember me, she would remember Alejandro De la Crux. *El Diablo.*

Next time I'd come for her, she wouldn't dare look me in the eyes like she had that night. I knew, next time Ana, my Andrea, would pray not to be seen, she would pray for me not to choose her.

But I already had, I had chosen her. For now.

"Nobody will touch you but me, until I want to fuck you. You are my whore, from now on. Do you understand, Andrea? My whore," I bent down and grunted the words into her ear, as I stayed inside her a moment longer, letting her feel my weight, my darkness. My poison was inside her now.

I watched her nod and felt her body shake, scared like she'd just seen a monster, like she'd been possessed by a demon.

It lasted only a few moments, the pleasure of having possessed her. As I pulled my trousers up, my mind was back on the target, back on seeking my revenge but I told myself that whore would do for the time being. I was going to fuck her until I got my hands on Andrea, the real Andrea.

I let my obsession guide me, I let my obsession become me.

CHAPTER 6
BUTTERFLIES AND HURRICANES

SEBASTIAN

No more lies, no more secrets, Andrea and I promised we'd always tell each other the truth, no matter what. We wouldn't let lies come between us, no matter how hard it was at times to come clean and talk about out past lives. I didn't want to let her down, I wanted nothing more than for her to be happy.

But I didn't think I could, really could pull it off, the not lying part.

I had built my life on lies. I'd used them to cope on the streets, lies had saved me countless times. And then all of a sudden, I wasn't telling them anymore.

Suddenly, I wasn't living the double life- the criminal, the fighter versus the undercover cop. I was who I really was, Sebastian Esposito, a man that had found his way out of hell and then jumped right back inside to help others.

But secrets, I was still keeping those.

When I arrived on the island, we'd spent our first night in bed, consuming each other's skin, legs and arms wrapped tight around one another.

We'd talked for hours and I had told her everything, the kind of man that I was and the story of my life. Yes, even the parts that hurt, the ones I'd rather lie about- the relationship with my non-existent mother, the beatings and executions I'd witnessed on the streets.

Andrea and I had never had time to really talk about us before, staying alive and running from Alejandro De la Crux the only thing on our minds. And yet it amazed me how we felt about each other, how we loved so fiercely even though we hadn't been completely honest from the beginning.

Sometimes you don't need words to know the truth. You just do. I knew it from the first moment I saw her that there was so much more to her than a pair of sad eyes and a broken smile. I'd fallen so in love with Andrea, I didn't need her to tell me her secrets to know she was worth fighting for.

Love is the biggest leap of faith. It's not rational, it's not perfect and you wouldn't want it any other way.

I know I never wanted Andrea to be any different, I took her for the way she was- so mysterious and reserved, magnetic and warm. I loved her when she'd open up to me and when she didn't.

Love is never perfect and it doesn't need to be. It just is and once you find that love so deep, so consuming, you just can't live without it. I longed to be with her, even when she looked so absent, her mind someplace else. I made sure I was always there, quiet and careful not to intrude, ready to hold her when she'd let me.

That first night in bed, we spoke the whole truth. I told her mine, Andrea told me hers.

I wanted to know everything about her, about her pregnancy with Eddy, about our son. She wanted to learn about my double life, my secret identity.

Breathing in her sweet scent, I found the courage to tell Andrea my story and tell her about the man that had saved me.

His name was Salvatore and he was a police officer in the small neighbourhood where I used to live in Naples, The Towers.

Those streets were filthy and dangerous, you could smell the fear, see the horror in people's eyes. Trouble was always around the corner, it took guts to patrol the area. If you walked around the place, you couldn't help but notice the desperation, the poverty.

The abandonment of the law. There was no law, but the laws of the criminal gangs.

It was easier to find drugs than milk and bread around there.

I'm not kidding, I know what I'm talking about. Sometimes I couldn't get my hands on food for days, but there was always cocaine or heroin in my house. There was always someone trying to sell me their shit, *'la via di uscita' 'the way out'* as they called it. The solution.

"Take this and you'll feel like you're in heaven," older kids kept telling me but I never took anything from them.

When the effects of the drugs wore off, those kids seemed just as desperate as I was, just as fucked up as before.

How did they know what heaven was like anyway, when we were all trying to survive, trying not to die in that hell we lived in?

They were just kids, only a few years older than me, but they were already doing drugs. Every day I looked at them and wondered.

How long before they get shot for playing the little 'gangsters game'? How long before they die? Who will end up in the crossfire this time? Me?

I wasn't afraid of death, when you see your friends lying in the streets in a pool of blood, a bullet in their heads, you know it's just a matter of time. You know you'll end up like them- no salvation, no way out.

Those kids had no future, just as I had none.

Salvatore took his work seriously. He dared to walk through hell, he dared to patrol those streets on foot.

The day he spoke to me, he asked me all sorts of personal questions and why I was smoking a cigarette at my age.

I remember gaping at him, like his question was the most ridiculous thing I'd ever heard. Smoking is something kids do at ten or eleven in those areas, a grownup thing to show others you are a man. A real man.

There was never any food around, but smuggled cigarettes you could find at every street corner. It wasn't a big deal I was a smoker and had been for a while. I was seventeen then.

"What? Am I under arrest or something?" I snapped, nervously.

It was the middle of the day, I was waiting for the bus and Salvatore's presence was ruining my business. I needed him to leave, immediately if I wanted to nick money from people's pockets there and on the bus.

Leave, leave, I willed him to leave me alone.

"You want me to arrest you?" he asked and I shook my head, squinting a little at him. "Cause that's what is going to happen if you don't stop pick pocketing people on buses and on the streets."

My mouth dropped open then and the cigarette twirled all the way down to the pavement.

I denied everything, even if I could tell he didn't believe a single word I was muttering, because he knew, he'd seen me, but he hadn't stopped me or taken me to the police station.

Why not? I couldn't understand why.

"You know what's happening now? Right now, this very moment?" he asked me after a few minutes.

The bus had come and gone, no people around us anymore, and I had told him a little about me, about my story. I was on the defensive; I was a loner and belonged to no gang. I had no money, no home, nobody to take care of me. And I needed to eat.

"This is your moment, you can change your life. But it's your decision to make. I am here to help if you want me to. I've had my eyes on you for a while now, I know you could become something. You are a smart kid."

Become what? I didn't understand at first, but then Salvatore opened my eyes to a completely new world.

I was in the gutter, swimming in human waste, but I could still choose who I wanted to be. Salvatore told me I could choose to be a criminal, like I already was, or I could choose to be on the other side, on the side of the goodhearted, the ones that tried to change that place and help those in need.

"You would be perfect undercover," Salvatore mumbled eyeing me and I didn't understand his words at first, but I trusted him instantly.

La via di uscita, 'the way out' those kids were talking about every day, it wasn't in the shit they were selling. It was Salvatore and people like him, the ones that came from outside the neighbourhood, the ones that wanted to change The Towers.

I followed him and he made me the man that I was the day I'd met Andrea. An undercover police officer. I was still living in the ghetto, I was still the same kid from those poor, filthy streets, only now I was fighting for the right side, I was helping the police.

In silence and in the shadows, I helped them take down one criminal mind at a time.

"You never tell anyone who you are, kid. Never," Salvatore told me when I started the process, my secret training, my secret enrolment. "You are Sebastian Esposito, the little thief, the little criminal. Find your place, stick to it. Make that you, you are a cop only when you report to me, other than that you are Sebastian," and Salvatore was right. That was the only way to survive and remain sane.

I never told anyone, no matter how long I stayed in one place, no matter how close I had gotten to a woman. I never said a single word about the real me and who I'd chosen to be that day at the bus stop.

I never told anyone, but Andrea. She was the only person that knew my story. Someone had saved me and had showed me how to save others.

I'd saved so many, before I'd met her.

No secrets, we agreed to be us, tell each other everything and then keep the past our past, choose our future to be different.

But one day I lied, I broke the promise.

I found out Alejandro had been released from jail on a spring afternoon and I' kept it from her. We had agreed not to look back, but my mind just couldn't rest.

Losing control was my biggest fear. Knowing where my enemies were, made me feel safer.

Only Alejandro wasn't where he was meant to be anymore. He was walking the streets of Rome again and for an instant I thought about telling her.

Then, Andrea and Eddy called out for me and started talking me into getting one of the white and black puppies a man was giving away in the town centre and I kept it to myself.

"Isn't she precious?" Andrea's eyes had lit up with excitement.

I just couldn't tell her, I couldn't. She was so happy, I lied because I didn't want her to lose that smile.

I kept the secret and we took the puppy home.

ANDREA

The nightmares started one day, out of the blue and for no apparent reason. Nothing had happened, no particular event had triggered them. We lived our lives like any other family on the island. But one late spring night, I woke up panting.

As I sat up in bed, I touched the corner of my eyes and notice they were wet.

I stared at my fingers in surprise, as my breathing slowly went back to normal. But the tears kept trickling down my cheeks.

The nightmare, it had felt so real.

Alejandro had found us, he had come looking for us at night and he had taken Eddy away. But not before pushing a pillow over my face, killing me in my sleep, impatient to hear my last breath.

It had been so dark in the nightmare, I hadn't seen Alejandro's face but I'd recognized his voice, his scent. Are nightmares meant to be so real? Is that what makes them so disruptive and painful?

For a moment it felt more like an omen than a nightmare. I couldn't shake it off, I couldn't move or speak or think of anything but the nightmare.

Minutes, hours went by but I was still sitting in bed, looking at my hands, glancing to the side from time to time, where Sebastian was meant to be.

The bed was empty though, he was at sea that night, awake and getting his hands dirty for us.

It was just a nightmare, I told myself the obvious and stood to fetch myself a glass of water.

It was my past, the living nightmare I'd run away from that came looking for me, that wanted me to fall back into the dark limbo of fear and loneliness. But I had been in that limbo and I had climbed out of it. I was safe, alive, with my loved ones and nobody could touch me, nobody could hurt us.

I knew the darkness would try to come back and claim me, I didn't understand why I was so stunned by the dream. Sebastian and I had talked about it so many times.

Look ahead, never look back. For our sakes, for Eddy's sake.

A sound, loud like something hitting the wall hard, made me tense. My head jerked towards the corridor, towards Eddy's room, and my hands began to tremble.

Without thinking it through, still shaken by the dream and good intentions aside, I grabbed a knife and started for his door but stopped dead cold halfway into the corridor.

Eddy stood in front of me, motionless, his eyes wide open like he had just seen a ghost. His breathing was fast, his stare empty and glassy.

"Eddy," I said but he didn't look at me. He seemed to be staring at something behind me- the window, the wall, but not me.

"Eddy," I called again and was about to take his hand when he started to speak.

"Blood everywhere," he muttered, tears rolling down his smooth, tanned cheeks. "Blood, blood. On my hands, on your hands, on dad's hands. He wants blood. He wants me."

I dropped the knife and went down on my knees in front of him, covering my mouth and stifling a cry.

"Eddy, baby," I said, looking at his steely eyes but he didn't turn to look at me.

He was there but he wasn't. He was sleepwalking, I realized a moment later, passing my hand in front of his eyes, seeing him neither blink nor flinch.

"He hurt my mommy," Eddy repeated four times. "The blood never washes away, never washes away, never washes, never."

I was in tears, right in front of him and I was seeing the damage for the first time. Eddy was damaged, like me, like Sebastian, and I had never noticed it before.

How stupid of me to believe I had managed to get one thing right, protect him from the horrendous life I had brought him into. Failure stood right there in front of me, I was crazy to believe I'd saved him from the truth.

"Come here baby," I said without even thinking about what to do next.

I had no idea what or how to deal with the situation. All I wanted was to hold him, close to my heart, begging for his forgiveness.

I'd ask him to forgive me one day, for not being brave enough to take him as far away as possible from his father from the very beginning.

I could have taken him away, given him to some family in another country and returned to Italy, handing myself to Alejandro and letting him take my life. It would have worked, it would have been okay, to let him take mine as long as he wouldn't take Eddy's. But I had hesitated, I had made a mistake. I could see it then.

Suddenly, Eddy looked at me, saw me and then searched the room a little lost. He was awake.

"Mommy, what are we doing?" he asked, as I tried to hide the knife.

"It's okay. It's okay, baby," I took his hand and pulled Eddy towards me.

He curled up in my lap and let me hold him tight.

"I called for you and you came for me. I had a nightmare," I told him and he tilted his head back to look at me in the eyes.

"Oh, no mommy. Are you okay?" he looked serene, not the child I had seen moments before. He had forgotten everything, he couldn't remember getting up from his bed, the words he'd said to me.

I silently thanked my lucky stars.

"I am okay. You are here, of course I am okay," I kissed his cheek, taking away the streak of tears.

That salty flavour on my lips reminded me of what my mother once told me about tears.

"They are your deepest sorrows. Let them out, let them all out. Clear your soul, lift your heart."

"Do you want me to sleep with you, until Sebastian comes home?" Eddy looked into my eyes again, smiling a little, being the brave little man that he was.

"Yes, please," I kissed him again and then we walked to my room, hand in hand, without switching the lights on.

The moon was high and full up in the sky, we could see the light shine through the blue shutters.

As we settled in the bed, our hearts settled too. A newly found rhythm, a newly found beat. I let him snuggle under my chin, let him find his place, my mind concentrated on the sounds of the night.

I wondered how deeply rooted his memories were, if it was just a temporary thing, if he would eventually forget.

Would the past affect him in the long run? Would it shape his future and who he'd become? How big was that scar on his soul? I wondered if it was just a coincidence- my nightmare, his sleepwalking. Or if it was all just an omen.

It's just part of who we are, our damaged souls are free to speak at night. They let us be during the day, but they come back for us at night when we let our guard down. We'll find a way to deal with the past. We will get through this, we will.

"I'll protect you mommy," Eddy mumbled, holding me tighter. "I won't let any monster touch you."

CHAPTER 7
THE MISSING PIECE

ALEJANDRO

To know where you're going, you must know where you're coming from. In this case where The Rat was coming from.

Naples, that's where I'd find my answers.

One morning I sat up in bed, knowing exactly what to do. I was tired of keeping a low profile, keeping my name clear. I had done everything the lawyers had suggested after I was made a free man.

For three months I had let my brother, my soldiers take care of my business, but I was tired of waiting, tired of standing there in the shadows.

By then, we were ruling The Market; we'd taken over a great part of The Ruins. Half of that goddam city of Rome was ours, but I couldn't care less.

One morning, I packed a bag and dressed in my finest clothes. As I adjusted the collar of my dark button-up shirt, I breathed in the smell of my favourite cologne and stared at the reflection in the mirror.

My hair was growing, Alejandro De la Crux stared back at me with a smug smile on his lips, like he had just won the fucking lottery.

I slid the chain over my head, the one with the family emblem, and let it dangle over my hard chest.

De la Crux, the cross, the rose and the snakes. I was going on a hunt, I was going to look for those snakes and that rose.

My rose. And seek revenge for all the wrongs they'd done to me.

I was Alejandro De la Crux, I stopped at nothing, looked everyone in the eyes, never scared of taking what I wanted. No matter the price.

What I wanted was to destroy the snake and take back what was mine by right.

My obsession and my son.

They couldn't have just disappeared, vanished into thin air.

I'm missing something. Something important.

I knew I was and I'd figured out where to look for that something, that missing puzzle piece.

My father was well known and respected in Naples, we had a couple of connections there. I used those to my advantage, I used them to find out more about Sebastian.

As time went on, my thirst for revenge kept growing, I kept thinking of ways to hurt him. My revenge had to be whole, complete.

Everything he owned, everything that he was, I wanted it to be mine. His city, his past life. I wanted to control it all.

I wanted to walk through Sebastian's neighbourhood and take it down with my own hands.

Study your enemies and learn everything you can about them, my father's words came back to me then. *You'll be ready to take them down, when you know them better than they know themselves.*

"I am taking soldiers," I announced that morning, telling my brother and my mother where I was headed.

I had contacted a man I knew down there already, I was good to go.

My family tried to make me stay, tried to make me see how all of that was taking me nowhere. My obsession, my revenge, they said it would be the death of me.

They didn't understand, they just couldn't. My thirst for revenge governed me, it was all I thought about, all I cared about. I'd be back only once I'd made sure those fuckers had suffered for their sins. Even if that meant losing time, wasting years.

"A man that shoots to kill, bears a heavy burden over his heart," my mother mumbled seeing me walk out of the door.

She was always so hard, so severe my mother.

'Donna' Filomena, as people on the streets called her, always walked around with her head high, no smile, her face dark and proud. Never saw the figment of desperation or worry in her eyes, on her wrinkled cheeks, on the sides of her full dark lips.

That morning she kept looking at me, like it was the last time.

"Don't let that burden be the death of you," she mumbled.

I heard her, but I was out on a hunt and couldn't care less what she meant, if her words were of any use to me.

Go to Naples, find that the missing piece. I cared about nothing else.

I wanted to find that trail. Follow it to the very end and take my risks.

Two months of going back and forth to Naples, before I could actually find something on Sebastian, something useful.

Drug traffickers there knew my father, knew how we operated in Rome and offered their help. I was lucky, they were greedy. It was easy to buy their silence and their information. I sent them cocaine, the finest cocaine from Colombia, and they opened all their connections to me, one in the police forces, too.

Ninety thousand euros of cocaine it cost me, to find what I was looking for, and it was worth every single penny.

The inside man in the police force handed me a file. A to Z on Sebastian Esposito. I knew his background, his addresses, his meaningful life on the streets. How many times he'd been in jail. What he'd been charged with. Who he had fucked, what he had eaten, where he had slept all his life. Every single fucking minute of his existence but not where he might have run off to.

The last official information on him was of the two months he had spent in jail, after I was arrested. Then nothing. I was back to the same place as before, back to the beginning of my search.

The pieces weren't all there, I couldn't understand what was missing, what was off with the whole story. But I was so close, I knew I was.

"Dig deeper, fucking look harder," I shoved those pages in the police officer's face up on the roof of a building, in the heart of The Towers.

The shithole where Sebastian Esposito came out of, my eyes scanned the dirty, rotten buildings of the neighbourhood and immediately I knew what I was looking at.

I knew what a ghetto was, I was the fucking king of one in Rome. But The Towers in Naples, was something else. It smelled like desperation and sin, the darkest and filthiest kind. From up there I could see it all, the scum, how poverty and broken dreams had violently ripped the life out of people.

Every night I watched small groups of kids on scooters deliver drugs across the neighbourhood. Fast money, dirty earnings. The kids weren't even fourteen yet, they were so young and so committed already. It was all about honour, respect and power.

Words can have a strong impact on kids.

"Honour your brothers. We are a family. Make people respect you. Show them how powerful you are. Hit hard, harder. Smash them with all your strength and take what you want. We are your family, we've got your back," that was what those kids were told and taught on the street.

Hit before they hit you. Take before they take from you. Honour your brothers.

Every night I watched those kids ride through the streets, chanting mottos and laughing at those that weren't part of their gang.

They felt invincible, part of something big. 'La famiglia'. The family, they were all brothers, all fighting for the same thing: power, money, success. *Fuck the law.*

It was all a game to them, until it wasn't and they threw themselves heart and soul into battles between clans, to protect their territory, the little crumbs bosses threw at them.

They were the perfect soldiers.

"I'll cut your throat if you don't find the information I am looking for," I turned to look at the police officer.

One look and he understood. No more "Mr. De la Crux you must understand."

No more "I cannot access classified information."

There was something there in those archives, he'd admitted it. He'd seen it.

There was a secret file on Sebastian, something coded. Maybe something he had done, something big that was not for the general public. Maybe something that could help me connect all the pieces.

Three days later, the police officer was back, less cocky this time, less friendly but with everything he could dig up on The Rat.

I never asked how he'd accessed the file, who he had to bribe, how much he was risking. I didn't give a shit, it was all there. What I'd had under my nose the whole time and just couldn't see.

Everything added up, why he was nowhere to be found. Why my wife and son were two ghosts.

I had been searching in the wrong places, looking for the wrong people.

"Well, well," I mumbled under my breath, rubbing my chin content. "Here you are."

My plan, my revenge played out in front of me, as I took the phone and gave all the information to friends. Friends of friends. Anyone that could help me find Sebastian with his new identity.

It took me a few hours, just a few hours and I knew where he was.

And so it begins.

PART 2
THE BEGINNING OF THE END

Vengeance is in my heart, death in my hands, blood and revenge are hammering in my head –
William Shakespeare

CHAPTER 8
THE DECISION

ANDREA

He came for me and I wasn't ready. I let him surprise me, I let him scare me, even though deep down I always knew he would come.

Like a constant, uncomfortable feeling at the back of my mind, Alejandro had always been there, lurking in the shadows.

I was too busy living, too inebriated by the beauty of our lives together on the island, that I let my guard down and forgot all about the darkness.

We all did.

It was like lightning on a hot summer's night. My nightmares came back all of a sudden, all together and I couldn't catch my breath. Their cold grip was choking the life out of me. I was given a choice, I had to choose what was right again and sacrifice everything else.

Our lives on the island.

One night, reality slapped me in the face, mocked me for my foolishness and reminded me I couldn't have it all. I had to choose and fast.

Love, the gut wrenching kind, the one that makes you walk around ten feet from the ground- the one that holds you and protects you when you are broken- I couldn't have that.

You can't have it all, you have to decide who you love more.

In a matter of seconds, I made my choice. I decided to protect the love of my life and give up everything else.

"It's up to you," Alejandro had the guts to tell me.

He put it all in my hands, like I was the one standing in MY way.

But really it was his choice. It was time to pay for running away, for leaving him.

I closed my eyes and took a step into the darkness.

The day he came, the whole island was celebrating the end of summer. Visitors from all over the country took part in the annual festivity.

The little cobbled streets were packed with tourists from all across Europe, sipping fresh beer and eating street food, as the music from the main town square played in the background.

That was where I was, in the town square, staring expectantly towards the stage, where Eddy and his classmates would soon perform their little play.

I remember Sebastian placed a hand on my back and kissed my bare shoulder, just a few minutes before my phone rang.

Our eyes met as he bent down again to whisper in my ear.

"You are a vision," his warm breath tickled my neck and I bit my lip, my mouth curling up on one side. "I can't wait to be alone with you tonight, my first night after a long time that I am home."

I nodded and turned his way a little, snuggling against his chest, just as the sea breeze started to pick up.

We were high on the hill, right at the heart of the island and even though there were a lot of people around, the air went from warm to fresh in an instant.

An omen. I should've seen the signs. I kept missing them.

"How about we stay up all night? I want to enjoy every second, I don't want to sleep," I purred against him and

Sebastian backed away a little, just enough to take a good look at me and smile.

"You only need to ask, Occhi Belli," *Pretty Eyes.*

I had gone from Sad Eyes to Pretty Eyes, because I was happy. Because of him.

Thanks to you, amore. My love.

"I am so glad you are not at sea tonight, you get to watch Eddy perform," I whispered, not wanting people to listen in on our conversation.

We were still hiding, we were still pretending we were other people, but I'd never felt so free to be me like that before.

My last moments of freedom, if only I'd known what was coming, I would have savoured them, held on to that life a little longer.

So many things I would have said to Sebastian. I feel as though I'd never told him enough just how much I loved him.

Forever in my heart, but life knows no such thing as eternity.

Everything ends and everything changes. And it's cruel we don't know when.

I can't help but wonder, how different it would be if we knew those were the last moments with our loved ones - our last smiles, our last words, our last embrace.

Our last kiss.

I don't remember what Sebastian said to me after that, I wish I could. I don't remember his exact words, but they were beautiful and almost made me cry there and then.

He told me I was his light, he told me I'd given him something he had never had before. A family.

He was my rock, when I lost my hold on things, I knew I could always rely on him. He was there even when I didn't want him to be, because he loved me in a way I never was loved by any other man. Unconditionally, for who I was.

I was that rose, the one on my back. My thorns were hidden- my depression, my nightmares, come and go, over and over again like a never-ending drama.

Sebastian was there every time, ready to hold me up, ready to love me no matter what.

"I am the lucky one, for having you by my side. You never want me to change, you let me be me. You never ask me for anything," I remember telling him this, looking into his dark brown eyes, seeing that spark -the one I had seen in that club many years back, when I had first met him.

He still looked at me that way, like I was a maze, a leap a faith, so deep but so worth the jump.

"Because you give me everything, without me asking," he kissed my head and held me a little, as the wind blew harder.

My back was naked, my white, long flowy summer dress whipped against my legs. I looked around hoping to see my parents any minute. They would never miss Eddy's performance, they would never miss their grandson's play.

I never saw them again. Maybe I will, one day when it's all over. When I'll be free again, in another life.

"Wait for me here, I'll be right back," Sebastian let go of me gently and promised it would only take him a minute, he wouldn't miss the beginning of the play.

I saw him disappear through the crowd of tourists and locals, to the left corner of the square. He seemed to stop at a stand, I couldn't see which one but I smiled, sensing he was onto something.

I was cold, but I wasn't shaking, not until my phone rang and I heard his voice on the other end.

"Ciao Andrea," he hissed my name with a certain pleasure, like a snake when it torments its prey.

That's just what I was, his prey. Alejandro's voice paralyzed me, a hard cold slap in the face. My heart must have stopped, shivers ran up my back and I suddenly didn't know if I was cold or hot anymore. I was terrified.

"Surprised?" he hissed again and my fingers reached for my mouth, just as I let out a sound.

I wanted to tell him I wasn't, because deep down a part of me always knew it was just a matter of time. A part of me had been dreading the moment.

The devil always comes for you, always hands you the cheque and comes to collect its winnings.

The words choked in my throat, I felt like I was dying. For a moment I wished I was, then I thought about Eddy.

"I took him, Eddy is with me," Alejandro spat out the words and the world started spinning, like I was going to throw up.

He took him, he took him. I looked around, looked through the crowd, behind the stage and saw nothing. My mouth made no sound, but my heart broke in a thousand pieces.

Too many people, too many voices around me, I couldn't see. I couldn't think. Breathe.

He took him, he took him.

My mind was in a loop. He had taken my life, my life. The only reason I was still alive, the only reason why I kept fighting the demons that haunted me at night.

I could fight all I wanted but this time, this demon wasn't going away. I wasn't dreaming, I was living the nightmare.

"Smile, love. Don't let anyone figure out what is happening or I swear to god you'll never see Eddy again," Alejandro snapped and I nodded.

I knew he could see me, he'd been studying me. For how long? How did I not notice?

"Please don't hurt him…" I whispered the words, breathing in and out fast but Alejandro didn't let me say another word.

"Listen to me and listen to me good because I won't say this again," he snarled. "You choose to fuck me over, you ran away with that son of a bitch and took my son away. But I am willing to give you another chance, you can choose again. For the last time Andrea, so choose wisely," he paused for what felt like an hour.

His words pierced right through me, daggers straight to my heart. I imagined him smiling, taking pleasure in my heavy breathing, in my silent sobs.

"What is your choice, Andrea?"

My choice, his words, I wanted desperately to believe his words, but I wasn't that naïve.

The devil lies, the devil controls. He doesn't give you a choice. He takes you where he wants. And that's exactly what Alejandro did. He took me, because he took my son, my life away from me and I had no choice but to follow him into the darkness.

SEBASTIAN

I made my way back to her, holding the blue stoned pendant in my hand. My jewel, my woman, I thought I held her tight, I thought I had her but Andrea was there only physically, my Andrea was gone.

She was so good to hide it or maybe I was too high on our love to see, see her change. I wrapped my arms around her and kissed her nose. She shifted a little and barely smiled, but she smiled nevertheless.

"I saw this, I thought it was perfect for you," I fastened the necklace around her neck and stared at it, how it dangled over her chest. Blue like her eyes, blue like the deepness of the sea.

"Beautiful and unique like you," I kissed her lips and she kissed me back, with abandonment and awe, I really thought I knew her.

It was her goodbye, her silent and hidden goodbye. Our last kiss.

"I'm running back home to get a jacket, I am cold," I was still holding her in my arms, her finger hooked around the back of my jeans, when she mumbled the words and I looked into her eyes.

She stared at me like…I don't know how to explain it, I didn't know what that look meant.

Tired? Andrea looked tired, yes. I convinced myself that was it.

Why didn't she ever listen to me? I smiled. I had told her about the jacket on our way out, but Eddy had been so eager to head to the town square, Andrea had shrugged it off and walked outside without going back for one.

"I'll be right back," she mumbled the words and squeezed my hand a little.

I took her arm and kissed the inside of her wrist, breathing in her scent. I loved to do that and feel her pulse, feel her body shake a little, as my lips brushed against her skin. She'd always giggle and complain it tickled.

She didn't giggle, not that time. Why didn't I see that?

I waited there for ten minutes, before grabbing my phone and calling her cell. I didn't even turn to watch her walk away from me, now I wished I had.

No, I wished I had fucking realized something was wrong, I was blinded. I didn't want to see, I'd let my guard down. I never really knew just how much a mother could sacrifice, how good she could lie to save her son's life.

CHAPTER 9

THE MASTER OF PUPPETS

ANDREA

I ran down the hill, seeing nothing, feeling nothing but heartache. I cursed my name for taking so long, I cried and screamed all the way to the boat.

Alejandro was waiting for me at the docks, his boat the only one still lit, everyone was at the town square.

Perfect timing, he had planned this from the very beginning, to perfection. I knew how twisted his mind was, I knew how nothing was left to fate or circumstances. Alejandro was the master of puppets and I was still his little doll- we all were- making me do exactly what he wanted. I had no choice. He had taken Eddy.

Let him be okay, let him be okay. Please, let him not know that Eddy is not his son, I prayed the truth was kept hidden. I wanted to lie, I needed to lie to play his game and keep Eddy alive.

If he'd ever found out the truth, about Eddy being Sebastian's son, god only knew what Alejandro would be capable of. He would have killed him in front of me, revenge was all he cared about. He didn't even care about Eddy, not really like a father should. I knew it was just a matter of pride and honour. He thought he owned him, owned us both.

"Andrea," he mumbled my name when he saw me stepping on his black yacht.

His men pulled me in, but I pushed their hands off me immediately.

Don't touch me, I wanted to shout in their faces.

They disgusted me, all of them. I looked around the boat, searched their consumed, evil faces and silently cursed every single one of them. They had no life, they had no soul.

Dead, they were all dead to me.

If anything happened to Eddy, I would make sure to remember their faces and kill them all. One by one. Or be their curse, the ghost that haunted their empty, meaningless lives forever. If there was any justice, any justice at all in this world or the next- in the afterlife- I would have it my way.

"I see you made your choice," he smiled, his eyes examining me closely.

I stared at him, my heart pounding in my chest, my breathing fast from running.

My biggest regret, my biggest mistake, he was back.

I hadn't seen him in so long, his hair might have been shorter, but the rest – his dark features, his arrogant posture, his piercing glare. Alejandro hadn't changed one bit, I don't know what I was expecting to see but what I saw was exactly the man I'd fallen in love with years back.

That smile, cunning demon that he was. My distress pleased him, that twisted son of a bitch.

"I did what you wanted. I kept my promise," my voice shook but I pressed on nevertheless. "Now you keep yours. Don't hurt anyone."

Not just Eddy, my thoughts went to Sebastian, to my parents. Alejandro had promised me he wouldn't touch them, if I'd choose to run away with him and not tell anyone. He promised they would all be safe.

"You did the right thing," Alejandro nodded, as he brought the cigarette to his crooked mouth, leaning back on the leather couch.

He took in a drag, my eyes stayed on the trail of smoke coming out of his lips.

Poison, poison him, I cursed his name under my breath.

"Where is Eddy?" I asked, my lips trembling as I spoke.

Nothing, Alejandro didn't answer me, he kept staring, taking in the sight of me, his eyes darting to my hair, my eyes, all the way down my body.

I suddenly felt cold and exposed, my arms wrapped over my chest. I held on tight to my shoulders, knowing I'd just stepped right inside the predator's lair.

"Where is Eddy?" this time I raised my voice a little, taking a step forward, my hands shaky.

"I did what you asked me to. I am here. Where is Eddy?" I yelled, this time launching myself forward, like I wanted to hit him, like I wanted to hurt him for everything that he'd done and was still doing to me. To our son.

Alejandro didn't even flinch, he just took another drag of his cigarette, as one of his men grabbed me from behind and held me in place.

"Let go of me!" I kicked and yelled, but my voice seemed to crash against the waves. We were at sea, sailing away fast from Folegandros, the wind cold and hard on my face.

Still I never closed my eyes, I kept them on Alejandro, hard. Pure hatred.

"If you hurt him, I swear Alejandro…" I cried and screamed, my legs still kicking the soldier behind me.

"You think I would hurt my son?" Alejandro stood up and walked towards me slowly.

Don't come near me, I smelled the tobacco on his breath as he spoke again, right in my face.

"Our son is alive and well, Andrea," he kept staring into my eyes, his lips almost brushed against mine, I feared he would move closer.

But he didn't. Alejandro just smirked and touched my hair.

I turned my head away, tried to free my hands, but the soldier was still holding me tight.

"You really thought you could get away from me, didn't you?" he groaned, tilting his head to the side, searching my face. "You really thought I wouldn't come looking for you? To finish off what I'd started?"

"Stay away from me," I screamed into the wind, refusing to look at him, but Alejandro grabbed my chin and forced his empty, dark eyes into mine.

I saw the flames of hell, I saw the perdition of his tormented, evil soul.

"I always keep my promises, Andrea. Always. Remember all the things I told you? Remember?" Alejandro said through gritted teeth.

We were so close, our noses almost touched, I fought the urge to spit in his face. I couldn't. I still had to see Eddy, I still had to make sure my son was okay.

"What did I say would happen if you ran away from me, huh? What?" he glared at me and I searched his face frantically, my pulse picked up.

What? My breathing became hysteric, as I started to realize what Alejandro was referring to.

"Don't you dare leave me, don't you dare run away from me. Don't forget I know where to find you, where to find your family."

"My parents…" I sucked in a breath and let out a cry, my eyes closed for a moment, just enough to imagine my mother's face, my father's smile. They were gone, I knew they were, my heart knew.

"Look at me," Alejandro roared while shaking me a little, I opened my eyes and spat the words.

"Megvàdolhatsz!" *May you be damned!* I screamed at the top of my lungs, but Alejandro didn't even flinch.

He held on to me tighter and shook me again.

"Blame me, Andrea. You can blame me all you want but it's your fucking fault," he barked. "You thought you could run from me, run from my punishment but you can't. You know why Andrea?"

His piercing dark stare cut through me, while his fingers moved down to my shoulder.

"Because I am right here, I was here the whole time," his finger tapped over my chest and I jerked away again. "I am deep like a wound, permanent like a scar, Andrea. You can't run away from me, because I am always with you, wherever you go. I am the devil lurking in the shadows. And the devil always comes to collect his possessions," his lips pressed hard on mine then and I closed my eyes shut, letting out a single, broken cry.

It was helpless, I was in his hands. I had handed myself over to him and in that moment I thought he could do to me whatever he wanted. It didn't matter, not anymore. I had lost everything- my parents, my life- everything but I still had to see Eddy, I had to keep it together for him. I had to make sure he was safe, I had to do everything I could to keep him from Alejandro.

"Mommy," a soft whisper, excruciating like the cry of a little boy, I heard Eddy's voice somewhere from inside the yacht and I suddenly felt like I could breathe again.

My heart, my love. I kicked harder and out the corner of my eye, I saw Alejandro nod, before his soldier released me.

I pushed everyone out of the way and stepped inside the boat.

"Eddy!" I shouted seeing him there, still wearing his play costume, shaking and huddled in a corner with a soldier watching over him.

"Eddy," I scooted him up and kissed his hair, his forehead, my arms tight around him, trying desperately to shield him from the rest of the people on the boat.

Don't look at them, don't listen to them, I thought closing my eyes shut, as I heard him sob against my chest confused.

"Where are we going mommy?" he asked looking up at me, his eyes red from crying.

Oh god I am so sorry, I let out a cry and shook my head.

"It's okay," I lied, because how could I not? How could I've hurt him more, by telling him the truth?

Where were we going? Back to the nightmare, back to being captive, back to hell. No way out this time, no hope.

Before I could say anything else, I felt his hand touch my shoulder, rubbing the bare, tanned skin, right where Sebastian had touched me- kissed me- and I jerked away, turning around to glare at Alejandro.

My eyes stayed on him, as I took small steps backwards deeper into the room, still holding Eddy tight to my chest.

Don't touch me, my stare spoke louder than words.

I was only there for Eddy, for my son.

As Alejandro's hand slowly dropped to his side, I took another step inside the boat and murmured:

"I hate you."

CHAPTER 10
HYSTERIA

SEBASTIAN

Her phone was ringing with no answer. I called her three times. The last time I tried, I was already halfway home, running down the cobbled road. I was running home, I didn't know why.

Cold drops of sweat rolled down my back, my muscles tensed. Something was off, I could feel something wasn't right, even though my head told me otherwise.

You're paranoid, maybe someone had stopped her on the way home or on the way back to the town square, Andrea was probably talking or walking back for the play.

I reached our house and she was nowhere to be seen. My legs picked up the pace, still holding the phone to my ear as it rang and rang and rang.

Click.

"Hello?" I said immediately, not hearing the monotonous ringing sound anymore.

My key turned the lock and I opened the door wide, into the dark empty living room of our house. I turned the lights on and looked around.

Empty, nobody was there. No sign of Andrea.

"Hello?" I said again, trying to control the panic in my voice, but my eyes went wide as soon as I heard a loud sigh on the other end.

"She's gone," that cigarette, throaty voice, the way the words slurred around his tongue, I recognized him immediately.

Alejandro De la Cruz, my hands curled into a fist.

"Where is she? What the fuck did you do with her?" I yelled into the phone, turning sideways, running through all the rooms. Nothing, nothing.

Andrea.

She was gone, he had taken her or killed her? Or… *My Andrea.*

"Where the fuck is she?" I yelled again and heard him laugh on the other end.

His chuckle, how he took his time to answer, long exhausting pauses, I felt the urge to smash the phone to the ground but instead I gripped it, held on to it tighter and closed my eyes, breathing faster and faster.

"What do you want?" I asked and heard him laugh again.

"From you? From a worthless rat like you? Nothing. Nothing that is yours," Alejandro lowered his voice and pressed on. "I came back to take what's mine, Killer. My wife, my son. Do you really think you could take them away from me- a meaningless piece of scum, a rat, a police officer worth shit- and fuck me over like that? Tell me Killer, do you think I am a whore, that you can fuck me over like that?" he hissed and I closed my eyes shut, biting my lip hard.

I tasted metal, fear and pain, as drops of blood trickled down my mouth.

My son, my son, he had taken Eddy, he had taken them both.

"If you lay a finger on them, I swear…" I roared, punching the wall in front of me.

"What? You swear, what? You think you can threaten me, Killer? You think you can tell me what to do? You can't do shit. You are nobody," he paused. "In fact you don't even exist anymore."

I listened in, as I paced the room, brushing my hair back, not knowing what to do, where to go. Were they still on the island? How long had Andrea been missing? *Twenty minutes.* No boats were at sea, maybe I could still stop them, find them.

Just as I was about to walk outside the house, I heard his voice again and his words ripped away every last bit of hope left in me.

"We are far away already, we are at sea. I am not going to lie to you about where we are going. I am taking them back to Italy with me. Why am I telling you all this, Killer?" Alejandro paused. "Because you can't come after us. I made sure you wouldn't. You see, Sebastian I had time to figure things out. I had all the time in the world after you dumped me in prison. Time to make my revenge perfect. I thought about everything."

Sebastian Esposito, the undercover cop, didn't exist anymore. Alejandro had accessed my files, bribed every police officer he could in Naples and had the man in charge of my missions, removed. No more double life, no more secret identities. I existed as the criminal, as the offender of my undercover missions. I was the Sebastian Esposito that was sent to jail, the one that robbed, the one that had assaulted and done all the shit I had been accused of, just to make my job plausible.

"If you set foot back in Italy, I will kill you. I have my soldiers, my friends, friends of friends after you. You come near us, I'll kill you. You are a criminal there, I will have you arrested for stalking and attempted homicide. I don't know, what could be more fun?" he snickered in the background and added. "You see my thinking, Killer? How elaborate my revenge is? I could have killed you, put you out of your misery. Instead I left you there alone, to spend the rest of your life with regrets and knowing I took everything away from you."

Eddy, he doesn't know. He doesn't know he's mine.

My chest felt lighter, it was the only thing that kept me sane, allowed me to keep it together. For him, for Andrea.

"If you think I'm going to sit here and let you get away with this …" I started to say but his laughter muffled my words.

"I already have, Killer. I already have."

"How do I know you are not bluffing? Let me talk to her, I want to know they are okay," I said and he laughed again, the grumbling sound of his voice almost drove me crazy.

"Whether they are okay or not, is none of your concern. They are mine and I will do with them as I please, Killer. Every single thing that I want. For my pleasure, only for my pleasure," he hissed the last words and I paced the room, covering my face.

"No!" I shouted, "No!!! You son of a bitch, I'll kill you. Do you hear me? I won't rest until I find you!" but the phone went dead.

"SON OF A BITCH!" I smashed the phone against the wall and threw everything that was in front of me.

Vases, chairs, plates, picture frames, they crashed to the floor as I let out another cry and yanked at my hair again.

I opened my eyes and I saw blood everywhere. I imagined Andrea being hit, slapped.

Raped.

"NO! NO!" I shouted and went to the terrace.

In the darkness of the night, I shouted her name over and over.

"ANDREA!!!!!!!!!!!!!" I pulled my hair, searching the shore, feeling helpless.

My eyes filled with tears as I called out for her, slumping to the floor, holding my face.

"Eddy," I cried out. "No… no, god no!" I kept both hands over my eyes and dug the nails into my skin, as I broke down into pieces.

I would have ripped my own flesh apart, if it would've stopped my heart from hurting, if that would've brought them back to me. But I was alone, they were gone. Forever.

I am going to feel sick...

I don't know where I found the strength to pick myself up, but I did. I managed to stand up again and walk back inside, trying to think, trying to reason with myself.

You can get them back. You can save them.

I scanned the place for something, clues, ideas. *Think, think!*

I walked around the house grabbing stuff- a knapsack, water, a knife.

"I'll kill that son of a bitch, I'll kill that son of a bitch," I kept saying, walking fast through the living room, silent tears rolling down my cheeks, as I slowly came to terms with what had just happened.

I had let my guard down and now they were gone. Just like that, under my very nose, Alejandro had taken them away from me. My family, the very essence of my life.

I have to find them, my head kept telling me over and over again.

Out the corner of my eye, I saw the pieces of our lives smashed on the floor and I bent down to pick up a picture. Me, Eddy and Andrea on the beach, under our house. Together.

My fingers brushed against Eddy's cheeks, around Andrea's beautiful warm smile.

Our home, the memories we had together, I had thrown them everywhere, I had let Alejandro destroy us.

It's my fault, the thought haunted me as I held my face, my bloodied hands began to shake.

I'd had the chance to kill him and I'd failed. I'd let my emotions, my love for Andrea and Eddy, get the best of me and I hadn't finished the job.

A bullet to his head, I promised myself I wouldn't fail again. Not this time. No matter how things turned out, I was ready to die. But I was going to take Alejandro with me to hell.

I slipped that picture into the bag, along with the things I needed for my journey back to Italy.

That was where I was going, back to my country, chasing the past. There was nothing else I could do, no time to waste. I'd wasted too much already.

I ran down to the docks, to the wooden sheds we used as storage near the fishing boats.

"Come on, come on, come on," I mumbled, my hands thrusting through all the junk in there.

Fishing rods, nets, boxes of tools, I went through them all until I found it, the small compartment, an opening in the wooden floor.

I pulled the lock open and slid my hand into it. The hole was too deep, I had to lay down on the floor and dive in with my shoulder to reach for it, but I did. I grabbed the black tied-up bag and tore it open, as fast as I could. All that I had kept from my past life was there. Money, passports, a knife, my gun.

A thud, a muffled sound, like when something falls on a carpet. I barely heard it but it stopped me cold.

Left, I turned immediately and saw the shadow of a man reach out for me in the darkness of the shed.

Fuck, I dived to the floor, taking the man down with me, grabbing his arms and rolling to the side.

It was too dark to make out a face, but I recognized the metal sound of a gun as it hit the wooden floor.

Shit, I punched him in the face, once, twice, my blows fast and hard.

He hit me once, right bellow my neck and I yelled in pain, but I pinned him down nevertheless, pushing all my weight onto him. I was stronger, broader and a walking human rage. The Killer was back.

Nobody can stop me.

"Who sent you? Who?" I took his arm and twisted it until I heard it crack.

Broken. The man cried out and I cursed under my breath.

"He sent you to finish the job, didn't he?"

Alejandro. That son of a bitch, that coward.

"He sent you to die," I said and pulled him up, wrapped an arm around his neck and squeezed it tight. So tight, the man kicked and tried to break my hold, to catch his breath but choked out a cry.

Choke, choke.

I held him in place, nearly snapped his head off, but then two arms grabbed me from behind and I was pulled away, fast.

"What the fuck…" someone else was there, another man.

How many? Armed?

I tried to look around, but it was too dark. I kicked out at nothing and no one in particular. I tried to turn but the man I'd pinned to the floor was now standing up, coughing and holding his arm in pain.

I caught sight of his worn out, bruised face thanks to the light filtering through the wooden cracks in the shed, just as he launched himself at me.

His fist slammed into my jaw, I cursed.

"Figlio di puttana!" *Son of a bitch,* he yelled and told the other man his arm was broken.

"Take the gun, shoot the motherfucker," the one behind me yelled.

I tried to headbutt him but he dodged the blow and the one with the broken arm kicked me in the stomach.

Pain shot through my ribs, I coughed and tried to catch my breath.

No air, the blow had sucked it out of my lungs, my chest filled with fire.

"The gun!!!" he shouted again.

"It's on the fucking floor somewhere," the other one said.

Breathe, think, I thought as I tried to catch my breath.

I didn't know which part of the shed we were in, I didn't know what was behind us or to the side. All I knew was that I had to take them down, I had to smash their heads in before they smashed mine.

My chest still aching, I pushed backwards with all the strength I had left in me. The pain became almost unbearable, I cringed searching for air, but I didn't stop.

"Son of a ….!" I let out a wild roar, as we went to the wall.

The man hit his head with a loud thump and shouted, his grip loosened around me for just an instant, but I didn't hesitate. I pulled away, turned and banged the man hard against the wall, my hands twisted around his neck.

I banged him against that wall once, twice, then I dropped him to the floor and hit the other man, as he tried to grab me.

Not this time, fucker.

I punched them until they weren't moving anymore, until they stopped fighting. It was no use, they didn't stand a chance. I wasn't myself anymore, I was The Killer and I was ready to do anything to save my family.

No mercy, no doubts.

The ropes in the shed came in handy. I tied Alejandro's men up so tight, I saw their wrists turn red in just a few seconds. I didn't care, I wanted them to regret it, I wanted them to curse the day they were born. Coming after me had been a bad idea, their death sentence.

I found a light and then some tape, I covered both their mouths and then threw water over their heads.

In just a matter of minutes, they were both awake and glaring at me, as I slid in the cartridge and pointed the gun at their heads.

"Call him," I said to the first one, the man that had tried to hold me back.

He glared at me, as I held up his phone, the one I'd taken from his trousers.

"Call him, tell him you killed me and I'll let you live," I said and removed the tape from his mouth.

The other one started to shake, his right arm slumped to the side, bloody and broken.

"Fuck you," the man spat on the floor and I punched him in the face.

No, fuck you!

He let out a cry, blood running from his nose.

"I'll tell you one more time and one more time only: call him and tell him you killed me. Now."

"Go fuck yourself," he spat out again and I pointed the gun to his head.

I smirked but my face hardened. *Wrong answer.*

"See you in hell," I pulled the trigger and the man's eyes rolled back, his head slumped forward.

I stared at his lifeless body as it hung over the ropes, while the other man let out a scream. The sound came out muffed by the duct-tape.

I ripped it off and stared at him attentively.

"You want to go next?" I asked and watched him shake his head, shaking to the core.

An easier one to break.

"Call him, tell him you killed me. Now."

He nodded and I held the phone to his ear, he was still shaking as it rang and when Alejandro's voice answered the call, I saw the man's eyes go wide.

"It's done," he simply said.

"Good," I heard Alejandro say on the other end.

It was so quiet all of a sudden, I heard the chuckle, the satisfaction in his voice, I wanted nothing more than to rip that smile off his face.

I will.

"Stay away for a while. Report when you get back," click.

The phone went dead and the man looked at me expectantly.

"I've done my part," he stuttered and I nodded.

He had. He'd done exactly what I'd asked but it wasn't enough. Not enough to save him. Not for me, for the man I'd become.

You let him go, he'll come after you and try to kill you. Kill him first.

"Good little soldier," I kept nodding as I stood up and placed the phone in my pocket. "But I lied," I said and aimed the gun to his head.

"I did what you asked," he cried out, his eyes darting to the side, to his friend's lifeless body.

That's going to be you in a couple of seconds.

"Do you know who I am?" I asked, pushing the gun against his temple.

The man closed his eyes for a moment, as tears ran down his cheeks.

"They used to call me The Killer, I could take a life with my bare hands. I thought I'd left that part of my life in the past. I'd become a good man, a merciful one. Then you came here and tried to fuck me over. You tried to kill me," the man whimpered as I carried on, the fireworks from the town square lit the night. "You came to war… and you lost."

I fired the gun, never taking my eyes off him.

Dead, I took his meaningless life and didn't feel a single thing. I looked at him and saw Alejandro, I saw my enemy, my fight.

The war.

As I picked up my knapsack and cleaned my face with a piece of cloth, I realized I wasn't myself anymore. What happened that night changed me forever. Sebastian Esposito was gone, dead, he left with Andrea on that boat together with Alejandro. I was The Killer now and I would stop at anything, I wouldn't let emotions interfere with my mission ever again.

Kill everyone in your way, kill them all and don't stop until you find them, I promised myself, I promised Andrea and Eddy.

I promise.

I cleaned up and headed out of the shed, locking the door behind me. Then, I walked to the harbour and found the boat I was looking for at the end of the docks. The head fishermen saw me and waved, as he ordered his men to hurry up, it was time to sail out to sea.

"What are you doing here, *Malaka*?" *Asshole.* He laughed and I jumped on the boat. "It's your day off."

"I know, I need a ride," I said and slapped hands with him.

I must have looked horrible, I could feel my cheek pulse where that fucker had punched me.

"Are you okay?" the fisherman asked and I nodded.

"I need to go home," I simply said and he eyed me for an instant before nodding.

"Welcome aboard, man."

Then he walked to his control station and the boat slowly moved out of the harbour.

I kept my eyes on the coast the whole time. I could see the house, our house. Lights were off, no sign of life inside. No life left for us there on the island.

No happy ending, my eyes hardened as the island slowly became just a haze in the dark mist.

Just memories, all we have are memories Andrea.

Our life together flashed before my eyes. Happiness lasts only for the blink of an eye, sometimes I wonder if I hadn't imagined everything, if it hadn't all been a dream. Then I'd remember something Andrea or Eddy had said to me and it's like I could feel their touch, their laughs and the sparks. I could feel the sparks, it was all real.

Come back to me, I looked down at the black water and felt breathless, like that darkness was calling my name, telling me to give up. And just jump, end my life. My life was over anyway, oblivion was taunting me.

You will never see them again.

You will never get there in time to save them.

But then I looked up and caught sight of the coast, of the land we were leaving behind, and I felt it again. Hope, I wasn't too late, I could save them. I could get them out of there and set them free.

I let that hope guide me through the dark night, holding on tight to our memories together.

I didn't know If we'd ever find our way back to the island, our way back to our life there and it didn't matter. I wasn't coming back, I knew this was the end. For me. There was nothing I wouldn't do to save them, nothing. I'd give up my happiness, sell my soul, agree to torture, death. I would have died for them. Anything to save my wife and son.

I'm coming, I thought as the wind picked up at sea.

I was going after them, I was going to kill Alejandro De la Crux. I had nothing to lose. I was dead without them anyway.

Without you I am nothing.

CHAPTER 11
PRISON OF GOLD

ANDREA

Have you ever had that feeling, an uneasiness inside you, when waking up from a dream? A dream so wonderful and perfect, you twist and turn in bed, feeling so stupid for even thinking it could be real?

For a moment, I thought it was. Sebastian, Eddy and I, our happy ending felt so real.

Two days since I last saw him, I closed my eyes, holding Eddy in my arms, as our last words to each other replayed in my mind.

I hadn't even had a chance to say goodbye, he wouldn't ever have let me go. Sebastian would have never understood. There wasn't any other way with Alejandro. I couldn't have let him leave with my Eddy, with our son.

Please forgive me Sebastian, I bit my lip and held back a tear.

My heart broke for us, but I kept my shoulders straight as the car stopped in front of the De la Crux mansion early in the morning.

It was dark and cold, the sun still to rise, but it didn't matter. I could see the mansion clearly, I remembered those walls, I remembered the loneliness I had felt living there. Being used, feeling lost. I knew what I was walking into.

I'm back.

My prison stood before me, eerie and imposing. The chains would be tighter this time, soldiers would be on my back night and day.

I wasn't escaping, not even if left unattended. Eddy was the deal breaker, I couldn't risk his life. I knew better, this time I knew I couldn't run away. You can't escape from someone like Alejandro, the devil always finds a way.

Marrying him, I had struck a deal and all I could do was learn how to live with the regret. Find out how to save Eddy. Maybe my life was over, maybe I was nothing more than Alejandro's pretty doll, but I could still be a shield, between him and Eddy.

I will live to protect you, I kissed his hair and marched up to the front door, Alejandro right behind us.

Like a silent prayer, I asked God to give me strength.

Life carried on before my eyes, mine didn't. I was back to where it had all started, sacrifices had been in vain, hearts were fooled, hopes were crashed.

I tossed and turned at night, holding Eddy in my arms, never letting him go. He never stopped asking questions, he never stopped trying to understand what was happening. How could I have told him the truth?

"Why did we run away from the island?"
"Where is Sebastian?"
"When can we see him?"
"Is he coming for us?"
"Why did we leave with dad?"
"Is he going to hurt us?"

A six-year-old looks at you expectantly and you know you'll have to lie. You'll disappoint him anyway, whether you tell him the truth or not. The best I could do was lie, tell him what I knew he could cope with.

"We had to come back home. Sebastian will come one day, but Eddy please don't talk about him in front of your father. He won't hurt us," I tried to smile, but my hands were shaking, my nerves were failing me.

Lie to survive, I hated myself.

If it hadn't been for Eddy, I would've shoved a whole box of tranquillizers down my throat and wait for death- sweet, careless death.

I had nothing, no more dreams, no more secret wishes. I let life happen around me, without interfering, without taking a stand.

Empty, my mind, my heart they were completely empty.

What else was left for me to do? When you take away someone's dreams, someone's hopes, you take away their will to breathe and fight. I wasn't fighting, not physically, not with myself anymore, not even with Alejandro.

When we walked back into that house one morning at dawn, I left my heart and soul at the door. I gave it up and in a way it was liberating. I stopped hurting, blocking everything that wasn't about Eddy. What was going to happen to me? I didn't care.

But Eddy, he was my only worry, my only thought.

Slowly, as the days went by I started to think of how to save him, planning his escape. It was too late for me, but not for him. Yes, he was damaged, I saw that for the first time when he'd sleepwalked around the house on the island. The house where we'd once been happy, together, with Sebastian.

Sebastian, I shook away the thought immediately and squeezed Eddy's hand tighter.

Eddy was damaged, he had cried all night as we had travelled back to Italy, sobbing out questions, avoiding Alejandro's stare, hiding his face against my chest.

It was true, my dreams had been crushed, but slowly my mind had started creating new ones. And they were all about Eddy, on how to get him safely out of there, out of Alejandro's life.

The secret I had been keeping for six years- the identity of his real father- I would take it to the grave with me.

And that secret, that lie, was going to help me get my son out of Alejandro's hands. He didn't care about anyone and anything, a man like him would put a gun to his brother's head without blinking twice.

But Eddy was his blood, Eddy was his future or so he thought. That was going to be my weapon, my deadly secret move against Alejandro.

I had soldiers around me all day, every day. I had no gun, no chance of running away. My battle couldn't be physical, my rebellion would be emotional.

Chaos and doubt, I wanted them to spread like a disease, like venom in Alejandro's mind and soul.

I was going to put up the best resistance I could manage, until I had the chance to send Eddy away, make him disappear somehow. Even if that meant I'd have to give him up, give up to the idea of seeing him become the man I was so desperately trying to raise.

My sacrifice for his safety. Anything for my son.

Every prisoner has a keeper. Donna Filomena was mine. She followed me like she was my shadow. From the kitchen to the dining room, then back to my room. Alejandro's mother was my personal guard around the house. She carried her weapons inside, ready to hit me. Her words.

"I never trusted you," she told me one day, as we were having breakfast.

I hadn't touched much of my food, just enough to keep me alive for Eddy- a piece of bread, a coffee and some juice.

My head was someplace else. I was watching my son play in the corner, a box of toys spread on the floor, and he made me smile. A smile of admiration, how children manage to pull themselves up and cope with problems. He couldn't help being a happy child, Eddy couldn't help hoping. Another thing I was going to have to preserve was that hope in him. He deserved to believe.

A tiny smile spread across my face, as I heard him laugh from the corner. A tiny smile, the first one in two weeks, but Donna Filomena wouldn't allow it. She was there, ready to fire, to strike me, to put me in my place, on my hands and knees again.

"I never trusted you and the influence you had on my son," she spat the words out, keeping her face straight.

Her coffee cup was back to her lips a moment later, like she hadn't just spoken to me.

Nobody spoke to me, if not to tell me where to go, what to do. Alejandro was keeping his distance from me, I hardly saw him in the days that followed our arrival.

From the guards I understood he was busy with his business outside of Rome. I prayed he wouldn't come to me, that he'd stay away and I'd be numb if he ever touched me.

"You don't know me, Donna Filomena," I murmured, as I stopped smiling immediately. It didn't really suit me anyway.

"I know you. Women like you," her voice came out cold again.

She wanted me to believe she was indifferent to me, but I could tell she wasn't. "You are a liar, you are a traitor. You are not the sort of woman my son needs."

Liar, traitor, I let her accusations wash over me, not letting them settle, but my pulse quickened just at the mention of lies. I was a liar.

"I'm sorry," I mumbled staring at her.

She looked up to me and wiped her lips with a napkin before speaking again. Her brown eyes and dark skin reminded me of Alejandro, but the way she moved, the way she spoke, her temperament was different. She was a woman of pride and honour, she was quiet and sneaky, the kind of woman that moves in the darkness, betrays you when you least expect it. My secrets, I feared for them with Donna Filomena at my back.

"You are sorry?" she questioned me.

"Yes, I am sorry I didn't run away far enough," I said and we stared at each other in silence- my cold blue eyes into her dark fiery ones.

Two women fighting a battle, two women and their weapons. *Two liars, face-to-face.*

"You think you did something honourable? Running away like that? Taking a son away from his father? Do you know what that does to a man? His wife and his son, fleeing? Leaving him to rot in jail?" she shook her head as she spoke and squinted at me.

Hate was the unspoken word, but Donna Filomena made sure I could feel it- all the hatred she felt for me.

You have no idea, I wanted to scream in her face, *no idea what it was like to be married to Alejandro, what he did to me when we were living in this house. How he'd abused me, used me and what he threatened to do to me when I left him.*

But I eyed Eddy and saw that he was still playing, serene and joyful with his toys, I took a deep breath and told her something else instead.

"I did it for Eddy. What was best for him. Look around you, Donna Filomena? Is this life? The life my son, your grandson deserves? What life is this? We have guards with us all the time, we drive around town with a bullet proof car, because Alejandro has been threatened so many times. Eddy is going to school with soldiers, he can't go out to play with the other kids. Tell me, Donna Filomena, is this the right thing to do? Come back here? Is this the life your grandson deserves?" my voice failed me at the end but I took another breath and pressed on. "I did what was best for Eddy, I wanted him to have a better life. He's not like Alejandro…"

"And who is he like? Like you?" the edge in her voice, I let it drop. I didn't question it, didn't answer her question. I simply shook my head and went on.

"If you care for Eddy, you'll see that this life is wrong. This life is going to kill him. And it's going to kill Alejandro one day, you know that."

She knew, the way she was looking at me, I could tell I had touched a soft spot but one thing a woman like Donna Filomena would never do, is show that your words had had an impact on her.

Her face stayed the same, composed, serious.

"For some reason Alejandro wants you by his side, for reasons I will never understand. You are an obsession, his weakness. He wants what he can't have and that's why he wants you, because you'll never truly be his," words flowed, like I wasn't really there in front of her, like she was talking to herself more than to me.

But then her eyes seemed to find a new focus, they were back on me, vivid.

"You will be his death, Andrea. I know you will."

ALEJANDRO

"Scream, I want to hear you scream," I twisted her hair around my arm and pulled, as I pounded into her. "Scream, Andrea. Tell me you're mine."

"I'm yours," she tilted her head back, opening wide and I groaned louder, filling her up.

If only it was you, if only it were true.

"Fuck," I cursed, staying inside her a few moments, before rolling to the side.

Her arms snaked around my back and that was when I usually took a step away from her. That time was no different. My whore tried to keep me close to her body, but I was already up, walking away naked, my hardness still pulsing.

In the dim light, I found my clothes and slipped my shirt on. My whore was still on the hotel bed, staring at me with wide, bright blue eyes, waiting for me to speak again.

She knew all too well she wasn't allowed to say a word to me, if not spoken to. My whore knew how to behave, she was well trained. I fucking loved that and hated it at the same time, resistance, rebellion- I wanted her to be more like my Andrea, the real Andrea.

Fucking sick motherfucker, I thought as I slid my pants on and pulled the zipper.

"Dress," I ordered and she scooted up in the ruffle of sheets, picking up her panties. "The car will take you back to my brother's club. Still no fucking with clients, Andrea. Do you understand?"

"Yes, sir," she nodded and slipped on the short, red dress she had on before.

I had almost ripped it off her, the eagerness to fuck her hard had clouded my thoughts.

Two weeks with my wife and son in the house and I'd been away, I'd kept my distance from them. From Andrea. I'd dragged them along with me and left immediately after, my attention was need elsewhere. Naples.

My trips had become more frequent, the clans there asking about me, buying my cocaine. I knew it, once they'd tasted top quality junk like mine, they couldn't go back to the shit they had been selling before.

With the help of two influential families, I was starting to rule the underskirts of that city.

Everything, I'd taken everything I could from there, my revenge was almost complete and I had a surprise for Andrea, for the real Andrea.

As a crooked grin spread across my face, my whore walked to stand in front of me and I took a good look at her, one of the last times if not the last time I'd see her.

Blonde messy hair, the hair of someone that had just been fucked hard, consumed and used by a sick, twisted man. Me.

I was leaving her, leaving my demons to haunt her, I was sure my whore would never be herself again after I was finished with her. My roughness was going to be her torment, my demands her nightmares.

Forget someone like me, someone that had possessed her like I had? She wouldn't. Never. I had fucked her for months, released my rage on her. I owned her, she wanted me to own her because I'd broken her and she didn't know how to put those pieces back together. She didn't know how to be without me.

How old was she? Twenty? I'd ruined her for good.

I was done with my whore, my wife was home, I had found my real Andrea. All I had to do now was take her, it was that easy. She was mine again. Mine to possess.

"When will I see you, master?" her shaky voice asked, more like a plea.

A plea that would cost her, she knew I would punish her for speaking to me but she had spoken anyway, because my whore had felt the distance I was putting between us. She knew it wouldn't be long before I'd dispose of her.

"You spoke to me," I groaned and grabbed her wrist. "You know better than to speak to me."

She nodded and sucked in a breath, knowing what was coming.

"Get down on your knees," I ordered and pulled down my zipper.

CHAPTER 12

ALL THAT IT TAKES

SEBASTIAN

"I can't wait for you to come home. I can't wait to wake up to you," Andrea sealed her wish with a kiss, my lips moved with hers. "Wake me up when you come home, I want to make you breakfast."

I looked into her eyes, lost myself in their beautiful shades of blue, and cupped her face.

"I want YOU for breakfast," I teased and she giggled, placing a hand over mine.

That sound, that giggle. So warm, real. Straight from the heart.

She told me she wanted to live, live US to the fullest and never miss a thing.

Neither did I.

"Promise me you'll be here when I come back," I said and she smiled a little.

"Sebastian," Andrea mumbled and I nodded, waiting for her to carry on with her thoughts.

Were we saying goodbye? It was dark outside.

"Wake up, Sebastian," Andrea said once and I shook my head a little, squinting my eyes.

Wake up? What…?

"Wake up, Sebastian," she whispered and smiled, touching my cheek. "Wherever you are, wake up my love."

My eyes snapped open and I sucked in a breath.

Windows, hard, dark seats. We were still moving, the train still had to stop.

It was just a dream, another one. I had had so many in the past few days, all about Andrea and Eddy.

Her smile, I saw it every time my eyes closed. Sometimes I imagined her in our house. Other times walking barefoot on the sand, Eddy running ahead, calling my name, eager to play with me, to spend the little time I had with him.

Time, I wish we'd had more.

I ran a hand through my hair and my eyes darkened. How many days since they had left? A week.

I lost track of time, I measured it in train stations, stops along the way. The sun rose and set over and over, the train crossed borders, while I kept drifting in and out of sleep. My dreams were all about them.

Andrea and Eddy.

I saw them everywhere, took them with me every step of the way. I was trying to do the impossible; go back to Italy, careful not to end up under Alejandro's radar or the police's.

Where are you, Sad Eyes?

I rubbed my face, as we crossed deserted lands, sunk in my seat, trying not to attract attention. I kept as low key as possible, changing trains every time I could. I had to wait for the night to travel, so I could take the least busy routes, less people in my way. Less authorities.

My journey seemed endless, the road to Italy long and winding. I had no idea what lay ahead for me, once I'd crossed that boarder. All I knew was that my identity, my real identity had been wiped.

I was somewhere in Montenegro, when I took the phone out and thought about calling my superior in the police. Useless, his phone was dead.

"Fuck," I cursed under my breath, dialling another number. His office.

Another man answered and I hung up immediately, not knowing who I could trust, who was Alejandro's inside man.

There was no way I could get a hold of him, the only man who knew who I really was in this world. I was alone.

Running a hand through my hair, I slumped lower in my seat, feeling sleep creep over me once again. It was still dark outside, I still had a couple of hours of peace, before having to hide all day again.

I turned to one side, then to the other, putting my feet up on the seat in front of me.

The carriage was empty, it was so early in the morning, the sky was pitch dark.

That's when I felt it. An itch behind my back. No, lower than that.

My pocket.

I slipped a hand in and took out a small piece of paper. The writing had been scribbled fast, just a few sentences, a note. A goodbye note.

Her hands in my pockets. Andrea.

My eyes grew wide, wider as they took in her last words to me.

"He took Eddy, I have to go. I can't let him take Eddy. Please forgive me, Sebastian. Don't try to stop me, don't look for us.

You were right. There is no happy ending for people like us, but Eddy will have his. He will. I promise you this.

We will meet again one day, someplace else. I will wait for you there, Sebastian. I'm yours.

Andrea"

I closed that piece of paper and held it tight in my hands, I pressed it to my forehead.

How did I not realize? How did I not see? My jaw tensed, as I fought back the tears.

In the silence of that carriage, I promised myself I wouldn't stop until I found them.

Till my last breath.

I would get them out of there and set them free forever.

I'm coming, I'm on my way, Sad Eyes.

After switching trains six times, I finally made it to Croatia. I continued my journey by foot for a while, eyeing the horizon. I looked at the sea and imagined Italy. I told myself that if I looked hard enough, I would see the coast. Italy was right there, in front of me. I had almost made it.

As I sat on the bus hours later, waiting to depart and cross the border to Italy, I wondered where they were, my son, my Sad Eyes. What were they doing?

Please let them be okay, I prayed but dark thoughts haunted me day and night, thoughts of Alejandro playing with my son, teaching him to be like him.

A monster.

Finding out he wasn't truly his son.

He'd kill him, I closed my eyes and took a deep breath.

That piece of scum forcing himself on Andrea, touching, violating her.

He's going to hurt her, I ran both hands through my hair and nearly pulled it all out.

He had hurt her, I knew he had. No matter how fast I tried to reach them, I knew it was too late. When the moment came to protect her, I had failed. I hadn't been there.

No matter how fast I tried, I knew irredeemable damage had already been done.

My Andrea.

My fingers dug in my scalp and I swallowed hard. It was all my fault, I hadn't finished the job when I'd had a chance. I'd failed to save her, I'd failed her and my family.

The agony ripped me apart, tore me in half.

I covered my eyes, hid behind my fingers for a few moments, trying to come to terms with my loss. Right when I felt I had everything, I had lost it all, to a demon.

"Passport," someone touched my arm and I jumped a little.

Had I dozed off? For an instant I felt lost, but I quickly realized where I was.

Still on that bus, still waiting for it to move out of the platform. Still at the Croatian border.

"Passport, please," the man- a police officer- asked me again and I nodded.

My hands dug inside my bag and I took out my ticket, my fake passport and my hope. I put it all in that man's hands.

Read it and give it back, I willed him, smiling a little, apologizing for being so slow. I had fallen asleep.

The man checked me out, checked the passport, then my picture again and kept the document in his hands, as he studied me closely, eyeing my belongings.

"Wait here," he barked and walked to the door.

My pulse quickened as I watched the end unfold before my eyes.

From my passenger window, I saw the police officer hand my passport to another one. Their fingers brushed against the picture, they examined the stamp, all the info closely.

Come on, come on, I thought, one hand already on my bag, the other one on the empty seat next to mine.

The policeman kept his eyes on me, as the other one called someone up on the radio and read the numbers.

AI76659Y, I read his lips. My passport number.

FUCK! My eyes darted to the front of the bus. Then to the back, where the other door was. It was open.

By the time my eyes were back on the police officers, I saw the one with the passport in his hands say something fast to his colleague.

FUCK!

They both turned my way but I wasn't there.

With a jolt, I was at the back door, out of it in a second, bag behind my back, running fast and crossing the highway.

I crossed it, never looking back, never thinking twice. That was the only way to escape, the safest way to cross the border. Through the woods on the other side of that damn highway.

"Stop!" they shouted behind me, I heard them running.

They were close, they were on foot, cutting through the trees and bushes like me. But I was faster, it was the fear that made me faster. I wasn't afraid of being caught, I was afraid of being held up, of wasting time. I had no time to lose. I was late already, late for Eddy, for Andrea.

My legs were quick, I crossed the woods in sharp bends, never following a straight line. I ran through brambles – their thorns digging into my skin, into my face- and I never stopped, not until I had lost them. Not until I had crossed the border.

I made it to Italy, tying myself under a truck at the last gas stop in Croatia. I couldn't risk being caught, being shot to death. It wasn't my time to die. Not yet, I had to find my family and kill Alejandro De la Crux. I had to make sure that fucking bullet crossed his heart for real this time. I was going to be there and I was going to make sure. Then and only then could I rest in peace.

CHAPTER 13

TORTURE

ANDREA

The devil lurks in the dark, until he knows he can take you down. Until he's sure you're in his hands.

I was in his hand, I had nowhere to go, nowhere to hide.

Alejandro came into the living room one evening before dinner, my whole body shook with fear seeing him again. Like I wasn't expecting him, like I wasn't ready.

You are crazy, I wanted to scream to myself.

How many times had I held Eddy at night, secretly hoping to never see him again, hoping that someone would kill him- one of his enemies or one of his men backstabbing him?

How many nights had I gone through never closing my eyes, too scared he would come to me? Because I knew he would. Sooner or later.

It was sooner than expected.

Alejandro crossed the living room slowly that evening and eyed me warily, until he reached Eddy, who had suddenly stopped watching cartoons. He was looking up, his big blue eyes too young to fear the man, the monster, the heartless demon staring down at him.

Without saying a word, Alejandro tossed his black jacket on the couch, shooting me a glance, I couldn't look away from. I was terrified of what it meant. His dark, small eyes looking up and down my body. I froze.

So did Eddy, he didn't move an inch. He just stared at the man he thought was his father, solemn, no smile on his lips, but with kind eyes. He couldn't see what I saw.

He will, he will.

"Ciao, Eddy," Alejandro said and sat beside him, not on the floor, but on the couch.

"Ciao," Eddy's voice was low, but steady.

I straightened up in my seat, not sure what to do, if I should've run over and hugged him, shielded him from Alejandro and whatever he wanted to say or do to him.

What if he found out? What if he knows about Eddy? My pulse picked up, doubt kept haunting me.

That is the thing about secrets. They don't just hurt those in the dark, they wreck the keeper too. I was barely holding it together, but the fear of losing Eddy was slowly eating me up inside. I never knew what to expect from someone like Alejandro.

"I'm sorry I've been away. I'd like to talk to you," he said and Eddy nodded, pulling up his blanket, so it covered his chest.

Was he cold? Scared?

I don't even remember standing up, but I found myself walking towards them, until someone grabbed my wrist and stopped me.

"Let go of me," I said, pulling my arm but the soldier didn't loosen the grip. "You are hurting me," I said through gritted teeth, but he didn't even look my way.

The man in black with no soul- one of Alejandro's little puppets- was all eyes for his master. The master of soulless men. The devil.

"Release her," Alejandro mumbled and I was granted freedom, for the time being.

I touched my wrist and resumed my walk towards my son but two soldiers stepped between us.

My lungs filled with heat, I felt the flames burn inside of me. Those puppets, those heartless men were keeping me from holding my son, keeping me from taking him in my arms.

Eddy, I looked down at him and saw he hadn't moved, not one bit.

His blue sad eyes just searched mine, watery and frightened.

"Eddy," I stuck my arm between the two men and reached for him but they pushed me back, told me to step down and keep my distance.

Distance? From who? My son?

"No," I spat in their faces, but still they didn't react. They just stood there like hard, cold marble statues in my way.

"Mommy," he whimpered, seeing me try to fight my way through.

Please don't cry. Please don't let him shed another tear for all this, I bit my lip and held back my own.

"What does this mean?" I asked, looking at Alejandro.

"Silence," he barked, keeping his eyes on Eddy.

He took one of the stuffed animals on the floor and started tossing it from one hand to another, slowly.

He's thinking, he's plotting something. I almost felt sick, panic making me breathless. I needed to know, I needed to take my son away from him. *Oh God.*

"I want you to leave us alone while we talk. I want a word with Eddy, just Eddy," Alejandro said, his eyes glued on my son.

I shook my head and whispered 'no' so many times, like it would make a difference, like he would listen to me.

Alejandro looked up and one of his men took me by the shoulders and started to walk me out.

He was right behind us, the devil, walking us to the door.

The devil wants what it wants. And he just takes it, like he took Eddy.

"Eddy, mommy is coming back," I cried out the words and smiled, a complete fool I was.

Why was I so desperately trying to protect my son from the horrible truth? As if my smile could defy him. It didn't. He was scared, he was sorry to see me cry. That smile was worthless, it didn't make Eddy feel any better. It simply confused him.

I wiped it off my face and glared at Alejandro – we were now face to face- and with the little voice I had left in me, I whispered my last words, pointing a menacing finger at him.

"If you touch him, I'm going to torture you, you son of a bitch."

He slammed the door in my face.

ALEJANDRO

Eddy and I stared at each other like two strangers, I had no idea who my son was, he didn't know me. The kind of man that I was and what I was capable of. To what length I'd gone to get him back.

Not knowing your own blood is like not knowing yourself. It rubbed me in a weird way, like I'd been deprived of something- a part of me, my future.

Nobody could take from me, nobody.

But Andrea, she almost did, I thought as I asked my son a few questions.

I listened to him, I was there to learn. Everything I could make out from those first moments with him, I'd take it and use it to build something. He was my son, the future of the De la Crux family.

Six years old was a young age for him to understand, but it wouldn't be long before Eddy would find out what his surname meant. Where he belonged in this world.

Next to me, he was MINE.

And nothing and nobody could stand between him and his destiny. His family.

Eddy was quiet, an observer. He studied me, just as much as I studied him.

He opened his mouth when he knew an answer, never risked saying something I wouldn't like hearing or something he wasn't sure of.

Not a single word on Sebastian, even when I asked.

"Did you like it there, on that island?"

"Yes, I did. It was perfect."

"What was?" I pressed on.

"Everything. The place, the people. I made a lot of friends. We had a beach and I went swimming almost every afternoon."

"With who?" I asked.

Silence.

"Why don't you want to tell me?" I asked again and saw him look down at his hands for a moment, before looking into my eyes again.

"Because I don't want to say things you don't like."

"What things?" I pressed on, keeping my voice low and calm.

Eddy was just a child, he had nothing to do with all the shit that had happened between me and his mother.

As I watched him hesitate, I told myself over and over again it wasn't his fault, none of it was. The only patience I had, I had with him. I left it all for him.

"I can't tell you," he mumbled under his breath, glancing my way again.

That look, those eyes, I recognised the sadness, like the one in his mother's glare.

"Why? Why Eddy?"

"Because I don't want you to be angry at me… I'm afraid of you, when you are angry," he didn't even hesitate.

He hit me with his thoughts, pure and simple. No filters.

My son is afraid of me, I stared at him not knowing what to make of it. I'd never showed him anything but kindness, never shouted at him, never did anything to scare him but I guess it wasn't about that. It wasn't what I'd shown him, it was what I'd done to his mother.

He sensed it, the hostility, the tension and the fear, all those feelings Andrea had for me. Eddy was breathing all of that and, in light of his six years of age, he'd decided I was the bad guy. And he was right, I was.

I told myself he was too young to understand, too young to see my side of the story. One day I'd explain how things worked in my world, what makes a man strong and powerful and what you must do to get some respect.

Or else… strike first, hit harder, show them who's the leader, cheat if necessary. Step over anyone that dares to cross your path. Stop at nothing.

That's how you get to the top, on your own terms, with your own hands. You use all the weapons you can find and fire all the bullets you need to. Anything is legit during war.

My life was a war and I was fighting one of the most important battles. Trying to take my son back, show him that I cared for him.

One day I'd tell him how crazy the idea of not seeing him, not knowing where he was or what he was doing, the thought of another man spending time with him, almost drove me absolutely, fucking mental.

One day Eddy would understand, what I'd done and why, because whether Andrea liked it or not, Eddy was a De la Crux and I was going to raise him like one, just like my father had raised me and Ramirez. Fight for four principles and four principles only. *Honour, pride, respect and power.* Eddy was going to be my right arm soon.

"Answer this, Eddy," I took him by the shoulders gently and he nodded, his blue eyes kind. "Did you ever call him 'dad'? Don't lie to me," I warned him.

Eddy shook his head.

"No, you are my father."

He wasn't lying, he was staring right into my face, no blinking, no hiding.

"That's right, I am. How do you feel about that? About spending time with me?"

"I don't know," he simply shook his head and eyed me expectantly.

"Well, you and I are going to do things together. I am going to teach you a lot of things. Do you like toy guns?" I smiled, trying to change the subject.

Eddy shook his head again and told me his mother never wanted to get him one. Guns weren't fun, not even toys.

"We won't tell mommy. I will teach you how to shoot one day, a real one," I kept smiling and watched Eddy debate whether it was okay or not to lie to his mother.

That bitch had brainwashed him, he was too good, too sweet. Too nice. But I had plans, plans for us all.

"I am taking you to a place soon, a new place. And I promise I will give you everything, all the toys you want. You name it, it's yours," I told him as I ruffled his curls. "I want you to be the happiest kid in the world, I want you to have everything your heart desires. Kids will envy you, you'll see. "I chuckled and added "You belong to a very important family, Eddy. You're a prince."

He scratched his head and went quiet, while figuring out what to say next. Eddy was very smart, clever, cautious. He was going to make a good leader one day, I could tell.

"Dad, are you going to hurt mommy?"

I took in a breath and studied him closely.

After so many years living on the streets, doing what I did for a living, I thought nothing could get to me, nothing but the words of my very own son.

Was I going to hurt his mommy? *Yes.* Had his mommy hurt me? *Yes.*

See, where I come from it's called payback, eye for an eye, my time to fireback.

Instead I told Eddy what he wanted to hear. A lie.

"No, I won't if your mommy behaves."

Too late for that, bitch. We had played a game, his mommy and I, each one of us had made a move and I had won. It was now time for her to pay up.

"Okay," Eddy nodded, but didn't sound sure. "I will tell her to behave and I will be okay wherever we are going. I don't want anything…just please don't hurt mommy."

I opened my mouth to speak but the words got stuck in my throat.

Please don't hurt mommy, he said. *What about what mommy did to me? Taking you away from me?*

"Okay," I choked out in the end.

Another lie, I was starting off my relationship with Eddy with deceit and it was all Andrea's fault- my head kept telling me. I knew there was a slight chance my own blood would grow up hating me, despising me for what I'd done to his mother. But it was a risk I had to take.

Because I wasn't going to let Andrea off like that. She couldn't be forgiven.

No fucking way.

CHAPTER 14

THE DAY SHE BEGGED

ANDREA

My body stopped shaking when I was let in the room again. Twenty long minutes later.

Eddy was on the floor, playing with his toys, his attention back on the TV screen, Alejandro standing in front of one of the windows.

I rushed to my son, doing my best not to scare him, I kissed his hair and breathed in his scent. Cookies and chocolate, that was what Eddy smelled like to me since he was born. Pure sweetness, just like him.

But for how long? How much time do I have until Alejandro's venom poisons him?

I glared at Alejandro as he walked towards us on his way out – something had come up, he was needed in his office. He didn't even look at me. He was out of the room and I was back inside, holding my son tight to my chest, watching cartoons with him.

My eyes were glued to Eddy, I was desperately trying to figure out if something had changed, if Alejandro's words had affected him somehow.

Does he look different? Sadder? Hurt? Is he hurt?

His hands, his arms, his chest were okay, my eyes scanned him quickly. What had they talked about?

I found the courage to ask him later, after dinner when he was playing in the bath and he told me his truth, all of it and with pride.

"I told dad he could keep the toys, I just wanted you to be happy. I didn't want you hurt."

Oh my god, Eddy. I nearly cried into his wet hair there and then.

Sebastian would be so proud of you. Your real dad, I thought and then I wondered if my truth would ever come out, if Eddy would ever end up knowing, if I would ever get a chance to explain he had the blood of a good man running in his veins.

A man that loved and accepted us for who we were. A man with a kind heart, strong and protective. A man that would never hurt us, that never wanted anything more than to see us happy.

My soulmate, your father.

I kissed his hair again and smiled.

This kiss is for you, Sebastian. I hope you feel it, wherever you are.

Eddy was sleeping soundly when I heard a knock on the door.

Half past nine, I checked the time and thought it was maybe Donna Filomena checking on us. She sometimes did that at night, her visits had become more frequent, as my body had become thinner.

The two things were related, I knew that for sure. I saw the way she kept staring at me lately, weary, anxious, like I was a bomb ready to explode, ready to starve to death. I would never, ever do that, leave my Eddy alone in that house with them, to raise my son with hatred and corruption.

No, never.

I opened the door and breathed in a breath, as my eyes adjusted to the sight of Alejandro. He stood there shirtless, his tattooed chest bare, except for the long family pendant dangling down his neck.

"Let me in," he ordered, his hands tucked in his trousers' pockets.

My pulse quickened, my heart thundered in my chest, like it was screaming at me to run fast. Run where? I was trapped.

I backed away, not knowing what to do, my eyes went to Eddy before I spoke again.

"He just fell asleep," I whispered and took in a breath, the air suddenly felt heavy as he stepped inside the room.

Alejandro nodded, his stare lingering on Eddy.

Then his attention was back on me, his little eyes invasive. They studied me carefully, from the hem of my robe to my ankles, then all the way up to my hips. They felt rough on my skin.

"In there," he hissed, pointing to the bathroom door.

I turned slowly and took small steps, closing my eyes, walking into the darkness. My entire body tensed, sensing the danger, knowing what was waiting for me behind that door. *My punishment, my long-awaited sentence.*

Alejandro had come to finish what he'd started years back, behind that shed. Only this time nobody was going to save me, nobody was coming to take me away and I wasn't going to scream. I couldn't risk my son waking up to a nightmare, seeing his mother hurt and broken. Alejandro knew I never would. He'd trapped me.

He grabbed my shoulder and pushed me against the wall. My head banged against the tiles and I let out a soft cry.

"Shut up," he grumbled in my ear, holding me in place.

One hand went for my neck, while the other one pulled my robe open and snaked under my shirt, fast.

"No," I sobbed.

"Shut up," he growled and I closed my eyes, whimpering the words of a song, the one I sang every time I'd gotten hurt as a child. The *Soothing rhyme*, my grandmother used to call it in Hungarian. I wanted it to work, I wanted it to take the pain away.

Please take me away.

His hand slipped down between my legs and I jumped, I tried to fight it, but he wouldn't stop.

Stop, stop!

I sang those words again and again, keeping my eyes shut, telling my mind to run out of there, go someplace else, but Alejandro groaned in my face, making sure I could feel him, smell him.

Tobacco and liquor, he'd been drinking. I wanted to scream.

"What is it, Andrea? Huh? You used to like it a little rough," he hissed, tearing my shirt open, pressing his lips to mine. "You like to be fucked like a whore, don't you?"

"No," I said turning away, trying to escape from his grip. "No, no."

"No? No what?" he hissed again pulling my panties down, biting my chin.

"Don't. No," I cried softly, shaking my head. "Please, stop." I pleaded.

Please.

There it was, the word I promised myself Alejandro would never hear me say. But in the end, I pleaded.

I begged him to stop again and again but Alejandro just laughed in my face.

"Now you say please, huh? You fucking bitch…" He grabbed my wrists and pressed them up against the wall.

Everything happened so fast. His hands were everywhere. One grabbed my thigh and pulled it up roughly, spreading my legs apart.

"No," another cry, I turned to look away as he groaned against my cheek, pushing his body hard against mine.

I couldn't move, I could hardly breathe, his erection pulsing with life against my clit.

"Please… please don't," I whimpered, hearing him groan again.

But he didn't stop, his hand travelled between my thighs instead.

Please, oh please, God no, I cringed, his fingers digging so roughly inside me, I begged him to stop again.

"You can plead all you want," he grunted.

Then I heard the zipper of his trousers and my legs gave in.

"You forgot who you belong to, Andrea," he pulled my hair a little, forcing me to look him, straight in the eye.

El Diablo.

Don't look at him. Don't break.

"You are MINE," he said, just before it hit me.

The heat, his skin burned like the flames of hell against mine.

I breathed in and out and cried, as I felt his hardness push inside me, I nearly screamed, it made me sick.

That look in his eyes, a combination of rage and pleasure, for taking my body, for taking back what he'd claimed as his.

I just want to forget all about it but I can't.

Once the devil possesses you, tries to take your body and soul, he comes again and again, any time he wants, he waits for you at night, he lives in your mind forever.

"Remember this?" he moaned. Another thrust, I closed my eyes shut. "Look at me," he groaned but I didn't listen.

Don't listen to him, don't.

"You used to like me inside you, remember? How many times you begged me not to stop? Huh? Remember this, Andrea?" Another thrust. Deeper, it burned.

He moaned against my lips, I closed my eyes and tried to shut him out, but I could feel him staring at me, at the tears rolling down my cheeks, at my bruised chin where his teeth had sunk into my skin.

"I hate you! I will never forgive you for doing this to me," I cried out, shaking to the core. "I will never forgive you, never, for doing this to me. Never, never," I whimpered.

I opened my eyes and looked at Alejandro. He was still inside me but he'd stopped moving. So I told him the words I knew would hurt him, I knew would hit him hard. Words, the only weapon I had.

"I'll never be yours…" I cried, shaking my head. "Never. I'm Sebastian's. No one else's."

"Shut the fuck up," he pushed his forehead hard against mine, clenching his teeth, and I stifled a cry.

My skull pressed onto the bathroom tiles, I nearly screamed.

He's going to kill me, he's going to kill me.

I shut my eyes tight and prayed he'd take my life fast.

No more pain, please, please God. I couldn't take it anymore.

Then everything stopped.

I felt my body lighter, no weight, no pressure on it. I wasn't pinned to the wall, I couldn't feel him inside me anymore. Alejandro had taken a step back, I saw his jaw twitch, as he pulled his trousers back up quickly.

My death, he's going to make it slow, I thought as I stood there in silence, scared of making the slightest sound.

But I couldn't stop shaking and stammering under his glare. Nothing comprehensible, just fragments of thoughts, broken words.

"Aleja…." I started to say, trying to close the robe.

"Shut the fuck up," his fist flew forward, hitting the tile next to my head.

I covered my mouth and bit back a scream, slipping down to the floor.

He stomped to the door, eyes red like blood.

"Clean up and get fucking dressed, you are coming with me tonight."

And then I was alone again, on the bathroom floor, picking up what was left of me.

I reached the toilet just in time to vomit.

CHAPTER 15

THE MAN IN THE MIRROR

ALEJANDRO

"*I will never be yours. I'm Sebastian's,*" Andrea's words replayed in my head.

I slammed the door shut.

The hell you are!

Obsession grows like a seed inside you, it feeds your rage, until it possesses you, controls your mind. I wasn't thinking straight anymore, I was blinded by my obsession. By Andrea.

"Goddam it," I punched the dark red wall in my room, once, twice, until my knuckles turned red.

Blood dripped to the floor and I just stared as it crawled down my fingers. I felt nothing.

I should just fucking killer her, the veins in my neck pulsed harder and I twisted my head, shaking the thought away.

No, no. Too easy, too soon. She's mine, I told myself and then cursed.

I made it to the bathroom, before my hands turned burgundy and washed it all away.

My eyes stayed on the red streaks running down the sink for a moment, until I caught sight of my reflection and froze. I took a good look at the man in the mirror, the man I had become.

Who the hell are you? What the hell have I become?

I couldn't fuck her. I couldn't rape her. What the fuck was wrong with me?

She hated me. I made her sick, I disgusted her. Fuck.

What the fuck am I doing? What the fuck do I want? I wanted her to fear me, yes so she wouldn't try to screw me over again. Fear my punishment, my rage.

But I wanted Andrea to obey my every word, worship me like I was a freaking god. But hate?

You killed everyone she loved, she hates you. Sometimes my mind, the part of me that was still thinking straight, would snap me back to reality.

Yes, I had. I had taken everything away from her, so she'd have nobody left to rely on besides me.

So she'll be yours, the darkness snickered in my ear.

Only she never would, I'd just realized. I could take her body, but Andrea would never be mine. She'd never be the obedient pretty wife I wanted.

"I'm Sebastian's. No one else's."

"Motherfucker," I shouted to the man in the mirror.

I couldn't look at her without seeing him, that rat, touching her, violating her. Not just that, I couldn't forget that abandonment, that look in her eyes, his hands all over her.

I wanted her to look at me that way, to feel that pleasure with me and no one else. She was mine, her body was my temple, my hands were the only hands that should've made her feel like that. I had fucking married her, not that son of a bitch. She was mine to satisfy and possess.

My obsession had gone beyond reason. I wanted what I knew I couldn't have and still I kept thinking about how I could get it. I wasn't listening to my mind, I was guided by rage.

Another man had taken what was mine and there was no way I could change that.

Every single time I would lay a finger on her, I knew I'd imagine him, fucking her, taking pleasure out of my wife.

Fuck, I kept my hands in the sink and my eyes on that reflection in the mirror.

Another thought, another doubt.

"Don't hurt mommy," I hadn't forgotten Eddy's plea, the lies I had fed him. Did he believe me? Did I believe in what I was doing?

Yes, yes I do. I wanted revenge, this is it. I am letting doubt, I'm letting my son and a dirty whore control me. I am hesitating, I never hesitate. I never blink or think twice.

I never did. My hand was always firm, I never let anyone change my mind or tell me what to do. Maybe I had started to realize that taking back my wife, making her the woman I wanted her to be, would take longer than expected.

Time, it's always a matter of time and patience. When I was in prison, I seemed to have so much of it, but now I wanted it all sooner, now.

I finished cleaning up, convincing myself I needed to stay calm and focused. Andrea was going to give herself to me, eventually.

Sooner or later she'd see there was no other choice but surrender. Maybe I could use Eddy. I could use drugs.

I could, make her forget, make her not care.

I slipped on a burgundy button-up shirt and dark trousers and styled my hair, taking one last good look at my reflection in the mirror.

Yes, I recognized that man again. Alejandro *"El Diablo"* De la Crux. I felt focused and determined.

Strip her bare, destroy her hopes and dreams. Take it all away. She'll stop fighting when she'll lose faith, she'll hand herself over to you. She'll be yours, again.

I pressed my lips to the family pendant and sealed the deal. I always got my way in the end. Always. I still had a few cards up my sleeve, I was anything but done with her.

ANDREA

In the darkness everything looks the same, I took comfort in that as I listened to my son's breathing. Eddy was sleeping soundly, peacefully, sprawled on my bed, like we were home.

Like back in Folegandros.

In the absence of light, I pretended we were still there, I remembered when it rained hard, when the storm picked up and we were awakened by the wind.

How many times we'd waited for Sebastian's return worried, holding on to each other in bed like we were now, listening to the storm, listing all the things we loved about Sebastian?

He was strong, Sebastian was kind and quiet. He was patient but impetuous as well, when he knew something needed to be done. Sebastian hated waiting but waited when it was worth it.

"He waited for us," Eddy would say proud.

He had, he hadn't given up on us.

What about now? Had he given up on us now? Were thoughts of me and Eddy haunting him, like thoughts of him were haunting me?

'Is he looking for us?' I held my face and cried some more.

I told myself it was because of what had happened in the bathroom before, with Alejandro. Instinctively, I kept my legs tight together and tried to ignore the mark he'd left inside me.

Deep down, at the heart of my soul, I knew I was aching for Sebastian. I hoped he wasn't looking for us, risking his life again to try and stop what couldn't be stopped.

This time Alejandro would have him killed, he'd had too much time to think, too much time to plan. He would see Sebastian coming.

But I could still dream, couldn't I? Dream of him looking for me and Eddy, not giving up on us.

In the darkness everything looks the same, I kept telling myself to pretend I was waiting for Sebastian to come back from fishing all night. I imagined him walking into the room, lifting me up in his arms, complaining about how thin and light I was, kissing my hair and telling me I smelled like wildflowers, my skin smooth like the petals of a rose.

Someone knocked then and I took my battered body, my deprived soul to the door.

I opened it just a few inches, telling myself whoever it was, whatever was waiting for me on the other side of that door, I had to feel nothing. No emotions, no feelings. Maybe it was Alejandro, coming back for me, coming to finish what he'd started.

"Donna Filomena," my eyes were barely open, I felt exhausted, but I had cleaned up and dressed like Alejandro had requested. And I hated myself for obeying.

"He's waiting for you downstairs. I'll sit here with Eddy until you come back, in case he wakes up," she told me and I nodded, thanking Donna Filomena for her kindness.

She never smiled, I wondered if she was broken too, for living so many years in that house, with the men of her family. I could see she was just as poisoned as them, but she was also a woman. A mother. She understood that side of me, at least.

"I'm doing it for Eddy," she wanted me to know. I already knew.

"Thank you," I said again and walked out of the room, head high.

Makeup covered the bruises on my body, the marks Alejandro had left on it. My body, I had no control over it. Not anymore, it was Alejandro's to do with as he pleased. My legs shook at the thought.

When he comes for you, go back to the island, pretend in the darkness, I told myself to be brave and show him nothing but disgust.

"Why do you keep doing this? Why put up this resistance? Why make it so difficult for everyone? You came here with him, you left your country and married him. He chose you, don't you see, Andrea? It's done," Donna Filomena kept her voice low but to me it felt like she was screaming the truth.

Because it was just that, the truth. Alejandro's truth. I had no say in his decisions. He'd chosen me years back and I'd fallen for him, letting the devil take my soul. I was doomed and I knew it.

I believe in the right to say no. I believe in the right to decide for myself, not obey, I wanted to tell her all that, but I kept quiet.

She wouldn't understand, Donna Filomena had been living in hell for too long to see anything but damnation. She would continue to live and eventually die in the pit. The idea of being someone's possession was too deeply rooted in her but not in me. Never.

Till my last breath, I will always fight back, somehow, with my own weapons, with whatever I can find. I'll lie, ignore, backstab if needed. I'll never give up, I'll never give up for Eddy.

No, Donna Filomena wouldn't have understood.

"You can ask me to lie to my son, smile and pretend everything is okay, Donna Filomena but you and I know that nothing really is. I can't pretend to be what I'm not. I'm not a doll, I'm not what Alejandro wants me to be," I took in a breath and held back from saying the rest, from saying the things Donna Filomena wouldn't understand.

I am Andrea Szerov, I am Katerina Kochenov. I am still that girl on the island, the one that likes to dance, that loves to play the piano. A woman who speaks up, that can't be ordered around and expect to smile and be happy, when someone tries to break her wings. I'm the woman who married Sebastian Esposito, not the woman Alejandro De la Crux wants me to be. I'm Sebastian's, no matter where I am, no matter how far apart we are, I am his.

Donna Filomena stared at me for a moment in silence. Then she moved in closer and whispered to me, like she was afraid of anyone listening in.

"Then I am afraid it can't end well for you, Andrea. My son is the spitting image of his father, no resistance will work with him. You are a mother, Andrea. Think about your son."

A dark omen and the words of a mother, the only thing Donna Filomena and I had in common. We were both mothers, both worried, both trying not to go crazy and save our sons.

I didn't trust myself to speak for a few moments after that, I simply nodded as she stepped inside my room, passing me by. My hand reached out for her arm then, I touched it and Donna Filomena stared at me, her eyes unreadable. I saw her take in a deep breath, fearing my next move, my next words to her.

I had something to say, something I knew she would understand.

"If anything happens to me, you have to promise me you'll take care of Eddy. You will do your best, you will protect him, as much as you can," my lips trembled and the grip around her arm tightened, when Donna Filomena looked away, refusing to meet my eyes.

I wouldn't hear of it, my fingers dug in her arm and she looked at me, finally looked at me, her eyes wide as Donna Filomena came to terms with Alejandro's sickness. His obsession, me.

All the bruises, the marks, the scars on my cheeks were staring back at her.

Your son's doing, his sickness.

"You have to promise me, please," I begged and got down on my knees because I had no one to trust, no one I could ask for help if things were to go wrong for me. I had to make sure someone would look after my son, my Eddy. She was his grandmother after all or so she thought. That lie, I grabbed onto it, my only hope.

Donna Filomena's eyes widened, but I couldn't make out that look.

Was it pity? Sorrow? I wasn't sure and didn't care. My son's life kept my heart beating, my mind sane. He was the only thing that mattered.

"I promise," she jerked her arm away and helped me up quickly, maybe worried soldiers might walk by.

I nodded, adjusted my black dress and walked barefoot, shoes in hand down the corridor.

I turned once and saw her stare at me, how fragile I looked, how I dragged my beaten body through the house. Then she walked in and I made my way to Alejandro, my legs weren't shaking anymore.

Whatever was waiting for me, I knew Eddy would be fine. I knew, Donna Filomena would help me, because she was a mother and mothers understand the pain, they can't ignore the heartache.

In the darkness everything seems the same. Step after step, my feet touching the red burgundy carpet, I imagined I was walking down to the beach, walking on the sand. I imagined Sebastian's boat making its way back in the harbour.

I could almost smell the sea.

CHAPTER 16
DISORIENTATED

SEBASTIAN

Just outside Venice, I washed my face and changed my clothes in a café. Four hundred euros was all I had left after I'd paid the truck driver that had smuggled me in through the border.

I scrubbed and scrubbed my black face, slapping it a little, hoping to stop my eyes from closing. Even if I didn't want to admit it, I needed a safe place to sleep. I hadn't slept more than two hours in a row, for days. My body told me I had to rest, my mind screamed to move, to be fast.

Faster Sebastian, faster.

There was no time to waste. No money to waste either. I needed it to travel to Rome.

An airplane would have been a stupid idea but not a speed train. I could have boarded that without having to show a passport. I was in Italy, I was Italian and only an authority could check and find out my ID was fake.

Get up, you're not tired. Move, I pushed myself up in front of that mirror, in the bathroom of that café.

Coffee and food, I would use them to keep me awake.

With my knapsack over my back, sunglasses on my nose, I walked out of that place and into the train station, bought myself a one-way ticket to Rome on the next speed train. Four hours and I would be in Rome. Back to where it had all started. Where my life had changed.

Don't give up, Sad Eyes. I am almost there.

She told me more than once, but I remember this one time in particular. It was cold and windy outside. I was teaching Eddy how to read the clock, he was nervous, he wanted to learn so fast. I remember wrapping an arm around his neck and telling him to be patient, to keep trying and stay calm. Haste can only lead to failure, haste makes you do silly things, I knew it all too well.

Andrea sat there at the piano without playing, listening in to our conversation, gazing at us in awe.

That look, a soft smile played on her lips, but I recognised the sadness in her eyes. Andrea was thinking about the past, there was always a dark shadow about her when she did.

I left Eddy on the couch, playing with the clock and walked over to her, smiling mischievously. I was about to sit when Andrea told me out of the blue how I had changed her life, from the moment we'd met.

She had found hope, a reason not to let go, to surrender to the idea of being a possession. If a stranger like me had seen her, really seen her for what she was deep down, if she'd managed to escape her life for a few hours, she could find a way to escape forever. Nothing was lost.

"Why do you love me?" She asked, never looking away from me. "What do I have to offer you? Why am I worthy of you, of your sacrifice?"

I heard the doubt in her voice, the shadow of her past was making it hard for her to see. Why did I love her? How could I not?

"Why is the sky blue?" I smiled, leaning a little closer. "I just do, Pretty Eyes. I love every single thing about you. Even when you doubt yourself, that's when I love you the most. For never being scared of being you," I cupped her face and Andrea let out a deep breath. "I'd fight for you all over again because you are worthy, so worthy, Pretty Eyes. You are the reason I'm still here, alive."

"Thank you," she said and kissed my hand. "You changed my life, made it worth living."

I changed her life. Andrea had no idea how much she'd changed mine.

Before I met her, I had just finished up two years of undercover work in Naples. Before that, thirteen months of undercover work in Sicily. They moved me around, I got my hands dirty here and there, enough to report to the police.

Do you have any idea what it's like to be two different people at the same time? To lie every single day of your life? To do things, nasty things to fit the part and then live with the fear of being exposed? Any minute, any moment, someone could find out who I was, someone could have betrayed me.

I lived side by side with drug traffickers, killers, real ones, not fighters like me in a ring. I'd dodged a few bullets, risked my life on the job. Sometimes the fear of being exposed and killed in my sleep, would keep me up at night. Sometimes pills were the only solution, just to get my mind to rest, to stop from worrying.

Andrea had changed all that. She and Eddy had been my salvation, I never wanted more than to be myself, just me and live for them, for us. I had a family, 'the nobody' from the dodgiest neighbourhood in Naples had a family. A reason to stay alive, to keep fighting.

I had to find them.

ANDREA

The enemy studies you, looks for your weaknesses. The enemy listens in and smiles cunningly, until he learns how to take you down.

That's when he strips you of your certainties, of your dignity, he takes hold of the situation and then goes in for the kill.

That was what Alejandro was doing to me. He was trying to shake me, trying to make me feel alone and out of place. He was, I wasn't imagining it and I wasn't crazy, even though I was starting to lose my sanity. He wanted to take away all my confidence, so I would have no one else to go to but to him.

We rode in silence in the car, my eyes never left the seat in from of me. It was black and white, the head of one of the guards sitting at the front leaned against it.

I never turned to look at Alejandro, but I felt him staring at me, even though I'd let my blonde hair down, to cover up my neck, my face as much as possible.

Give him nothing, nothing. Not your attention. Not even a look.

My eyes wondered outside only once the car had stopped and I didn't have much time to think then. The car door opened and a soldier let me out, but I stood there without moving next to the car, until Alejandro walked to stand beside me and my entire body froze.

The whole world froze.

The fight club, we were standing in front of the fight club, that very one. It had been years, it felt like it had all happened in another life, but my eyes, my heart recognized the place where it had all begun. Where my life had changed forever.

The night two damaged souls met, the night we found each other, my first night with Sebastian, the night we loved each other so much, we made Eddy.

I bit the inside of my cheek, swallowing back all my emotions, my tears.

I couldn't break, not now.

Alejandro took my arm and I jumped, like I had forgotten all about him.

You are nothing, nothing compared to Sebastian.

If only I could've shouted those words to his face, maybe on my death bed I would. If given the chance, I would one day.

"Move," he grunted and I followed him to the door.

Inside the music was loud, two fighters were on the ring and it was packed.

Nothing had changed, it looked exactly like it had years ago.

Everything is like it was, I was a prisoner again, my guards were different - Alejandro himself was there- but I was Andrea Szerov, the girl with Sad Eyes, lost and broken. *Again.* Only Sebastian wasn't there, he was lost too.

Why are we here?

Panic rose in my body at every breath I took in the smoky, seedy club. My mind was racing, had he found out something? But how? Nobody knew. His old soldiers had been killed, nobody knew. Nobody saw us.

Had Sebastian told someone without telling me?

Oh my god.

"Sit," he ordered, like I was his little dog.

I glared at him, despite my good sense, but took a seat on the stool and he ordered us drinks quickly, with just the gesture of his hand.

The bartender, a girl in a sports bra with a lip piercing and snake tattooed on her arm, served us two glasses of whiskey and greeted Alejandro with a smile.

She knew him well, he had been there before. How many times? Why?

"Drink, all of it," he ordered me and I took a sip, two, three. Not because he told me to, but because I needed it, to keep my nerves in check.

"Do you know what this place is?" he asked, the edge in his voice made me shiver.

Lie, pretend you don't.

"A fight club," I said staring into his eyes, being careful not to blink or hesitate.

Anyone that avoided his stare, Alejandro thought was liar. So I made sure not to mess it up, by looking down.

No, I don't know where we are, I don't. I don't.

I'd learned to lie so well, it scared me sometimes how two faced I could be. Lies were my weapons, Eddy's salvation.

"Not just any fight club," he hissed and shivers ran down my back.

I put the glass on the counter, so that he wouldn't see my hand shake, and I turned his way again, without saying a word.

"This is where Sebastian fought, ate, slept, fucked every woman that set foot in this place, bar girls included. This is where that scum of yours moved his little dirty hands. This is where he was the fucking king, The Killer," Alejandro told me.

His words like poison, he wanted me to feel uncomfortable, he wanted me to feel his loathing for him. How he'd stressed the fact that Sebastian had fucked other women, that he was dirty. Not worthy of me.

"I bought this club, it's mine. The whole goddam place, every single thing that happens here happens because I say it can. And not just here, Andrea. This isn't the only thing I took that was his. These years you were gone, I had time to think. Death was too simple, torture would have been gratifying but revenge isn't just about immediate pleasure. I wanted it to be whole. I want it all, Andrea,"

"I don't understand," I stuttered and began to shake.

Eddy, a shiver ran down my spine. *He made me leave the house,* maybe that had been his plan all along. He had found out the truth and was having him killed.

Donna Filomena lied to me, it was just an act. They are killing him right now.

I nearly cried there and then, but Alejandro spoke again, his lips curled in a cruel smile.

"Where's your Killer, Andrea? Where is he? I'll tell you. He's gone. He's not coming for you, he's not coming to save you," he hissed, licking his lips, leaning on the bar counter, his eyes running up and down my body, my skin went cold.

Don't shake, don't react. He was no power over you, no power.

"I am moving you and Eddy down to Naples. We are going to live there from tomorrow onwards. No more Rome for you, you won't be allowed outside if not to take Eddy to school and go to church. Why Andrea? Because you are mine and I will do with you whatever the fuck I want. I OWN YOU and everything that was Sebastian's. This goddam place, you and soon, very soon Naples and the place he was born, will be mine. All mine. I won. I have my hands everywhere, I even bought Saint Catherine's Institute and had it knocked down," he moved closer, his fingers brushed against my arm, I shifted in my seat. "Soon I'll be king of his filthy, little neighbourhood. I am selling my shit to his friends, some are already dying because of drugs. Don't you see, Andrea? I'm destroying his everything, he doesn't exist anymore," he hissed in my face, as I still managed to look him in the eye, the sick man that he was.

He's completely crazy.

"You lost, Andrea. Nothing else you can do but surrender to me, to your destiny. You belong to me," he paused and stared at the tears running down my cheeks.

Sebastian would have stopped them, Sebastian would have moved the world to stop me from crying. Alejandro reached out to touch one of the tears and wiped it off my cheek, like it meant nothing, the sign of the weak.

Stop crying, I scolded myself. *That's exactly what he wants you to do, he wants you to lose hope, he wants you to surrender.* But I couldn't hold back the tears any longer. I was breaking, one crack at a time and then fast, all at once.

He looked at me attentively, his face hard as he moved in for the final kill.

"Surrender yourself to me, Andrea or I'll take Eddy with me to Naples and leave you to rot alone, a prisoner in my house here in Rome. You'll never see him again, never."

No, I gasped, my breathing picked up, panic surged through me.

"What kind of man are you?" I sobbed the words out, holding his cold glare, his arrogant smirk.

A man that cheats, kills, tortures. A man that uses a child to take what he wants.

"What did I ever see in you?" I shook my head and cursed the day I fell into his trap- the gentleman, the exotic man on a business trip.

I'd sold my soul to a man that smothered me with attention and presents, he always smiled and asked questions. He wanted to know me, how amazing a man that finally listened, interested in what I had to say, not just my looks.

Wrong, Alejandro asked and listened only to use that information against you somehow, someday. He never did anything without a reason. I knew that now, only it was too late.

"I was what you needed. I gave you what you wanted. I changed your life, you ran away with me because I treated you like a queen. I made you feel alive and I took care of you, gave you a new life. A pretty amazing life. You had everything you asked for, Andrea. I loved you like you were my fucking queen, but you went and threw it all in my face."

I shook my head, I dared cross him again, uncaring of the consequences. I needed to say those words, right to his face.

Now or never.

"You never give without wanting something back, Alejandro. I wasn't a queen, I was a prisoner. You kept me in that house, like I was your pretty pet. And you expected me to be grateful. You took my freedom away and thought presents would fill up the emptiness I felt inside of me," I took in a breath and felt my eyes fill up with tears again. "You took my life away, you tried to destroy me day by day, like you destroy everything and everyone that gets in your way. You used me, treated me like I was an object. You hurt the people I love, you took them away from me. And you still talk to me about love, Alejandro? You really think you love me?" I searched his face and shook my head again. "If you loved me, you'd let me go. You'd let me be. You'd care for all the pain you've caused me."

He moved closer then, I froze in place but didn't look away.

Don't stand down. Show him how strong you are, I kept my eyes on him, nowhere to run, no sense avoiding his glare.

"What about the pain you caused me? What about that, Andrea? You never once did what you were told. Always fucking contradicting me. You ran away from me and took my son with you," Alejandro searched my face, stressing each word one by one, using them like sharp blades. "Do you know what it was like all those years in prison? All I kept thinking about was you and Eddy and how I had to find you. I cared about nothing else. I had to take you back, I wanted my revenge and now it's almost complete."

He paused for a moment, as the crowd grew rowdier and rowdier. The fight was almost over.

At the far back where we were sitting, I took a glimpse of what was happening on the ring. I could barely see one of the fighters, he was on his knees, trickles of blood running down his neck and arms. The other one stood right above him, one hand on the fighter's shoulder, holding him down, preparing the final blow.

"Finish him!!!" someone shouted and gave way to the chorus.

"Finish him! Finish him!" everyone yelled.

It was hard to see the fighter on the ground but I could tell he was now lifting his arms up, in defeat, begging his opponent for mercy.

He's surrendering, I thought as my breathing picked up.

"Finish him! Finish him!" the hungry crowd kept shouting, ignoring the man's plea.

The fighter closed his fist, drew back his arm and prepared the blow. I closed my eyes and then heard the crowd cheer.

When I opened them again, I saw bets being paid, people cheering and drinking, moving to the side as the winner exited the ring, with a triumphant smile, both arms up.

But my eyes were all for the man still in the ring, on his tired beaten body sprawled to the ground. He was breathing fast, his face swollen and purple.

"Look around you, Andrea," I turned to Alejandro and we locked eyes again. "There is no forgiveness, no peace, no way out of this. You have nowhere to go but home with me. Surrender yourself to me, Andrea. All you can do is follow the rules, my rules. Give yourself to me or I'll take Eddy away from you. I swear you'll never see him again."

Eddy is my life, I didn't need to say it for Alejandro already knew, he knew too well a mother would do anything, anything to keep his son safe and close to her heart.

I'd rather die than be apart from Eddy, the only reason I'm still alive, my last connection to Sebastian, I closed my eyes and began to shake.

Alejandro would come again, he would come and take me, my body and this time I wouldn't scream. I wouldn't cry, beg. I'd let him do to me whatever he wanted, waiting for the moment it would all be over.

When he's done with you, think about Eddy and forget everything else, forget what has happened, I told myself I would do it, I would do anything for my son.

Then, I opened my eyes and saw Alejandro staring at me, waiting for my answer, with the look of someone who knows he's won the battle. Just like that fighter in the ring, I could only raise my hands and surrender to him. That was all I could do.

Nobody is coming to save me.

As I nodded and watched him smile, I told myself I had to be quick, I had to make sure my plan went a little faster. Get Eddy out of his hold, no matter what.

"You won't disobey me, you'll do everything I say," he said. "Start now, say 'Yes, Alejandro.'"

I swallowed hard, my face hardened.

Lie, lie Andrea. Play his game, make him believe he's won. I swore on my son, someday my lies would be the death of Alejandro.

"Yes, Alejandro."

I raised my hands up in defeat, harbouring my betrayal.

A few days later we moved our things to Naples.

CHAPTER 17

THE FIGHT CLUB

SEBASTIAN

"Stay out of trouble, keep a low profile. If you master the art of being invisible, you can study your enemy, make the right move and come out clean. No rush, no hesitation. Stick to your plan and act as normal as possible. Don't stand out but don't stay away from people either. Don't do anything to draw attention," my superior's words kept coming back to me- Salvatore's way of introducing me to a new case.

Every time he'd moved me around Italy, we'd go over the same notions.

Keep quiet, be invisible, listen and pretend you are not listening. Lie but remember your lies.

As soon as I set foot back in Rome, I did my best to walk around the city centre looking like a tourist. Sunglasses, hat and scarf, my beard a little wild, I covered my face and the tattoo on my neck and made sure to stay under the radar. Any radar, both police and street gangs.

I took alternative and longer routes, I spoke to no one, I tried to mesh with the surroundings.

I walked all the way to The Market, back to the old hood, because there was only one person that could help me find Alejandro De la Crux. The man that had welcomed me to The Market years back, my once manager and only friend, *Joe.*

If he was still there, if he was still alive.

The last time I'd seen him was after one of my matches on the ring. We'd spent our winnings on alcohol and women at my old place. Then, I had kept him in the shadows about Andrea and my job to protect her.

A couple of phone calls, then nothing. I had thrown that phone away.

I didn't know if I'd find him there but I walked into the club nevertheless, after making sure the coast was clear.

No mafia, no street gangs.

I kept my face straight, my pulse picked up at every step I took deeper into the place. I was afraid someone would recognize me. Nobody did.

My hair was longer, I'd tied it up behind my head, I had a beard. After years at sea, my skin looked darker, thicker, older. I looked so different, nobody even looked at me twice.

Me, The Killer. I had once ruled the club, I couldn't have walked in without being stopped by someone for a chat, a drink. Women would purr dirty things in my ears, rubbing their bodies against mine.

The first thing that hit me was the smell of smoke and sweat. Then as I passed the ring, my nostrils filled with dried up blood and spilled alcohol. I'd forgotten all about that stench.

As my eyes adjusted to the dim light, I walked to the bar and took a seat at the far end, in the shadows.

"What can I get you?" the woman shouted over the music, over the loud men chatting around the ring.

A fight was in session, all eyes were on the two men up there.

"Vodka," I said, really wanting rum instead.

Too risky, always change your habits, never have anything in common with yourself, to be someone else means to create all the background and side story around the character, I told myself. That was exactly what I was doing. I was creating another character, another identity to cover up my old one.

Lie to survive.

The young girl served me the drink, glancing my way once or twice, before she moved to someone else along the counter. All the faces behind the bar were new, I didn't recognize anyone except one. Joe.

It took me a few moments to figure out it was him, but my eyes never left him from that moment on. My stare followed him across the room, as he moved to talk to the men betting in one corner of the ring.

Joe was a small man, not a single muscle in his body but his brain. He was short, well dressed and sneaky. When something interested him, he always rubbed his hands together, while grinning. Betting, women, drugs. You name it, he had his hands in it.

He seemed the same to me in a way except for his face, I couldn't stop staring at it.

White, thick scars, his whole left cheek was covered in scars. Burn marks.

Whatever had marked his skin, it had been big and round and the surface had been smothered all across his cheek, from his ear to his chin.

He had two faces, Joe. His right side, was old Joe. But the left side, was just pieces of him, the story of how things had gone wrong.

The mob, he'd been punished for something.

I sat there all night, eyeing him, waiting for the right moment. Eventually he went to the bathroom and I followed him down the corridor.

Joe saw my reflection in the mirror when I walked up behind him, but he kept washing his hands. He didn't recognize me, he didn't really SEE me. Until I opened my mouth to speak.

"Joe, it's me," I said and he turned quickly.

He squinted, mumbled something and then cursed my name.

"What the fuck," he mumbled at first. Then his face hardened as he gave me another look. "Sebastian?" his eyes narrowed. "What the fuck do you want?" he growled and tried to get past me, but I moved to the side and blocked him.

"Fuck off, out of my way," he growled again and pushed me a little, but his weak arms couldn't do anything to me. I didn't move one bit.

"Joe," I tried to grab his arm but he jerked away. "I need to talk to you," I said but he shouted in my face, catching me off guard. I backed up a little.

"You want to talk to me??? Now you want to talk to me? You left me here to rot," he pointed a finger at me, then to his face, back to me again like he was silently telling me something.

His scar, it was about me. It was all my fault. Who'd burned him?

Alejandro, I gaped, suddenly realizing what had happened to Joe.

"You disappeared, you didn't tell me the truth. I thought we were friends. I thought we had a deal."

"I couldn't tell you," I tried to speak up but he moved closer and spoke again, lowering his voice.

"You left me here, alone. You screwed up and they came for me. Two, three times asking me to tell them where you were hiding. How the fuck did I know? You never told me where you were going," he pointed to his face again. "You know what they do to people like me? Look at it, look at what they do to people like me. I see it every single fucking day. Go away," and he pushed me again, I lifted my hands, trying to calm him down, but still I didn't move out of his way.

I couldn't leave, I couldn't go away. This wasn't about Joe or about me. I was there for Eddy and Andrea, I needed Joe. I needed his help and I didn't know if an apology would buy me forgiveness, but I was willing to try anything.

"I can't, Joe. I can't go away. I'm sorry man," I shook my head and lowered my voice.

He was the angry one, he was the one that shouted and had all the right to.

I wasn't, I was just desperate. I needed his help.

"I can't talk to you, I don't want them coming back," he kept glaring at me as I stared at his cheek, carved with lines and holes, hard and rough as if it was sandpaper.

The heavy hand of the mob, when it comes looking for you, when it comes with demands.

"Nobody knows I am here. Nobody," I said and nodded. "Please, Joe. I need five minutes and I'll disappear again. Forever."

Before he could say anything else, I told him he was right, I had screwed things up, but I needed to talk to him, somewhere private, somewhere nobody could see or hear us talking.

After a few minutes, I don't exactly know why but he agreed.

"Let's get the fuck out of here, before someone sees us. The last thing I want is my right cheek fried up too," I let him through and followed him upstairs, back to my old room, back to the place I had spent the first night with Andrea.

Only now there was no bed, it was empty, it looked more like an office. Joe's office, he was the man running the club.

"They are going to fucking kill me, if they find out I am talking to you and not telling them," he grumbled nervously and set a packet of white powder and a rolled-up bill on the desk.

Cocaine, he hadn't changed one bit.

"Fuck…fuck," he mumbled and leaned forward to take a line in.

Then he flung his head back and rubbed his nose, closing his nostrils, not wasting a single bit of that junk.

I watched Joe breathe out relieved, his hands weren't shaking anymore, his jaw seemed to relax.

"I need this to keep my shit together," he said.

"That 'shit' is going to kill you," I told him what I used to back in the day, but he cut me off immediately.

"Well, something will sooner or later," he snorted out. "I'd rather this, than a bullet to my head, Killer."

I couldn't argue with that, in a way I knew what Joe had said was true. Sooner rather than later, death would come knocking on his door, demanding his soul. He could only hope the end would be bittersweet. He could only hope it would be the drugs, rather than the mob.

"I was trying to keep you out of my business, trying to protect you. That's why I never called. Never said a word about me that wasn't necessary."

"They came for me anyway, Killer. You can't hide from someone like De la Crux, you can't fuck with him, without getting fucked over. He's the devil for fuck's sake," Joe pushed his hair back and licked his lips, while I saw him relive the fear and terror of those moments.

His jaw twitched, his eyes stared ahead, wide.

"Things are different now. The Market isn't what it was years ago. Look around you, when you walk down these streets, watch your back. The De la Crux's family is everywhere. They own it all, this place, this part of Rome is all in their hands. They took The Ruins too," Joe told me, as he pressed the side of his nose and leaned down to sniff another load of that junk.

He filled in the blanks, told me what had happened since I'd been gone. Ramirez De la Crux, Alejandro's brother had taken charge of the family business, until Alejandro was made a free man. The trial had been a joke, they'd bribed whoever they could and punished the traitors. Alejandro walked out of prison thirsty for revenge, ready to destroy and rule.

"The execution, that's what they called it. I heard they punished everyone that testified against him, they were either killed or disappeared mysteriously," Joe paused. His hands, I kept looking down at them, how he couldn't stop moving them. He couldn't sit still.

"I've seen some pretty fucked up things, Killer. I don't know how I fucking made it here, how I'm still alive… Alejandro gave weapons to a couple of small street gangs in The Ruins, waited for the war to break out. He watched them kill each other for the territory, then he stepped in at the very end and took the place in his hands. People were either with him or against him, those that didn't want to obey him, he shot them in the head. I saw that, I fucking saw it with my own eyes."

Joe ran a hand through his hair and swore, taking out more cocaine from his pocket. He lined it up on the desk again and carried on.

"He knows everything, Killer. He knew who I was, he knew that I knew you. The first time he came for me, you'd told me you'd gone to Naples, back home so I told him that and he let me go."

When I had taken Andrea and Eddy with me to the Institute, I thought and kept quiet, I let Joe talk, didn't dare interrupt. I needed all the information I could get, anything to help me find them, help me work around the security, the soldiers around Alejandro. Maybe Joe could help me get to them, he always knew everything going on in the underworld.

"Then, he was arrested, you disappeared and he sent his men for me," Joe went on, but I couldn't help but notice him shiver. "The first time they came, I was lucky. I only got a few punches, a couple of kicks in the stomach, a broken rib."

"Shit," I mumbled under my breath, my hands curled into a fist and I looked away from Joe.

"Then they came again and again. Until one time, just before De la Crux was set free, they did this to my face," Joe pointed to his cheek, to the scars that wrecked his face. "I had nothing for them, nothing new. They didn't believe me or maybe they had orders to just fucking kill me, since I was so fucking useless," he spat the words out and lit up a joint, his hands a little shaky again.

"Do you know what skin smells like when it burns, Killer? It smells disgusting … like failure… you can hear it, feel it as it breaks, as the flesh opens. They pressed my cheek onto the fucking radiator of their car. One push, a matter of seconds, just enough for the flesh to crack up and bleed, then the same fucking questions about you, where you were, if you'd called. Then back onto that radiator. Five times. I screamed and kicked, spat out blood. Five times, the burning flames of hell wrecked my goddam face. During those last seconds I remembered you telling me something a while back, about growing up at The Towers, I told them where you lived in Naples. Not just that, I told them you used to fight in a club down there. That made them stop, but I thought they'd shoot me anyway. Instead they kept me alive, I think they knew you'd come. You'd try to call me or something," Joe looked at me, straight in the eye.

And that's exactly what I did.

They knew, of course they knew. There wasn't anything I wouldn't do to save Andrea and Eddy, Alejandro knew better than to underestimate me.

Only he knew I was dead, he thought his men had killed me.

He won't see me coming, I told myself taking in a deep breath.

It was my turn to lurk in the shadows, my turn to wait patiently for the right moment. make my move. To strike at him, hard.

I'd use his own methods, his own weapons, that's the only way to fight the devil. I wasn't going to let anything stop me.

Till the very end, I wasn't planning on running away, no happy ever after for me. Life had fooled me once, I wasn't going to fall for it twice.

No, I was on a mission, I knew what I had to do and the price I'd have to pay. My life, for my wife and son's freedom.

I will break every single bone in your body, Alejandro. You'll pay for all the pain you are causing them and when I'm done with you, you'll beg me to kill you.

My only doubt was Joe's role in this. I wasn't too sure asking for his help had been a good idea, trusting a man like him, a creature of the streets like me.

He was still in that dump, still struggling to stay up, hoping to survive, at the service of the powerful dark forces that controlled the city, the De la Crux family.

"Why the fuck did you come here?" he shook his head, as if reading my mind. "Why did you bring me into this again? Fuck," he cursed under his breath and looked away.

I leaned to the side, followed his stare and made sure he'd look at me in the eye again.

"You've got to help me, I need to find him," I said and Joe's eyes went wide.

"I can't help you, you made a mistake, just…just leave," I saw the panic in his eyes, as he stood and pushed his hair back. "Don't you get it? He's going to find out I spoke to you, he's going to kill me this time."

"He won't, I was never here," I stood too and walked to him, as Joe started to pace around the room nervous.

"If he comes, I won't keep your secret. If he asks, I will tell him I saw you," Joe was honest with me, maybe for the first time in his life.

In the end, fear had made him an honest man.

"I know," I said and took him by the shoulders, looking down at him, at how small and fragile he was. He was half my size. "I'm not asking you to cover for me. All I'm asking you is to tell me where Alejandro is. I need to find him."

"Why? Why didn't you just stay away. He won, he took his family back. What the fuck did you think you could do?" Joe almost shouted in my face.

It's not his family, it's my family, I thought but swallowed down the truth, my secrets. Those secrets were what kept Andrea and Eddy alive.

Keep feeding those lies.

"That woman and child… he's going to hurt them," I told him but he shook his head at me again and grunted.

"Why the hell do you care? All this for pussy? Don't tell me, Killer. That's his son, his wife. Have you gone completely crazy? What is the matter with you?" Joe said and mumbled something under his breath, I feared he'd smell something so I told him, I had to tell him, one small truth. That I was a cop.

"Fuck me," his mouth dropped open, as he listened to my story.

I told him I was from The Towers, yes, that was all true. My past life, my troubled upbringing, the violence and abuse, it was all real, that was me. A part of me at least. I wasn't proud of myself, I wasn't proud of my past, but I held my head high as I told Joe how I'd made it out of the streets, the ghetto, only to go back and save people from their cruel fate, to fight crime from the inside.

"I can't leave two innocents in Alejandro's hands, I just can't," I said and Joe covered his mouth, rubbing his lips as he thought things through.

He's considering it, I thought.

If I knew Joe like I knew I did, he was probably thinking his way out of all that shit. He was assessing the situation- Alejandro was a gangster, a very powerful one, but I was a cop.

If he'd played his cards right, he'd buy his way out of the streets, without losing his other cheek.

"I can't protect you," I had to tell him, I had to be honest. "I can't right now, I need to sort out this situation first. I need to get those two out of Alejandro's hands. There's a child and a woman at stake."

Joe nodded. He understood, he understood the situation perfectly and knew he was fucked, even more now. He knew I was asking him to keep one foot in two shoes, play the game between me and Alejandro, a very dangerous game, where anyone could lose his head.

I was ready to lose mine but only after I'd found Andrea and Eddy and sent them somewhere safe. Then, they could've done to me whatever their sick, twisted minds could come up with. I wouldn't have cared. I'd served my purpose.

I was willing to sacrifice anything for them, my Andrea, my son.

Why do I love you, Andrea? Because I just can't help it, like one can't help breathing. To me your life is worth more than my own.

"I know he goes down to a stripper's club, just off The Ruins," Joe told me then, his eyes a little glassy, his stare fixed on something at the corner of the room. "Memento, it's called."

Alejandro De la Crux went there every two nights, to meet with his whore.

"Rumours say he calls her Andrea," Joe eyed me then and my stomach clenched, my fist tightened. "But her name is Ana. She knows where he is, I don't know. I swear it's the truth, man. He's not at his family house. His mother and brother live there, but he's not there. She's the only person that's last seen him. You won't be able to talk her, it won't be easy. Soldiers escort her to work and drive her home. Don't ask me to do it for you, man," Joe told me.

I wasn't going to, I assured him that was all I needed to know.

"Thank you," I looked straight at him and nodded. "I won't ever come here again, you have my word, but I won't forget this, Joe. I won't, thank you."

We slapped hands, I held his tight and took one last glance at his scar, my scar -the one I was responsible for.

Guilt, another burden to take with me. Another sin.

"A police officer?" he cursed under his breath and smiled. "You fucking fooled me, Killer."

I chuckled and headed to the door, without saying another word. I was already thinking about my next move. The stripper's club.

"You are fucking crazy for doing this, he'll have your head."

I turned and smiled, hardly but I smiled, my eyes dark as I thought of how to get back at Alejandro, how I wouldn't go down without a fight, without taking him to hell with me.

"I'd rather him have my head, than have that woman and child."

CHAPTER 18

THE REAL ANA, THE FAKE ANDREA

SEBASTIAN

Alejandro's obsession had a face and it stared right back at me.

Ana, the first time I saw her I knew immediately who she was.

Tall and thin, blonde hair and blue eyes, Ana was younger than Andrea but the resemblance was so astounding that it made me sick.

She wore her hair down, never tied up. She wore white most of the times, hardly any makeup and her thin lips had just a hint of red. Just like Andrea.

He's a sick motherfucker, my jaw twitched, my hands burned, as I followed her to the club one night and watched her get out of the car. I caught sight of the tattoo behind her back and my eyes went wide. There it was, the rose.

I shivered. She had a rose tattooed on her back, just like Andrea.

Sick, twisted motherfucker, I rubbed my face, my eyes closed a little as I waited for her to walk out again.

I hadn't slept in days, I hadn't slept two hours straight in weeks, since they'd left the island.

Sometimes my eyes would close during the day, I'd drift in and out of sleep, and for just a fraction of a second, I thought I'd hear my son's voice.

"Wake up," my mind would scold my body then, for even thinking it could rest. No resting until I found them.

My eyes would snap back open then and I'd grieve all over again. My grief for Eddy and Andrea seemed never-ending. One step closer and two steps backwards, it felt as though I'd almost made it every time, but one second too late.

I'd managed to sail away from the island safely, escaping Alejandro's men. After days of travelling, afraid of being caught and slowed down, I'd made it to Italy, then to Rome, only to realize they weren't there. Not in the De la Crux's mansion.

No matter how fast I was, how hard I was trying, Alejandro wasn't easy to track down.

What if I'm too late? I shook away the thought and tried to keep my eyes on the target.

He will pay for everything he's doing to you, Andrea, I thought, my eyes back on Ana.

I steadied my breathing, walked around the area, staying in the shadows where it was safe, in those dark alleyways around the club.

My time will come, sooner than later. I'm almost there, I kept myself awake, I kept my mind focused.

I fed myself lies, convinced myself I'd get there in time before he could hurt Andrea but my guts, my guts weren't buying it.

I was late, I knew I was but I was going to get her out of there. I was going to get my son out of that sick bastard's hold.

For two days I kept in the shadows. I studied the situation, I wrote down times and places, trying to figure out a routine.

For two days I followed Ana everywhere, Alejandro's men never left her side. Two with her at all times, two always waiting in the car.

Alejandro's security had been increased. If Joe's information had been correct and Alejandro had messed around with the balances of other clans to gain more territory, he had more enemies now, he needed to watch his back like never before. I wondered if he'd found out I wasn't really dead or if Joe had betrayed me and he knew I was coming for him.

On both nights, Ana was driven to the strip club at eleven p.m. sharp.

"You are crazy. You can't get in there without getting into trouble, man," Joe had warned me, tried to make me see reason, face my limits, but I was beyond crazy at that point. I was desperate.

For the third night in a row I was following her, I walked to the club, wearing a white shirt and black jacket.

Hiding behind my beard, I smiled as I handed money to the man at the door.

I a.m. just a horny, sleazy bastard, I kept my face as relaxed as possible, while the man gave me the change and hardly looked at me.

I walked through the door with a gun secured behind my back. I had to take it with me, I had to be ready in case things went wrong.

My feelings for weapons hadn't changed, I still hated the sight of them, hated to use them but this wasn't just a fight, this was a war, the fight of my life. I was ready to shoot, bite, punch, kick, cut throats.

I was a soldier and I let my love for Andrea lead me to war.

Whatever it takes. Whatever it takes to save you, Sad Eyes, I thought as I walked into the place.

The music was loud and hypnotic, I couldn't even hear my own thoughts. 'Firestarter' by Prodigy was on, the lights were dim but every now and then rays of blue and white lights would cross the room and for a moment you could clearly see the faces of the dancers on stage.

I recognized Ana, swinging around her pole, hardly looking down at the men gawking at her. She swayed to the music, letting her body get carried away. She danced like she wasn't there, like she was dancing to her own music, ignoring her surroundings.

Ana was untouchable, nobody could lay a finger on her and I made sure to keep my distance.

One man to the right, two on the left, I sipped my drink and searched the room, looking her way every now and then.

The soldiers pushed back a couple of men. They'd tried to reach out for her, as Ana slid down to the floor at the end of her performance.

Too many coincidences. She looked like Andrea, she stripped like Andrea used to.

Alejandro's obsession had a face and a name. That name was Andrea Szerov and Ana was just a woman caught in the crossfire.

As I watched Ana take the money from the floor and make her way to the black curtain on the side of the stage, I gulped down the last of my drink and walked to the back of the room.

Now or never.

It was between two and three am, when Ana took a break from work. She ventured outside for a cigarette in the dim alley behind the club, the one just off Via Veneto, the posh, elegant street in the centre of Rome.

The club was well hidden from the crowds, but it had quite a unique clientele; rich, business men came in and out, dressed in designer suits, smoking the finest cigars, drinking the best rum and whiskey money could buy.

Fucking the prettiest girls, taking advantage of their situation.

I'd seen the strippers, I didn't need to take a closer look to notice they were all from Eastern Europe.

Drug trafficking, human trafficking, I recognized the hands of the mob behind the two. I'd seen it happen so many times. Traffickers promised those girls a job, a new life in Italy and they made sure that they would cross the borders from Albania, Ukraine, Poland without a glitch. Sometimes they even got them to smuggle drugs into the country, hiding it inside their bodies.

The higher the stake, the more dangerous the game.

A long time ago I'd seen one of them die in Naples. Girls were being moved out of a van and into another, when they'd found her corpse. She'd fallen asleep at some point during the trip, not a single whimper, not even the slightest request for help. She died in silence, far from her family. A skinny redhead, with pink nail polish and thin necklace around her neck. She must have been eighteen or twenty.

The stash of cocaine they had hidden inside her, leaked into her body, killing her, crushing her dreams of a new life. She was thrown into a lake nearby, large rocks were tied around her ankles, so nobody would find her.

The girl with no name, the one of many that vanish into thin air every day. Another victim of the mob, another broken life.

She died thinking life had been unfair to her, that she had missed her chance of a new life.

Wrong, she'd been the lucky one. She'd escaped a life of torture, slavery and abuse. She'd lost her life but she'd kept her dignity. Death isn't the worst thing that can happen to you when you are in the hands of traffickers.

Once they reach their destination, those men strip the girls of the little possessions they still have on them; phones, money, identity cards. They rape them, one by one, over and over, until they don't have the strength to fight back anymore, until they're controlled.

"You are nobody without me, you try to runaway I'll kill you and your family. You are a whore. No phone calls, no money until I say so. No talking to anyone. You are who I say you are," I'd heard the threats time and again, seen the stories unfold before me. I'd reported back and was moved along.

Some organizations like that had been dismantled, traffickers arrested, but I'd never forgotten, never truly moved along. One group was handed over to justice, while so many were still operating, still violating and abusing women. How could I have ever moved along?

When you see the amount of pain and roughness I've seen, you can't carry on like nothing's ever happened.

I saw that pain in Ana, behind the sunglasses she wore during the day, behind the small, empty smiles and glassy eyes.

She's human meat, I thought just moments before the little black door opened and Ana stepped outside, white fur coat over her pale, long legs. Alone, no guards.

It was now or never.

"Ana," I stepped forward and watched her jump, the cigarette in her mouth almost fell to the ground.

"Who…" she said, grabbing the cigarette and stumbling backwards, her back to the wall.

"I'm not going to hurt you," I raised my hands and then placed my finger over my lips, looking sideways, but making sure my eyes were back on hers a second later. I needed her to see that I wasn't there to do her harm.

I slid my hood down, so she could see my face clearly. I could be trusted, but I knew she wouldn't believe me anyway. She'd probably been hurt by those she'd turned to for help.

I stopped, kept my distance and lowered my arms.

"What you want? Who are you?" the words came out disconnected, she still had to learn the language, the accent was strong. She hadn't been in Italy long.

In the dim light I could see her panting, as she hugged herself tight, keeping the fur coat closed, her hands shaky.

"My name is not important but I know yours. You are Ana," I wanted to say 'you are not Andrea'. I knew they called her that, Alejandro De la Crux's orders.

Her wide eyes just stared at me for a few moments, before her shoulders pulled away from the wall and I watched her body relax a little.

I hadn't touched her, I hadn't come anywhere near her and that was enough for Ana to know she wasn't in danger. Not immediate danger anyway.

"You must go. I am not allowed to talk. Nobody can talk to me," she whispered, her accent made every word sound deeper, darker.

"I know that too, but I need to talk to you. Someone is in danger, do you understand? Danger," I looked into her eyes, so alive, so intense. So different from Andrea's, the real Andrea. Hers were younger, scared, not as fierce and determined like my Sad Eyes.

"Yes," she nodded and kept her cigarette in hand, letting the wind burn it off, never taking a single drag.

Ana was smart, she knew better than to take her eyes off someone like me. I had the face, the looks of a gangster, a soldier, maybe a trafficker.

As she eyed me from top to bottom, I sensed she was trying to figure me out. Was I who she thought I was? One of them? I wasn't.

"But I can't. I work. I go back," she pointed to the door and began to stutter a little. "The soldiers, they notice I am gone. They come for me."

I saw the panic flicker in her eyes but I reassured her.

"Tell me where and when," I said and pressed on. "Please. It's important, I need to talk to you. Danger," I said the word again, making sure Ana was on the same page.

She finally took a drag, eyeing me from top to bottom again, giving me a sideway glance, her cheeks a little red from the cold wind.

"When I finish, two hours. I go home, you leave first. Meet me there, in house," she took out a tissue from her pocket and scribbled the address with the pen I'd handed to her.

I didn't need it, I knew where she lived, I'd been following her for two days but I didn't tell her.

Instead, I took the tissue and nodded.

"You didn't see me," I backed away, stepping out of the light, back into the darkness. And I waited.

CHAPTER 19
THE WIFE AND THE WHORE

The darkest hours are the ones you're not sure you'll live through. As I sat in Ana's apartment, hiding in the shadow, I eyed the door nervously, my watch, then the door.

What if someone noticed? What if she told the soldiers?

Fear makes you doubt everything and everyone, yourself included.

Ana had probably doubted me, just as much as I doubted her but I had to hope, I had to keep hoping she'd walk through that door alone and willing to help me. Still, my eyes scanned the place quickly, searching for a way out in case things went wrong.

Living room window has a balcony, I realized moments later, finally releasing the deep breath I'd been holding for what felt like ages.

Everything in that place looked new, refined, expensive. Not the house of a stripper, not even the house of a classy stripper like Ana. It had leather couches, carpets and oil paintings. The furniture was old style, golden touches everywhere. Not the house of any common whore, but the house of a mafia whore.

I looked down to my hands, to the picture Eddy, Andrea and I had taken on the beach, and tried to calm down, to steady my breathing. That smile, those eyes, my son and my wife, the only thing I'd taken with me from our house on the island. The best part of me, the happiest moments together.

Before hell broke loose.

The sound of the lock startled me, I jumped right up, slipping the picture in my pocket.

Ana walked in slowly, locking eyes with me immediately. Her back to the door she stayed there at the entrance, not saying a word.

"Are you alone?" I voiced my thoughts and saw her nod. "Did you tell someone?"

"No, too risky," she whispered the words. "I don't know what to tell. You don't tell me your name."

She was right, I hadn't but she'd trusted me anyway. She was so young, so naïve.

Anna walked across the living room and switched on the light near the window, then the one in the bathroom.

"I do what I do every night," Ana told me. "The soldiers sleep down," and pointed to the street.

She was right. She had to do her thing, so nobody would suspect, nobody would notice that night was any different.

"What's your name?" she asked, taking off her coat, setting it on the couch.

With the lights on, I saw the place perfectly for what it was: a love nest, a place to keep a lover, a whore, ready for when her man, her master would come for her.

"Sebastian," I said and kept my back to the wall, the farthest from any window in the room.

"Sebastian," Ana tried the word on her lips and then walked to pour herself a drink.

Vodka for her, I settled for nothing but she handed me a drink anyway- vodka for me too from the smell of it. I just tossed it down and let the liquor burn my throat, my stomach.

"I never have guests," she smiled a little embarrassed, as she watched me gulp down the drink. "Nobody talks to me, nobody wants to speak."

You are untouchable, I simply nodded.

"You are the first person that talks to me in a long time," she mumbled the words looking down at her hands. Then her weary blue eyes were back on me.

"How do you know me? Why you here?"

"It doesn't matter how. I am here to help you and I am here because I need your help, too," I said and sat opposite her.

Ana bit her lip, her eyes were so wide, they kept looking away like she wanted to say something but just couldn't. Or maybe she didn't know how, not in my language. So I spoke for her.

"Is this apartment yours?" I asked but I already knew the answer.

She shook her head.

"It's my 'Padrone'" *My Master's,* I nodded. "He put me here, he comes for me. I am only his. Nobody can touch me. Not until he says so. I can't speak to anyone, dangerous for me and you," Ana warned me, I was getting into trouble, putting both our lives at risk.

I knew why danger hadn't stopped me from looking for her but I didn't know why she'd agreed to see me, to put her life in danger.

It's survival, the strongest human instinct. Ana wants to live, she wants to escape, to be free.

"I'm here for Alejandro De la Crux. And I am here for Andrea."

The real Andrea.

Ana's jaw dropped open. She covered her mouth for a moment, before swallowing hard, her eyes locked with mine.

"I know he calls you that," I said and didn't wait for her to nod, I didn't need to.

Joe had told me, the rumours, Alejandro's sick obsession.

He had a whore, he'd picked one that looked like his ex-wife and he liked to do to her everything that crossed his mind, everything he could never do to the real Andrea.

"Master tells me what to do, what to say, how to behave. I never say no, me scared," her voice came out a little shaky.

"Where is he? Where is Alejandro?" I asked and Ana closed her eyes shaking her head.

"I can't speak, I can't. Master will come, he will know," she kept shaking her head, as her eyes closed. They snapped back open as soon as I took her by the shoulders.

"I need to know, Ana. I need you to tell me where he is or I can't help you, I can't save them," I slipped one hand in my pocket and took them out, my family, the reason why I was still standing, still fighting.

Ana stared at the picture, her fingertips brushing against the two foreign faces- Eddy and Andrea. Her eyes rested on the woman, the woman that looked so much like her. Andrea, the real Andrea.

"This is her?" she looked up at me, her eyes a little watery. I nodded.

"He kidnapped them. I need to find them, I need to stop him. He will hurt them both, Ana. Do you understand what I am saying?" I paused, catching my breath, watching her nod, her eyes terrified. "I need you to tell me where he is."

"I can't," Ana shook her head, looking from me to the photo, then back at me.

She was still incredulous, shocked to be face-to-face with her nightmare, Alejandro's obsession and her doom. Andrea.

But I saw her eyes rest on Eddy's smiling face too. She just couldn't look away from him.

"I want to help you," I said but Ana didn't let me carry on.

"You can't. Master will be back. He will know I spoke. Nobody knows where he is, I know. He said when…" Ana went quiet, her breathing became fast, steady and her eyes watery.

"What did he say? Ana, please. I need you to tell me, I need you to help me. He's going to hurt them, he's going to hurt them like…" *Like he hurt you,* I was going to say but couldn't.

Ana covered her face, her body shook a little, but she kept her tears in place, where I could see them, in her young blue eyes. She glanced back at me and her voice broke.

"Nothing you can do. They doomed. Master devil, he evil."

My gut twisted, my muscles tensed. All that I'd feared was coming true. I knew what Alejandro could do to Andrea, but I needed to ask. I needed to hear it and from who, if none other than the woman that had felt it before her.

"What did he do to you, Ana?" I whispered.

I asked the question and she gave me the answer, handing me the heavy cross she'd been carrying on her back for so long. She'd been held captive, she'd been told to keep her mouth shut at all times; no talking, no sharing, no friends, no calls.

Ana was Alejandro's little toy and nothing else. Not anymore.

"You disobey, I will torture you, Andrea. I will cut you, hit you and fuck you until you cry out blood. I won't even stop then. I will keep hitting you and fucking you until your last

breath, do you understand? You are my whore, Andrea. My whore." Ana sobbed out the words, one by one. She told me he'd raped her, every time, anywhere he wanted to, her body just another toy in his hands. Until she'd given up, handed herself to him, without fighting back.

She was to keep quiet, unless he'd order her to say something, to say that and just what he'd asked.

Alejandro had wanted her to play the part, the part of the loving wife, the one that never questioned, doubted, like a little servant. She told me he'd forced her to blow him one night, the only words out of his mouth the whole time had been: *"Fuck, Andrea. You are mine. You like it don't you, I will make you like it. Mine, you are mine, Andrea. You like it don't you, I will make you like it. Fuck."*

He'd filled her mouth up and then he'd pulled her hair, forced her to look into his dark eyes and say she was his, that she'd liked it. That she wanted more.

Ana covered her face and said something I didn't understand, in her language probably, a plea, an agonizing sob.

"Ana," I touched her shoulders, her body kept shaking as I spoke. "You need to tell me, where is he? Do you know? Please."

My eyes searched hers as she nodded, the sobs less violent now. She had finally spoken to someone, she'd finally spoken her truth.

"When Master came last time, ten days ago he said he'd be back in two weeks. I no speak, no clients, I'm still his. Only his. He would be back, but not every night. Not every day."

I listened and tried to understand, Ana had stopped talking.

"Why? Why not every day?"

"Because," she almost whispered the words, the slap she tried to make it gentle when nothing was, nothing was gentle in our world. It was brutal and fucking unfair, but still Ana tried to make it sound less harsh.

The truth killed me, just like I knew it would.

"Because Master in Naples. Master live there now."

I gaped and breathed heavily, we were both shaking now or maybe it was just me.

"Naples?" I murmured.

"He said he had his wife now," Ana's lips trembled, her voice broke, her heart broke again for me, for how I was hurting. "He was going to Naples but he'd be back. He's coming to take me, to fuck me? Or kill me? I don't know. I'm sorry."

Her hands went to her face and she cried, leaning against my chest, letting all the tears come out. She'd been keeping them inside for so long, they held every slap, every deep thrust, every 'No' she'd kept secretly in her heart, the one's her lips weren't allowed to voice.

I held her tight, I owed her that. Another broken life, another broken soul.

I will make sure he pays, I wanted to tell her as I held her tight, while Ana let all the pain out.

"I don't want to die," she cried against my chest. "Even if it hurts, master hurts, I never want to die."

"You won't," I was quick to say and didn't let go of her, not until the tears had dried up.

When the sobs became less and less, I took her by the shoulders again and made sure she saw I wasn't joking. I wasn't lying.

"Take this," one hand dug in my jeans' pocket and took out a roll of notes.

Half of the money I still had on me, that was all I could give her, it was enough to get her started.

"Take this and run. Run as far as you can, change. Hair, name, clothes. You are not Andrea, you are not Ana. Go home or find yourself a new home, don't stay here."

She shook her head but my hands gripped around her shoulders tighter.

"I promise you, I promise you I will make him pay. Every single thing he did to you, Alejandro will pay. With his blood," and then I stood, I paced the room, my mind racing about what I had to do next.

Naples, that sick motherfucker took them to Naples. Why?

"What do you do? Where do you sleep?" Ana asked me, as I buttoned my jacket and stood by the door, ready to leave.

I had to move, fast.

"I don't sleep. Not until I find them. I won't stop until I find them," I said and Ana stood too, making her way to me.

"Stay, sleep here a while," she gestured to the couch but I shook my head, refusing her offer. I had no time to sleep, no time to waste and a train to catch.

"Thank you but I need to go and so do you, Ana. You need to go. Find your way, find the moment. Run. Run."

She nodded and just as I opened the door, Ana walked over and dropped to her knees. She kissed my hand, resting her forehead against it for an instant, before looking back up and whispered:

"Niech cie Bog blogoslawi," *God bless you.*

CHAPTER 20

NEW GHETTO

ALEJANDRO

How many people in this world? How many souls? Different skin colour, different habits but we all have something in common. We all eat, sleep, shit, fuck and beg when our time comes. We complain about our miserable lives, for one reason or another, then when the end is near, we take it all back, we suddenly realize the dickheads that we were that whole time. We grab hold of the last thread that keeps us alive, our nails clinging to that misery, that life we've spat and cussed upon.

"Ti prego, no," *Please, please no.*

I breathed in deep, looking down at the man, straight into his frightened eyes. Nothing made me higher, nothing made me feel so powerful than holding someone's life in my hand.

Click, I pushed the cartridge in and the man shuddered. He cried louder as I loaded the gun.

"No please, no," he kept shaking his head, his hands up in defeat.

You can beg all you want.... I thought, one hand on the family emblem, the other one tight around the gun.

My men were right beside me, they'd seen me do this before, since I'd stepped in my father's role, and almost every day since I'd set foot in Naples. I'd been there three weeks already, I'd hunt down almost every single one of them. Everyone that had been friends with The Rat.

"I will give you money every month," the man said, pulling desperately at his hair.

Money, as if that could have stop the bullet, the one with his name on it.

No going back, it was all set.

I pushed the gun against his temple and he let out a guttural sound, the sound of a dead man.

"You think you are here because I want your money?" I snorted, my lips curled on one side of my mouth. "Look at me, do you think someone like me needs your money?"

"I will give you everything you need, I will be your slave. Don't kill me," he closed his eyes and cried some more, the stench of urine filled my nose.

That's what fear smells like. Blood and urine. His mouth was dripping blood; his pants were soaked in urine.

My men had played with him before, just for fun, so he knew who he was dealing with. But a gun to the head is a gun to the head, it changes everything, it's the end of everything. You almost regret pleading before, being kicked around. Pain means you are still alive, but a bullet takes it all away. Life and pain.

A gun to the head, it makes you do things you never thought you would. Anything, anything but death.

"I asked you nicely before, didn't I?" I snickered, looking at my soldiers for a moment, before my eyes darted to the man kneeling before me. "I asked you to stop selling your shit, to buy coke off me. And what did you say?"

The man shook his head, raising his hands up again, almost crying out the words.

"I have agreements with dealers…"

"I don't give a fuck. I'm taking over this area and anyone selling drugs here reports to me and only to me. Do you know who I am?" I smirked bending down a little, so we were face-to-face, my glare menacing, the man closed his eyes for a moment.

"Alejandro De la Crux," the man stuttered and eyed me frightened as I nodded, a hint of a smile still on my lips.

"Si, sono io," *Yes, that's me.* I searched his face carefully, making sure my words would be the last thing he'd hear, the last moments he'd bring with him to the grave. "Yo soi la muerte." *I am death,* I snarled in Spanish.

Then I stood up, brought the family emblem to my lips and kissed it. The man's cries grew louder as I looked back down at him, no smile on my face this time, the grip on the gun tighter.

Another one ready for the land of the dead, I was sending another one to the grave.

Once you stand in my way, you are just a dead man walking until I find you and make sure you are sent where you deserve. To hell.

"One last wish?" I asked but pulled the trigger before the man could say anything, the sound bounced off the walls of the old factory and his lifeless body slumped to the floor, face forward.

The last wish bullshit was my closing line, that meant I was going to shoot you, before you'd answer me. Why? It was my little present to the dead, they could take their wish with them to hell because that's the only place they'd be granted something. I wasn't going to grant them shit. I took their lives, didn't give anything back. Not even a decent burial.

"Take this piece of shit and dump him in the construction site nearby. Pay someone. Get them to pour cement on him."

"Yes, sir," my men were fast, they grabbed the body and dragged it to one of the cars.

I walked slowly to my SUV, my driver was inside ready to flee, but I took my time getting in and taking a seat, cleaning my hands and putting the gun back in the holster.

"You can't go around shooting whoever you please, not in my territory, not my people. This is not Rome," Gennaro, my father's friend and the leader of one of the strongest families in Naples, had advised me to keep my head down, my hands off the trigger and be cautious.

"The ones I am after are the same ones you cannot trust, the ones affiliated with an undercover police officer," I'd said to him and watched his face go pale at first, then turn red with anger.

That's right. A rat, I'd thought, seeing his stare harden.

Nobody liked the word rat, the word police officer. Nobody in 'the families' wanted a filthy, piece of shit in the armed forces, in their circles, their joints.

Three fucking weeks in Naples, I'd played my cards right. I'd brought in the good stuff, the best stacks from Colombia, and sold them to some of the families there. That shit was so good, those rich kids in Naples couldn't get enough. The demand was high, the price was kept low. We did the sums, broke the market.

Nobody had dared to cross me so far, I had Gennaro on my side, nobody could touch me. I was always with him, showing myself in public, making an appearance in the dirty streets of the ghetto with him.

"We could do so much together, Gennaro," I told him one day as we drove through Naples together.

He turned to look at me, waiting for me to carry on. He was interested, I was on.

"Just think if we sold this stuff in Naples, everywhere. I can get it cheap for you, good stuff. They'd all be buying from us. We could take the city in our hands," I didn't hold back.

Temptation was going to get me through, get where I wanted to. It worked.

We agreed we'd try to work to make it happen. He had to think about it, he said, how we could do it. I wasn't in a hurry, I was sure after trying the stash I'd given him, Gennaro would be eager to start our exclusive "collaboration".

"You're just like your father. Good businessman, fearless," Gennaro told me.

Greedy and vengeful.

"Stay by my side, we'll do great things together," he added and I smiled content.

I wasn't going anywhere, not until I'd gotten my hands on what I wanted. I was staying by his side, my name was starting to circulate amongst the crowd and I did everything I could to show people what kind of man I was.

Appearance is everything when you try to make a name for yourself in a territory. You need to show people you are the richest, the strongest, the most powerful and the most feared of them all. Feed the desperate, give them jobs, ask them to help you and pay them well enough to live. It buys you a throne, a fucking crown to wear on your head. Give the poor your crumbs, they'll make you a king.

Naples was perfect for that, poverty and ignorance made my world thrive. The city was easy to conquer, so much easier than Rome.

"What can I do for you, Alejandro?" Gennaro asked me, after seeing all the money we were making off the streets.

Our men had been working hard, pushing our stuff, staying clear of the police. We were doing great, earnings were good, I saw the opportunity and took it.

"The Towers, I want control over The Towers."

Gennaro thought it through, didn't say no to me, he knew better. He'd met my father and it hadn't taken him long to figure out I was exactly like him. A simple no wouldn't do.

It was when we spoke again a few days later, that Gennaro had my answer.

"Join me and my family at my grandson's communion next Sunday. Then we can talk about it, we can discuss it with the other clans. They will all be there," he told me and we agreed I'd bring my family along.

Perfect, we shook hands and I held back a smile.

Last thing I wanted was to show him how important The Towers were to me. Not that I was asking anyone for permission, I was going to take that fucking neighbourhood, no matter what.

It was done, already set in my head but it seemed clear to me how things worked down there in Naples; you must attend the right parties, the right dinners, you must meet everyone and show them your respects. Only then you can talk business and make your move, whatever that move is, but appearance is everything.

So I kept my intentions to myself and crossed the city streets by Gennaro's side, people bowed, lowered their stares, while I walked with my head high. Nobody dared to touch me, I was Gennaro Cannarsa's friend. He was the most powerful mafioso in Naples. Nobody could set foot in the city without him knowing about it.

"Lu diavol da' Capitale," *The Devil from Rome,* that was me.

I'd earned a new nickname and it suited me perfectly. I had the money, the power, the magic powder all of Naples was blabbing about and soon I'd have Sebastian's homeplace in my hands. I was ready to crush it, ready to rule it and destroy it, as I'd destroyed his life. As I'd destroyed him.

ANDREA

Breathe… I focused on my breathing, on the light coming from the curtains, on the sound of the cars going by. It was too early, it was too late. It was never right, it was never okay.

I focused on everything, on anything but him. How he moved inside of me, harsh deep thrusts, my body moved with them, lifeless, uncaring. I told myself it didn't matter, I didn't feel a thing. No pain, no hurt. Nothing. I was beyond hatred, Alejandro had taken that away from me too, along with my body and my dignity.

I didn't hate him anymore. I lived as if he meant nothing and punished myself every time I let his words, his actions hurt me.

No more, no more, I told myself and most days I'd straighten up and dragged myself out of bed. No matter how big of an effort, most days I tried to look my old self, I'd wash up and dress and smile when Eddy was around.

It's just me and you, I'd tell myself playing with him, pretending we were someplace else.

"Come my queen, I will save you from the fire," Eddy said one time, bracing a spoon and a lid from the kitchen, standing on a chair.

He'd look so fierce, so brave looking at me from up there.

How I'd wanted to reassure him that the queen would save her little prince. Maybe she'd lost her king but not her prince.

Instead, Eddy had stretched out his hand and I'd taken it, laughing a little I just couldn't help it. Those days when we were alone most of the time in that big, foreign house on the hill, I'd feel like we were us again, despite the soldiers, despite Alejandro's orders to keep a close eye on us.

Then there were days like that one, when the devil would come looking for me, when I was a prisoner, body and mind and I'd feel like a completely different person.

Meaningless and tired, trapped like a bird in a cage.

I let myself starve sometimes, I let myself stare in the same spot for hours, before Eddy came home from school.

When my son, my life, came back into that big house overlooking Naples, I was suddenly myself again. I'd smile, breathe like I really cared to be alive. I'd spend the day, cherishing his hand in mine.

He was growing, he liked to run ahead when we walked and my hand would feel empty and alone without his, but I smiled nevertheless because he deserved to see his mother smile.

I wasn't sure how much time I had left with my Eddy, how much time before Alejandro would get tired of my apathy, my close to death existence. Maybe he'd have me killed or he himself would kill me soon. I didn't want Eddy to remember me as the sad woman that raised him.

When I stared into nothingness, I was showing Alejandro how much he meant to me. Nothing.

He'd forced me to follow him to Naples, forced his body onto mine, making sure to leave a trace, carving his presence inside my flesh and bones.

He wants me to give up, he wants to break me to the point where I can't be fixed.

I wasn't going to let him think he'd gotten to me, that I was surrendering. I was ignoring him and from the way he kept glaring at me, I knew it was making him uncomfortable, unsatisfied.

Good, I stared into nothingness, giving him no importance and plotted my son's escape. The last thing I'd do, was going to get him out of there.

That's why I'd followed him in the first place, not just to be with Eddy. Not because I couldn't live without my son. No, not just that. A mother's love is deeper than that, reaches beyond selfishness. I followed Alejandro to save Eddy, to make sure he'd never get his hands on him.

Alejandro could touch me, but he'd never touch my son, I'd promised myself that, if it was the last thing I did.

It felt longer this time, but he stopped. He finally stopped moving.

"Look at me," he grunted at some point, words filled with frustration.

He was staring down at me, at my naked body between his silk, red sheets.

Alejandro stood and zipped his trousers, his tattooed naked chest moved fast, screamed out rage.

Had he been talking to me? Noise, he was just noise. It didn't matter, I wasn't listening anyway and I never truly would.

"Don't listen to the monster," my mother used to tell me when I was a child and was scared of the darkness at night. *"He wants you to be scared, he wants you to give in. Never listen to the monster, he's not real."*

If only that were true, if only I could make him go away with my silence, my apathy. As children they tell us monsters aren't real, then we grow up and smell the lie. They are, they are everywhere and they come back looking for you. They always do.

My head slowly turned his way, I showed him the emptiness of my eyes and nothing else.

"You're like a corpse," Alejandro's words grumbled like thunder, but I didn't jump. They didn't scare me.

Never listen to the monster.

"I am what you made me," I only whispered the words, giving them no tone, no emotion but Alejandro's face darkened and it looked as though all the emotions I wasn't feeling, he was feeling.

"I made you my wife, my whore, not a corpse," he snapped and I couldn't help but smile, I couldn't stop myself.

Never.

"You are wrong," I almost laughed the words out, giving him a pitying look.

That's when the thunder became a storm, his hands were on my throat in an instant, pushing me down on the bed. I didn't scream, I didn't fight him. I just looked straight into his dark eyes, showing him he was nothing but sound.

I'm not afraid of you.

Alejandro was a coward, he'd never kill me and he'd never admit it. He'd blown his cover, he wasn't invincible, unstoppable. He'd showed me his weakness.

Me and his obsession for me, I'd figured it out long time ago but deep down I always knew. His were just words, threats to kill me and have my head for leaving him. How many chances had he had? How many chances had he missed? Too many and Alejandro wasn't the sort of man to waste time.

No, he was a coward and I was his Achilles heel, his vulnerability. Me, Andrea Szerov, I was sure.

He'd never have killed me years back, behind that shed, because he'd wanted me, wanted me back. Alejandro knew that a dead wife, a dead obsession would mean failure, not having it his way. He wanted what he wanted and I'd silently taken advantage of that.

His hold loosened, but he kept me on the bed, as he searched my face, my empty eyes.

"Do what you like with me," I whispered and turned my face the other way. "I don't care."

Alejandro's hand moved to my face and squeezed it, forcing me to look at him again.

"Don't you ever look away from me, ever again until I say so," he growled.

"Or you'll hit me? Then do it, if that's what you want. Hit me, Alejandro. Hurt me. Then explain to our son what you've done. Make him hate you," I kept whispering my words, like the hiss of a snake.

Screaming wasn't the way to go, not for someone like Alejandro. He took pleasure in anger, in hatred. I wanted to hit him with my words, slowly like poison, with gentle soft blows. With what he wasn't used to, with the slap of the truth.

He jerked his hand away, my cheeks pulsed with life where his fingers had held my skin. I didn't flinch, I kept my arms along my body. Like a corpse.

Then Alejandro stood and started to walk to the bathroom but first he glared at me one last time.

"I made you my wife and my whore," he snarled.

"But not your lover, not your woman. That I will never be," I mumbled the words and took joy from his glare, as my words sank in.

I didn't have to say it, he knew it was true, he knew who I belonged to, who I longed for, the only man that could ever claim my heart and soul.

Sebastian, my lips refrained from whispering his name, but a sudden heat spread in my chest.

I pictured him, turning to look at me, as I walked down to the shore. I imagined him smiling softly, his eyes running up and down my body. Nobody could ever touch me the way he did, nobody could ever hold me how he'd held me.

I'll wait for you, Sebastian. We are stronger than this, stronger than anything. I will wait for you in this life and the next. Until my last breath, I'll be thinking of you, I'll be thinking of us on that shore.

My eyes closed for a moment, imagining his lips pressed on mine, his hands through my hair, the saltiness of his tongue.

"You are what I say you are, Andrea. You are mine, you don't get to decide," Alejandro hissed, bringing me back to reality, back to hell.

I opened my eyes just as he was about to walk away. "I will make you care," he added and disappeared in the other room.

I stared at the ceiling, suppressing my feelings.

Empty Andrea, you are empty. Don't give this man anything, not even one inch of your soul.

"You are coming with me today," he barked from the bathroom door.

I didn't care where or why. Not until he said:

"You and Eddy. We are going to a party. So be ready to go soon."

Eddy? I turned my head in his direction but didn't say a thing. I tried my best to stay calm, look unaffected by the news, but my whole body started pulsing with life. My temples, my chest, my stomach, the blood was back, the life was back, now I cared.

Why me and Eddy? Who's party? Why did he want us with him?

"We'll play a little game today," Alejandro said and my stomach twisted.

I felt like I was going to be sick, the twisted tone of his voice, the word game on his fowl lips, made my whole body tremble.

A game, with Eddy, every time he mentioned my son, I died a little, worried he'd figured something out.

"The family game, Andrea. You, me and Eddy will be a perfect little family today and show our respects to the other clans here in Naples."

He's taking us with him to handle his dirty business, he's making us part of his despicable life.

The blood thumped in my temples. Everything I always wanted to keep Eddy away from was coming back to haunt me.

We'd be forced to sit and eat with those people, killers, sinners and greedy gangsters, other families in the mafia and pretend. I didn't know how much longer I'd be able to pretend.

I'm running out of time, I thought as I listened to him dress and walk out of the room. I stayed where I was for a moment and went over my plan for the fiftieth time.

Don't panic, calm down.

Maybe Alejandro would make me care one day- care he was hurting me, care he was killing me slowly- but I was going to make him miserable. I was going to take his son away from him. I was going to make HIM care.

Be brave, don't listen to the monster. Kill him softly.

CHAPTER 21
WELCOME TO NAPLES, WELCOME TO THE NEW FAMIGLIA

ALEJANDRO

My father once was told you are friends with someone only once you've shared food with them.

Gennaro was my friend and he made sure everyone saw it. He sat us next to him during the reception and he'd lean my way every now and then to point out some clan leader or another.

"We call him The Sentinel, he knows everything that goes on, his eyes are everywhere. He knew about you before I told the rest," Gennaro informed me, eyeing the fifty something year old man greying at the sides, sitting at a table nearby.

"He owns the south eastern part of the city, he's my oldest ally and the most trustworthy of them all. He wants to meet you, he'd be more than happy to work with you."

I nodded and looked the man's way. He was staring at us, a glass of red wine brushing against his lips. He nodded my way and raised his glass. I did the same.

That was a sign, no matter where you were from, no matter which clan, city, country, that meant he was interested, business could be handled, that the deal could be settled.

Another greedy one after the finest cocaine, very good.

I drank my wine content, as Gennaro went over all the tables with me, each and every single one of them had some sort of clan or gangster from Naples and the nearby cities.

I listened in, until I realized Andrea was glancing my way, her eyes glum. The food in her plate sat there untouched. I looked at her, scanned her face, lingering on her cheekbones for an instant. She'd lost more weight.

She's fucking starving herself, I thought and glared at her, I ordered her to eat with a stare. I eyed the plate, then eyed her again and mouthed the word 'EAT'.

Not even the slightest interest or emotion crossed her face. Andrea picked her food for a while, bringing almost nothing to her mouth, her attention on Eddy.

He was playing with the other kids, they sat together at their own table, but he seemed a little distant, a little out of the rowdiness and commotion around all the toys that lay around the plates.

"What's wrong with him?" I asked, my voice low.

"He's not happy," she answered, her eyes never leaving Eddy.

"I'll get him a new toy," I mumbled and took a bite of the delicious roasted meat they'd just served us.

"That's not what he wants," she shook her head and drank some wine.

I glanced her way and my eyes traced along her long neck.

I felt the urge to bite it, her white skin so smooth and inviting, she'd braided her hair to one side.

"What is it then?" I pressed on, my tone impatient.

"He's homesick. Over the last few months he's been pushed around. Eddy doesn't like it here," Andrea whispered.

I turned my head her way and moved closer, her sweet scent filled my nose, made me dizzy as I whispered in her ear.

"His home is where I am, where his father is. I know what's best for us."

I stayed where I was, close to her skin and brushed my fingers on her naked back.

Andrea's body tensed, her face darkened as she kept her eyes on Eddy, avoiding my stare, like it didn't scare her.

Maybe it did or maybe it didn't, but I could feel her little body shudder, I could see her cheeks turn pale, as my hand snaked up and down her back.

What about now? Are you scared now, Andrea? My lips curled in a smile.

And when my lips touched her shoulder, she jumped in her seat but I was faster. I grabbed her dress and pulled down hard, so hard, I thought I'd rip it.

Where do you think you are going? I smiled, keeping her in place, and kissed her shoulder again.

"Are you questioning me?" I whispered in her ear.

Andrea eyed me cautiously this time but kept her stare just as fierce as before.

"This isn't about you or me or us. It's about Eddy, I'm worried," she paused. "You want him to grow up like this? With these people?" something flickered in her eyes. What was it? *Disgust, arrogance, hatred?*

"There are more guns, more soldiers in this room than in a high security prison. We drive around the city with a bullet proof car, Eddy is not allowed outside alone, he's not allowed outside at school. We live in fear, when we were living free before. He was happy, he was happy before."

"I'm giving him everything, I'm giving you everything. Anything you want you can have, money, clothes, toys every single fucking thing."

"Anything but freedom," Andrea's cold stare pierced right through me, I wanted nothing more than to punish her, slap her hard for talking back at me, for questioning me and judging my decisions, for being the fucking bitch that she was.

Shut up, you'll do what I say, I wanted to scream at her but we were surrounded by people, very important people and we were playing the part of the little happy family. I gritted my teeth and whispered again.

"My power has a price, Andrea. Just like your mistakes. Freedom is the price to pay," then I bit her ear and snarled. "Wait till we get home, I'll make you feel the price of daring me again, in front of all these people. Now shut the fuck up and smile, talk to the other women and speak to me only when you are spoken to."

My hand grabbed her and gripped her side, hard. I enjoyed the sight of her, shaking, in pain but resisting the urge to shout.

It was going to bruise, her skin was going to turn purple, her daily reminder she needed to keep her mouth shut.

"You can hurt me, Alejandro. I don't care, all I care is that you are hurting Eddy," Andrea said keeping her eyes ahead, on our son.

Before I could say anything back, Gennaro spoke again, inviting me to follow him and the rest of the leaders into another room for cigars and rum.

Another way to say 'to talk business'.

Andrea was fucking lucky I was needed elsewhere. I released her waist and saw her pant, breathing in and out frantically, like she'd been holding her breath. I took note of each and every tear she held in her eyes and smiled, leaning down to her.

From the outside I looked like a sweet, caring husband and she looked like an angel. We both were something else, something completely different from our appearance.

"I'll be back in a while. Our conversation is not over. When we get home, I'll make you regret every single word you said to me. I'll fuck you so hard, you won't be able to walk tomorrow," and then I moved down to her lips and kissed her softly, flashing a deadly smile at her.

Our glasses were still full of liquor when we settled in to discuss the deal. Gennaro immediately told everyone who I was, why I was there and what I had to offer.

"The finest cocaine at an amazing price. We all buy from him, we all have similar prices on the streets, no war against one another. The stuff is good," he gestured to one of his soldiers and a stash was placed on the round table in the room.

We were safe, Gennaro told us, the room had been searched for bugs, the restaurant was his. We were all free to speak.

Some of the men tried my shit, tossing their heads back in ecstasy, others tasted it on their fingers.

That shit was good, there was no questions about it but they all seemed very doubtful, they all looked at each other a little confused.

"What's in it for him?" one spoke up, his head nodding my way. "The price is so low, why?"

I smiled, lighting the cigar.

"Money, expansion of my trade and interests."

"What interests?" another one asked immediately.

I eyed Gennaro who took the matter into his hands.

"He wants The Towers, he wants control over it."

"That part is mine," a man dressed in a blue suit, crossed his arms over his chest and stared at me arrogantly.

The face of someone hard to deal with, hard to comply.

I've heard of him, they called him The Gipsy, he was a man that had made a name for himself. No family legacy, he just worked his way up and took control of the area. Prostitution and bets were his speciality. He loved to bet money on horses and underground fights. He was the man of The Towers, I looked at him and wondered if he'd met The Killer at the time. I wondered if he knew the truth about him.

I'm not the sort of man you want to cross, I kept smiling at him. I pitied him already, as he was going down.

"What makes you think you can come here, from Rome and take something that's ours? Who the fuck does this guy think he is?" another man said, pointing at me, looking around the room.

There were ten of them in total, most of them were quiet. The Sentinel just stared at me, his arms crossed over his chest too. He looked amused.

Who the fuck did I think I was? El Diablo.

"I am the man with the best cocaine, the best price in town. I am willing to sell it to you all, making you richer than you all are. I'm offering you peace. If you don't agree with these terms, I'll sell it to Gennaro and the Sentinel only. They'll break the market, they'll sell it cheap. We'll have everyone at our feet. Then, I'll take The Towers down anyway."

"What the fuck…" the man in charge of The Towers stood and slammed his fist on the table, then he turned to Gennaro and pointed at me again, his chubby face flushed.

"You allow this? We have a pact, a solid agreement and you let this piece of shit, this Spanish dickhead come tell us what to do, Gennaro? What the fuck is this?"

Gennaro raised his hand, telling everyone to calm down. To let me finish saying what I had to say.

I walked towards the man, the one that had what I wanted, my neighbourhood. It was mine already.

I stood face-to-face with him, my piercing dark eyes burned right through him.

"Do you want me to tell your friends how you had a rat in your neighbourhood and didn't tell anyone? Do you want me to tell your friends how the police have their names; they know all about their businesses because you had a filthy undercover cop in your area and didn't even realize it? How many people got arrested because of you? How do we know you are not a rat, too?"

"Ti amazzo," *I'm gonna kill you.*

The Gipsy went for my throat but the soldiers around us pulled him back. They pushed him down on the chair but he tried to fight them, tried to get free of their hold. He couldn't, he wasn't going anywhere.

Not so fast.

"What is this all about?" the others wanted to know, so I told them the story of The Killer. I told them how I'd found he was a rat, he'd been in The Towers for years, selling information to the police, telling them where they could find the stash of drugs, the money and giving names of the men behind the operations.

"They have your names. This was going on under his very nose," I pointed to the Gipsy. "He didn't do a thing about it, but I will. I promise you I will, I know all the people this rat has been in contact with, the people he was friends with in the neighbourhood. I know everything, I'll hunt them down, clean the place up and make it safe for us again to operate in. You have my word."

"Fucking let go of me," the man snarled, his face now pressed against the wooden table, the soldiers kept him down as Gennaro circled the table and walked to stand in front of him.

Gennaro stared at the others in the room and then leaned down to speak to the man in question.

"You failed. You failed us all. What happened with The Rat is a very serious matter, we could all go to jail for this. We could all blow up," the man didn't say a thing, he kept fighting the soldiers, so Gennaro ordered them to leave him alone.

The Gipsy stood up and faced Gennaro, eye to eye, breathing in his face, rage and resentment.

"I was always faithful to you, I never betrayed you, none of you," he pointed to every man in the room, but they all kept quiet, careful to question anyone or dare to intervene. "If what this asshole says is true, I will see to it. I will personally hunt these rats down and clean up the neighbourhood. It's my territory and it has been for years now."

"You have been my friend for a long time, Gipsy and that is why I'm not going to kill you. That is why I won't go hard on you, but you failed us all. We can't trust you," Gennaro said, then to the rest of the room. "We can't trust him to do the clean up."

I was silent as the others finally started talking, they mumbled amongst themselves, suddenly unsure of what to think or do. Unsure of the Gipsy, their long-term friend.

Loyalty in the mafia is just a matter of business and interests.

The alliance is solid until it's not anymore, it takes nothing to break the balance and everyone starts to question and doubt.

A rat! Betrayal! One word is all it takes and it's every man for himself again. Fuck the alliance, fuck friendship or 'la famiglia'. Money is more important, staying alive and out of jail even more.

In a matter of minutes it was settled: we struck the deal, my cocaine at a low price, my control over The Towers.

Everyone agreed, even though they still doubted me, sensing I couldn't be trusted, scared I'd want something else tomorrow, maybe something that was theirs.

I'd reassure them I wasn't after their city, after their shitholes. I wanted The Towers only. Mine was a matter of revenge, not greediness.

The Gipsy couldn't do shit. He had no say in our agreement.

We decided he could keep the rest of his territories, he could still be part of the alliance. He wasn't given any other choice but to hand The Towers over to me.

"Nobody goes after a man in the alliance, nobody. Gipsy, Alejandro, do you understand?" Gennaro said, forcing us to shake hands at the end.

He looked from me to the Gipsy and we both nodded, we both lied.

"Sure," I said and flashed my best smile, my most sincere appreciation.

The Gipsy simply glared at me, his eyes narrowed, not saying a single thing.

He didn't need to, his eyes did the talking.

He held my hand tight and tilted his head back a little, studying me closely, his cheeks still red from before, when he was held down on the table.

Watch your back, his dark eyes seemed to tell mine.

Watch yours, I glared back.

I knew better than to trust someone like him, someone from those filthy streets. I knew the Gipsy was already plotting my death.

Fair enough, but I'd be waiting for him.

I'd be ready to take him down.

CHAPTER 22
THE PIANOFORTE

ANDREA

"You are back early," Sebastian opened the door with a grin.

I smiled wide, trying to peek in our living room but Sebastian moved sideways, his broad shoulders blocking the view.

He was 'the view'.

I took in the sight of him, his strong arms flexed on the doorframe, a cheeky smile danced on his voluptuous lips.

So sexy, so cheeky, so Italian- he gave off passion and warmth.

I devoured him with my eyes.

"I came home early, I missed you," I smiled sweetly as my hands snaked around his back. I moved in for a hug and tried to sneak a peek.

"What are you hiding, Signor Esposito???"

Not a chance. Sebastian blocked my way in again and kissed me passionately. I lost all interest in what was waiting for me in there. He was such a tease, I let his big hands distract me.

"Close your eyes," he mumbled, staring into my half-closed eyes.

I pouted and he kissed my nose, once, twice. It tickled, he knew I loved it when he did that. I let out a giggle and complied.

Sebastian knew how impatient I was when it came to surprises. I was always restless, eager to find out, learn something new. He'd brought me back to life, I couldn't get enough of him, of us.

His hands gently pulled me into the house, I let Sebastian guide me. A few steps in and he told me to stop, to turn around, I knew I was facing the big glass window that led to the terrace.

"Now, you can open them, Occhi Belli," Pretty eyes.

I bit my lip and didn't wait for him to ask me again. My eyes opened wide and I remember laughing and smiling, not able to articulate a sentence for how surprised I was.

I covered my mouth, then looked Sebastian's way, then back to the black piano that rested against the wall, right next to the large window facing the sea.

A piano, he'd bought a piano. For me, just for me.

"Oh my god," I squealed with joy. "Where did you find this?"

"A man that lives two houses down from the harbour was selling it. I had to take it, it had your name on it, Pretty Eyes," Sebastian smiled and looked down at me, I slipped my hand into his, holding it tight.

"Do you like it?"

"Like it? I love it," I kept staring at the piano, not believing my eyes.

I could play again, I hadn't played since we'd left Rome.

"How did you buy this? It must have cost a fortune," I began to worry he'd spent too much.

Money wasn't a problem, he earned enough on the boats, while I had quite a few English students, but I came from a family of musicians. I knew how much a piano was worth and even a second-hand one had its price.

"It's done, mia bella signora." My beautiful lady.

We walked over to that wooden beauty, it was black and shiny. Sebastian had polished it, fixed a few things he said. The keys were perfect, he'd had it tuned when they'd delivered it that morning, while I was in class.

"I know it's a pretty thing to stare at but the man told me you can touch it and play it," *he went all smartass on me, I frowned at him but he kept smiling.*

Sebastian couldn't stop looking at me. I was over the moon.

As my fingers brushed against the keys, Sebastian kissed my shoulder, then moved to stand behind me and his lips trailed down my neck.

I pressed a key, he planted a kiss on my skin. I pressed another one, he kissed me again and again and again as I played a little. My giggles were lost in the music.

"I haven't played in so long, what shall I play?" *I asked, feeling his hands slide forward, over my waist.*

"Whatever makes you happy, it's all yours baby. You can start giving piano lessons, how's that?"

I nodded, keeping that warm smile on my lips. I liked the idea, I liked that Sebastian had thought about it, I loved his hands on me, his voice encouraging me to play.

"What shall I play?" *I asked again.*

"Whatever you want, baby. Whatever makes you happy."

I only had to think about it for a second.

"Gloria by Vivaldi" *and I played the first part, patient my fingers would warm up to the keys.*

"Beautiful," *he whispered in my ear.* "Everything about you is beautiful. What you do, how you do it. Your skin, your body" *he kissed my neck, my shoulder, while his hands trailed up to my breasts, I took in a breath and felt them slip up my neck.* "Your hands, your lips."

"Sebastian," I whimpered and started to turn, my hands off the piano, but he quickly took hold of them and gently guided my fingers back to the keys.

"No, Occhi Belli. Keep your hands on that piano. Keep playing it, I like to listen to you play." One hand trailed down my thigh, between my legs, I whimpered as the other one worked its way up again.

I kept my fingers on the piano like he'd asked me to, I kept playing while Sebastian played me. All afternoon.

"Do you like to sing?" I snapped out of my daydream, taking my eyes off the piano in the restaurant.

A man was playing it and singing a traditional Italian song.

I looked at the women around me, at the one that had asked me the question and shook my head, smiling embarrassed.

"No, I don't know how to sing," I said and self-consciously pushed a strand of hair behind my ear.

They were all staring at me. The women of those rich, powerful families studied me like I was the strangest, the most mysterious person they'd ever seen in their lives.

La straniera, "the foreign lady". *La moglie de lu Diavul,* "The wife of the Devil".

They knew only half of it. They knew nothing of me, my story.

"I used to play the piano," I regretted the words as soon as they escaped my lips, but it was too late, I'd revealed something about me and I now had their full attention.

Their heads turned, they spoke fast to each other, in slang I reckoned. I couldn't make out a word.

"That's lovely. A woman that plays the piano," a lady with ink black hair and green eyes smiled at me.

"Why don't you play something for us?" another one asked but before she could finish the sentence, I was already shaking my head.

No, I couldn't.

"Oh, come on," they insisted.

"I only play classical music, I don't have a repertoire for parties," I struggled to make my way out of the mess I'd jumped right into.

"Nonsense, we'd love for you to play. *La straniera suona per noi," The foreign lady will play for us,* the host- the mother of the child we were celebrating- announced to everyone in the room and I was invited to stand and walk to the piano.

My eyes searched for Alejandro, but he was still nowhere to be seen. I had no idea where he was or when he'd be back.

My legs shook, they nearly failed me but I made it to the piano nevertheless.

It was beautiful, long and white, pure white. Prestigious maybe, but all I kept thinking of was the black, old, smaller one Sebastian had given me.

If only I could have closed my eyes and relived that moment. I would have given anything, anything, for just one more time, one more song, one more moment with him.

"What shall I play?" I asked myself, like I once did with Sebastian.

"Gloria by Vivaldi," I imagined him whisper the words in my ear.

I nodded a little and let my fingers run along the keys.

To the good times we had, to when we were happy, to when our life was glorious and we needed nothing more than us. I played Gloria and thought of him.

For you, Sebastian. Don't forget me.

My hands moved on the keys- sharp, fast, harmonious. Gloria was joy, it was rebellion. I played for passion, I did it for freedom.

For the life that was stolen from me, I played like it was my last.

Gloria was the song I'd always played for Sebastian, every note reminded me of something, a word, a whisper, something he'd done, the sound of his voice when he called my name, when he called me Pretty eyes.

"Tesoro, Occhi Belli," Honey, Pretty Eyes. I smiled and kept playing, like he was there with me, listening, brushing his fingers down my back.

My cheeks flushed, my heart ached but I didn't stop. I focused on those memories, on that joy I'd felt with Sebastian.

Happiness lasts the blink of an eye. Then all you're left with are memories, you're left mourning those moments for the rest of your life. We all walk around looking for perfection, for success, but that's not what happiness is all about.

Happiness is home, it's feeling like you belong somewhere with someone. Not just laughter and smiles, but peace and serenity. Freedom.

It's having someone to hold you, it's holding someone back. It's feeling whole and never alone. I was never alone, I never would be. I'd always have Gloria, I'd always have memories of us, memories of Sebastian and our lives together.

I played it loud and strong, until my fingers began to hurt, like a rebel yell.

I love you, no matter where you are, my heart screamed. *Nobody can take those moments away from us. Nobody.*

I kept playing even when guests clapped their hands, overjoyed by my performance. I didn't stop not even when I saw Alejandro walk back into the room.

Freedom! I held his glare, his face was fuming with rage.

Yes, I was playing. Yes, I knew he didn't want me to, he didn't want me to attract the attention. He didn't want me to be anything but his wife, anything but his pretty doll. No initiative, nothing unless he said so.

Fuck you, my fingers danced over the keys until I heard somebody shout.

"Stop!" Eddy screamed at the door.

He'd been running outside in the garden with the other kids, I didn't even realize he'd walked back in.

"Stop!" he shouted again, running towards me.

I stopped playing, my face confused

What's wrong? What happened?

Eddy ran up to me and I opened my arms to catch him. Whatever was going on, I just wanted to hold him, hold him close to me, but he kept his distance, he stopped right in front of me with a look in his eyes I didn't recognize.

"What's the matter, baby?" I asked keeping my voice low.

He just glared at me in silence, as I tried to read his face. He'd never stared at me like that, I was confused.

"What happened?" I asked again and he shouted furiously, shaking me to the core.

"Don't play that anymore. Don't," I saw his little fist fly towards me but I didn't move.

I let him hit me, slap me in the face, punch me in the stomach, my eyes wide as I cried out his name.

"Please, Eddy. Enough, hush," I spoke to him in Hungarian, my lips trembled as I took his little arms and let the tears stream down my face, free. Unashamed. At least they were free to be.

"I don't want you to play that song. That was when we were happy, when we were with Sebastian. I don't want you to play," he shouted back at me in Hungarian, the words harsh, agonizing. "I hate this place, I hate it. I hate it."

"Please, Eddy. Hush, hush," I pleaded again and he gave in to me, to my broken heart.

He let me hold him, as I stood, my arms so weak from the lack of food, I thought I'd drop him and trip over but I steadied my walk and I gave out apologetic glances around the room.

Alejandro was by our side a moment later, his filthy hand pressing against my back, pushing me out of the room in a haste.

"I am sorry, he's very tired," he said to the guests and asked them to excuse us, we were just going to freshen up in the bathroom.

The chatter was full on in the room, I didn't care if it was us they were talking about. The only words that could rip me apart, really rip me apart were Eddy's.

"Clean him up," Alejandro ordered me around, controlling the anger in his voice for Eddy.

I nodded and told Eddy to follow me into the bathroom. On the threshold, Alejandro's hand gripped my arm. His devilish eyes sunk into mine, as he squeezed me tight.

"You cunt, you are lucky Eddy is here, I'd have slapped you and punished you here, now," he snarled under his breath. "Why don't you fucking keep that mouth shut? Why don't you fucking stay put in your place? Do you know the damage you just did in that room?"

His business, I'd ruined his perfect little business lunch. Of course, that was all he was thinking about.

Screw you!

He paused eyeing Eddy, sobbing on the toilet seat.

"Why do you fuck around with me? You like to be punished? Huh?" he shook me a little, I pulled my arm back, freeing myself from his hold.

I lifted my head, my spirits still high from playing the piano, from being myself again even if it was only for a moment.

"You still think I care, you still think you can hurt me, Alejandro. Fuck you. Fuck you. You'll have to kill me to keep my mouth shut, until then I am never going to stop fighting you. I can't help it because this is me. THIS IS ME!" I pressed a finger over my chest, over my heart, he just stared at me, his hands clenching at his sides.

I knew he'd never hit me, not in front of Eddy. He cared too much of what Eddy thought about him.

His eyes went to my little boy again, my little Eddy who was trying to dry his tears with a tissue.

No, he didn't hit me. Not with his hands. He punched me in the stomach with his words, slammed a dagger through my heart and hissed in my face.

"You want me to kill you? Is that what you want? Forget about it, too easy, too soon. I won't let you reunite with your Sebastian, not in this life, not in the next," he kept his dark eyes on me, as he mumbled the words. "Sebastian is dead. I killed that son of a bitch."

"No," my mouth opened to speak but nothing came out.

No, no, no. I cried, covering my face with both hands, then looked back into his soulless eyes. *Liar.*

I pushed my hair back and shook my head.

No, no, no. It's not true.

I wanted to scream, I felt as though I was going to throw up.

With a hand over my stomach, I tried to steady my breathing but nothing worked. Panic, I was having a panic attack.

Sebastian.

"You lied to me, you son of a bitch," my voice rose a bit, I'd forgotten all about Eddy just a step away from us.

Sebastian, I let out a cry, I imagined his body lying somewhere, his eyes closed. I'd never see those eyes again, never hear his voice again.

No, it can't be. Oh God no!

"You said you wouldn't hurt him, you lied to me. You son of a bitch," I spat the words out, uncaring if there were people around us.

I didn't care where we were or who heard me, a part of me was dying. A part of me had died already. *Sebastian.*

"You really thought I'd let him live? That piece of shit?" Alejandro hissed, his eyes flared with hatred.

My hands started to shake, my whole body nearly gave in. I felt as though I couldn't stay up, I couldn't do it.

Alejandro tried to grab my arm as I fell back and hit the wall behind me, but I pushed him hard, as hard as I could away from me, and I managed to stay up, while the weight of the world seemed to cave in on me. For Eddy, I managed to get up for Eddy.

Sebastian, I sobbed and cried, not listening to a single word Alejandro was saying to me.

My love, my rock, I'd lost a part of me. I suddenly couldn't breathe, it wasn't worth breathing anymore. I didn't want to live in a world without Sebastian, I didn't want to keep fighting in a world without him.

"Shut up!" I screamed.

Alejandro grabbed my arm again, steadying me.

"Don't you dare," he hissed and I spat in his face.

Die, die. Why don't you die? Dark thoughts echoed in my mind. I didn't ask God for forgiveness, I didn't ask God to put me out of my misery. I prayed for God to take Alejandro away, to punish him like he deserved.

Why? Why Sebastian, why?

Anger filled my lungs as he shook me again, snarling for me to keep my mouth shut and clean up our son. We'd finish the conversation at home, where he could punish me like I deserved.

"Whatever you've done to him, I swear to God you'll pay for it. This life or the next Alejandro. You are dead to me. Dead," I straightened up and walked into the bathroom.

I scooped Eddy up in my arms and we didn't leave the bathroom until Alejandro and his soldiers came for us, when it was time to go home.

"I hate this place too," I told my son for the first time.

No more lies, he'd sobbed under my chin and told me he hated when I lied. I never told him the truth.

"Only Sebastian tells me the truth," Eddy said and I held him tighter.

"I miss him," he whispered and I caressed his hair, breathing in his scent, cherishing that moment of truth.

I wanted to tell him everything, every single thing, what was the use of keeping it from him now? It was all over, I'd lost the will to keep going.

I almost did, but then I remembered the grand plan, the reason why I'd followed Alejandro to Italy.

To save Eddy.

So I looked down at him, at my life, my everything, at what was left for me to love of Sebastian, and smiled, tears pooling in my eyes.

"I miss him too. Every day."

PART 3
THE END OF EVERYTHING

And know that I am with you always; yes, to the end of time.
Jesus Christ

CHAPTER 23
STREETS KNOW MY NAME

SEBASTIAN

Time stopped.

I hear my mother shouting in the kitchen, throwing dishes everywhere. She's angry at me, I'm a 'good at nothing piece of shit', she's saying.

"Out all day and you bring this," she's tosses the coins I earned begging at a street corner, near a bakery.

I bite my tongue and swallow down the insults. I don't have the courage to tell her I used some change to buy a slice of pizza. Hunger made me do it, I'm only seven. I was hungry, so hungry.

"Strunz e'mmerda," Piece of shit.

No dinner for me, nothing. She screams at me to go to bed, my mother.

I don't say anything back, I disappear as quickly and quietly as possible.

I'm a mistake, I'm a piece of shit, I'm a hungry little creep. Mistakes don't talk, mistakes hold their breaths and should just be thankful they're given a chance to live.

I don't say anything back to my mother, even though there are so many things I want to say her.

Like I'm sorry I didn't bring enough money, for standing in her way, for making her life harder. I'm sorry I was ever born.

I'm sorry.

But I keep quiet, I can't say a single thing, not now. Not when she's like this. It's the drugs, it's not her talking. She needs another dose, I can tell.

Her eyes are wide and they move from side to side, frantically, desperately. She's in pain, aching all over, her hands shake.

Three, four men come in that night. They come and do their thing, I try not to listen in, but the walls are so thin, I can hear everything, and I don't understand any of it, but it scares me. Sometimes they make loud noises, sometimes nothing. I don't know what to fear more, the screams or the eerie silence.

I sleep in an old bed, the only other piece of furniture in my room is a wooden chest. It has holes and smells like mould, but it's the only space I have for my treasures, the things I find on the street and make my own. I take them home- toys, plastic things, old junk- and pretend it's my treasure chest.

I push that treasure chest in front of my door every night, it keeps the men out. Some try to come into my room, some have before I knew, before I knew I had to block the door to stop them.

I don't remember much of what happened, but what I do remember is that it hurt, for days. I couldn't move or walk without feeling the pain, it was low and deep inside me. The memory made me feel ashamed and guilty: I should have stopped them from coming in, I should have stopped them from hurting me like that but I don't tell anyone. I don't say a thing. Mistakes don't talk, they don't cause trouble. Mistakes like me should not have the right to be.

The mattress stops moving, I can't hear the springs anymore and I know the last customer will be out soon.

When they leave my mother seems happier, she counts the money twice and then runs out. Sometimes she doesn't return home until the following day, each time I wonder if she'll ever be back. Then she comes home, if I'm lucky she brings food, too. Those are the happiest moments for me, when she brings food. For once I don't have to worry about finding something to eat, hunger won't torment my sleep.

Via Napoleone 14, block 7, apartment 120.
I'm back in Naples, walking through those streets, the streets that know my name.
I'm standing in front of my old home, where my mother died on the kitchen floor one day and I was left alone- in an empty house without a table and chairs. Nobody around to dry my tears. Where I ate on the floor, bread crumbs and dust.
Time stopped. I can almost hear my mother's voice, her swearing, I remember the hunger, the abuse, the violence and all those men.
The Towers is just like it was. Nothing but tall building blocks, tainted with poverty and filth; no balconies, no dignity. Clothes hang from every window, there is no space inside for them, I know how small those apartments are.
I remember how sometimes during the summer, we'd ran out of water for days and be forced to wash up in the public fountains a few blocks down.
The streets where I am from have no dignity, no hope. People keep to themselves, everyone minds their own business. They are too scared to talk and the mob thrives on the fear.
Kids running down the streets, skipping school, are just new soldiers ready for sacrifice. Fresh meat, ready to do

anything, ready to brace a gun and shoot, for words like 'family' 'honour' 'brotherhood' 'money'.

When you have nothing, you don't care about taking risks.

The State abandoned you, you are left to wash yourself in the fucking public fountains. You need to get creative to find money to buy food, to stay alive.

Until one day a man dressed in fine clothes- smoking Cuban cigars, driving fast expensive cars- comes along and tells you that he can change your life, that you can have it all, you can be like him. Rich, powerful, above the law.

Not just food and water, suddenly you can afford designer shoes, motorbikes, the latest trends.

You can have it all, the world is yours if you do what he says.

When you have nothing and someone offers you everything, you take those damn risks with a fucking grin on your face. Till the very end.

What is the point of living a meaningless life like a worm, crawling in those filthy streets?

It's better to live a short life as a king, rather than a long life as fucking loser, this is what they tell you, those gangsters and their soldiers.

I nearly fell for their lies, I nearly braced that gun, took those risks.

The building has sentinels. At least two on the roof, a couple pacing the main entrance. I keep my distance, I pretend to look for something in my bag and stay right where I am, under the broken and torn bus stop. I try not to draw attention to myself, but I'm not worried. The sentinels are too busy smoking pot, laughing about something, probably one of their latest bravado.

Sentinels outside my old building, I can think of a few reasons why, but it takes me a while to really figure it out.

It's a brothel.

Each and every window on the West side has a coloured curtain: bright pink, red, yellow, green, blue. I count fifty apartments, two-bedroom apartments.

I swallow hard and watch the people walk in and out. Men, only men. Each one filthier than the one before him.

"You're looking for company, stud?" I turn to the sound of a raspy voice.

A forty something woman stands beside me, big brown eyes, tanned face and black hair tied up in a ponytail. Her nails are red, her dress short, tight around her waist and hips. She smiles at me cunningly and tilts her head as she takes a good look at me. Too much makeup, too much skin. Her face says she's tired and worn out. A prostitute.

"Maybe," I say to make her stay, to make sure she doesn't walk away.

I need information, I need someone to help me understand, why everything is so different even though I'm in the same filth- the same hell I came out of years back.

"Then I am your lady. I know a place," she stands in front of me and chews the gum in her mouth like she'd like to take a bite of me.

"In there?" I nod and indicate the building with my head, the woman eyes it and frowns.

"No, not there. I'm not in that business," she cuts off like that. I need more.

"Business?" I repeat the word, lifting my eyebrow.

"Straniero?" "Foreigner?" she asks but knows it can't be true.

My accent, the way I slur the words and 'sing' them out, the way only someone from Naples knows how to, the lady can tell I am from there.

I'm apparently unaware of something I should know about.

"No, I've been away for a while," I tell her and she nods, smiling again, looping her arm around mine, pushing me gently.

We start walking down the street, her eyes drift to the building again for a moment, before she points to a set of old, abandoned shacks.

"We can handle 'our business' in there," she winks and keeps walking, shaking her hips, emphasising the goods.

My attention is still on the building, my old home when we reach the shacks.

"What business goes on in there?" I ask as we step inside the place.

It's dark, smells like waste and as my eyes adjust to the absence of light, I realize it's full of junk. Out the corner of my eye, I can see old pans, sheets, bags of rubbish, diapers. It smells awful in there, but there is a little corner with a holed mattress on the floor and a pillow.

This is where she takes her customers. Where she lives, I feel like I've walked into my past. I imagine my mother, I remember the sounds from her bedroom. My stomach ties in a knot, cold sweat trickles down my neck.

I'm back.

I want to say something but the woman is already stripping, I feel the urge to stop it from happening but I can't blow it off like that. I need to keep the game going, I know how wary people in the streets are of foreigners.

If you are not a usual and you act strangely, you'll get nothing out of them. I need everything I can get out of her.

"Forget about that place. Let's worry about what we have going on in here, stranger. What would you like me to do for you?" she purrs, flashing her breasts a little, biting her lip.

I want you to tell me what the hell is happening here, I silenced my thoughts.

"I want company and I want to talk," as soon as my words are out, her face drops.

"Stronzo," *Asshole,* she mumbles under her breath and stops the whole seduction scene. "If you are here to waste my time, stranger…. I have none, no time to waste."

My hand dives into my pocket and I take out a fifty euro note. Red, new and silky. The lady stares at it, her eyes shining. I bet she sells herself for half of what I'm offering her. I can tell by the sparkle in her eyes. She's probably thinking of how much food she can buy, how long she could make that money last. I wonder if she has any children, more mouths to satiate beside her own.

"How much time can I buy with this?"

She licks her lips and manages to take her eyes off it, she's looking at me again now, a newfound stare.

Hesitation and suspicion, but also slyness. I am sure she's trying to figure out how to get more money off me, during our little 'chat'. That's another lesson you learn from the streets. You never know when you'll have a break, so when the time comes, you make the most of it, take advantage of it as much as you can.

"Half an hour," she mumbles and I know she's swindling me but I don't care. I need the information.

I just nod and take a seat on a what looks and feels like a chunk of wood.

"Tell me what happens in that building," I cut to the chase.

I'm too tired to play and try to mess with her, to pretend I'm curious. I can tell she'll talk, she needs the money.

"I don't talk to cops," she wants to clear the air immediately and I wonder why. Maybe because she doesn't trust the police, the government, she doesn't believe in justice. How can I blame her, if this is where she lives, where she eats and works?

"I am not a cop," I reassure her. *Not anymore, I am not.* "What is your name?"

"Maddalena," she tells me.

"Do I look like a cop, Maddalena?" I raise my eyebrow and she shakes her head, after taking another good look at me, my cheek still a little purple from the fight back in Folegandros.

"What do you think happens in there? It's a brothel," she says and tells me all about the families that once lived there, how they were kicked out one day, just like that out of the blue.

Soldiers came and gave them one hour to take their stuff and leave. Then the building was filled up with prostitutes all from the eastern European countries or African.

"When did this happen?" I ask and she takes in a breath.

"A few weeks ago."

A few weeks ago, when he moved to Naples, I think to myself.

I don't need to hear his name to know it's his doing. My old building filled with prostitutes, it's not a coincidence. Nothing is with someone like Alejandro. Still I have to ask.

"Who did this?"

She stares at the wall, then her eyes are back on me a little hesitant, like she's not sure she can trust me.

"He came from Rome, like a fury…" she carries on, I don't interrupt her this time.

"He made friends with important families, I know because some of his soldiers are my customers. Don Cristiano, Don Gennaro, Don Antonio. All the clans know him, he's powerful. He's been selling them his dope, rumours say he wants his little territory here in Naples. Some say he's taking over this place," she points to the building outside. "He started with that, so I lost my house, like many others. That's all I know. New clan, same miserable story for us anyway. We get kicked around, one way or another."

I listen to her carefully and watch her fidget a little, the lines on her serious face look deeper now, worry and abuse seem to have cut through her without mercy.

"I don't want to get into trouble, I shouldn't have said anything," she starts to panic a little, as she stands and starts to pace around the shack, I raise my hand and she stops.

"You won't get into trouble," I try to calm her, searching her face. "As long as you don't say a word, I won't say a word. Here," I hand her the money.

She takes it, looks at it for a moment and then hides it in her bra, like it could vanish any minute or someone could take it from her.

"Where does this man live?" I ask, hoping the money I gave her makes her feel safer, at ease. She gave me the information, I paid her off. Now I need the last bit, the most important part of it all.

Where can I find him?

"Everyone knows he lives on the Calliope, the hill that faces the sea. From his villa up there, he sees and controls The Towers. His sentinels, his soldiers are everywhere," the last part sounds like a warning.

I take note of it but don't show her the thing affects me. It doesn't. I know what I am fighting against.

"Grazie, Donna Maddalena," *"Thank you, Lady Maddalena,"* I pay my respects to her and she blinks at me like she hasn't heard someone address her like that in a long time. Like a lady, a real lady.

"Before you said you were from here. How did you get away? Where have you been?" she asks, her eyes still wide from my respects.

Trust works both ways, she wants me to tell her something for what she's told me.

"I was lucky, someone helped me get out of here. I've been everywhere," I tell her as I stand up and zip my jacket all the way to my neck.

"And yet you came back," I hear the edge in her voice, Maddalena wants to know, she's looking at me now like I am fool.

Why would anyone that has made it out of that place go back? Anyone in their right mind would stay away, as far away as possible.

"A word of wisdom from me Donna Maddalena: don't ever leave unfinished business behind. When you leave, leave for good, make sure you leave nothing behind. If you don't, you'll have to come back and take care of things," she starts to nod before I finish talking.

I am ready to go. I know where I am headed, it's not that simple though. I'll still need time, I'll still need to plan things well.

"If someone asks, I fucked you and paid you. This is our business, Donna Maddalena. Understood?" I ask and she nods immediately.

We've been in there for fifteen minutes, probably her average time with a customer. Before I step out, her voice stops me.

"What's your name, stranger?"

I slip my sunglasses back on, the sunlight hits my face as I turn to look at her again and say: "I'm a mistake. I have no name."

CHAPTER 24
THE HEART OF A MOTHER

ANDREA

The idea came to me the day we'd set foot back in Rome, although I'd never thought I'd see the day I could make it work.

I'd let things happen, kept quiet and observed everything that occurred around me. The idea seemed too risky, how could I get Eddy out of there? I was never left alone if not to sleep.

Windows had bars, bathroom cabinets were empty- no razors, no pills, no drugs. I was left to rot in my cage, no pleasure, just pain.

For weeks I tried to find a hole, a glitch, something in Alejandro's perfect schedule that could help me carry out my plan, my son's escape. He'd been very thorough, to the point of perfection. Alejandro was anything but a fool, he knew what I was capable of, how innocent I looked and how sneaky my mind was. I'd fooled him twice already, leaving him as his wife, then running away with Sebastian.

His obsession, he wanted to keep me on my hands and knees, watch me suffer.

The time never seemed right, I tried to convince myself it was impossible, but after days of agony, I found it. Eddy's way out.

The heart of a mother is the biggest force, the strongest force of nature.

It hides, lies, manipulates. It's as heavy as it is light, it shows all and nothing.

The heart of a mother waits for the right moment and is ready to betray to save its own blood, whatever the cost.

For the first few days, I watched Donna Filomena move around us, like a sinister presence in my shadow. Her pride was hurt, she'd told me I'd gone too far, I'd betrayed the family name, hurt her son.

She didn't like me, me yes but Eddy was a whole different matter. She didn't look at him the way she looked at me, she loved him. The same love that tricked Alejandro, I knew could fool Donna Filomena. I was ready to use it against her, manipulate her to get what I wanted. Eddy safe away from this nightmare.

The thought crossed my mind and at the beginning I discarded it, like I'd lost my mind.

It couldn't work, never, not in this world could I get someone so strict and unemotional like Donna Filomena to work for me, against her son.

Ah, but the heart of a mother is dark and heavy, cunning like a serpent, when the life of its own is at stake.

"You must eat, do it for your son," I knew she was falling for it, the moment she started to approach me, when we were still in Rome.

Donna Filomena had gone from spying on me in silence, to talking to me every day, sometimes helping me get Eddy ready for school or putting his snacks on the table for him.

I can't quite recall when her glares had softened, but they had. It must have been when Eddy had started asking me so many questions, when he'd looked confused and hurt by my constant lies or when Eddy's face dropped seeing I wasn't eating much or smiling like I once was.

Her apprehension for my health, or better still, for her grandson's wellbeing, had gotten to the point that she'd started visiting us in Naples.

For a day or two, then she began to stay longer, even though she constantly complained she hated the city, she hated the squalor, the misery of the poor neighbourhoods and missed her golden palace in Rome. Her heart though, I knew was aching for Eddy.

"I just feel like dying," I told her one day, after I'd walked Eddy to school accompanied by two soldiers.

Alejandro had just gone to bed after a sleepless night attending to this business- counting his money, fucking his whores.

I was left alone more and more, he'd just come and use me to get his point across, I doubted he felt any pleasure, I made sure to give him none.

Some days he'd stay away from me, other times he'd come to punish me for glaring, being too quiet or talking back. Alejandro would come to punish me for all the reasons in the world and for nothing. Because I wasn't behaving like I should have and my body was paying the price.

I am wearing my robe, putting things away in the kitchen, trying to focus on making Eddy's favourite snack, he'll soon be back from school. I keep myself busy and try to forget what has happened last night.

Another punishment, more bruises on my body for disobeying him, for talking back. The same nightmare over and over, the marks of the devil on my skin.

I'm trying to forget, trying to focus on Eddy, but my legs, my thighs are so purple, not even the longest robe can hide that.

I really don't want to hide anything, not to Donna Filomena at least. Only from Eddy.

I am playing a game – it's called manipulation. I'm playing my cards, using the only weapons I have. The strength of my mind, I'm using it to the fullest. I can't fight back, not physically, but my mind can and it will. I'm messing with everyone's brain. I hate them all, I want them to play my game. Donna Filomena is on the edge of my trap, she just needs a little push.

Look what he's done to me, I pretend to cover my purple thigh, but her hand takes the robe and opens it a little, her eyes look down at it, then they're back on mine almost instantly.

"Stop fighting, stop antagonizing Alejandro," Donna Filomena says to me, her eyes on the bruises once again.

The words of a woman in the Mafia.

Her son's hand left traces on my flesh and yet she is telling me to stop fighting him when clearly I'm not the one using violence. I'm not the one hurting him. Not physically anyway.

My eyes follow her stare, I look down to my legs and shake my head.

"Is this what you are going to tell your grandson when he'll begin to understand, when he'll start to notice the bruises? That his mother is antagonizing his father? Alejandro is a man that likes to hit his wife. He uses his strength to punish me."

"Do you want your son, a six-year-old, to see that? To find out what's happening, Andrea?" Donna Filomena stands there in front of me, her voice hard but not resentful maybe for the first time since I'd been back.

She looks worried, for her grandson of course, and concerned he'll figure out the hell I'm living.

She's falling. It's now or never.

"I won't need to tell him anything, he'll understand soon and I won't lie to him, I won't. This is what his father is like," I say and watch her shake her head.

"This is what you made him become."

I search her face and nod, my eyes a little glassy.

"What I made him become? It's my fault, I see," I bite my lip. "It's fair he wants me to smile, to laugh, to talk or close my mouth when he claps his hands? Tell me Donna Filomena, is that what you did with your husband? Did you prance around like a good puppy, stand there proud like a shiny toy for him to play with?" the words come out monotonous, no edge. I make sure she knows I'm not mocking her. "I am not like that. I'd rather die and I will, but I am not like that."

"You are a fool if you think this attitude is going to get you anywhere," she shakes her head and lets out a breath, a sign of exasperation.

We've talked about this before in Rome, the night Alejandro came for me, the night he came to take back what was his, in that bathroom with Eddy in the other room. I shiver at the thought of his body pressed against mine, his breath on my skin at every thrust. Sometimes the pain he's been inflicting on me over the past few months surges through me, all together, all at once and it feels like it's going to choke me. Then I shut my eyes tight and push it away, with all the energy I have left in me.

No, no. I can't let it get to me. Not yet. *Eddy, think about Eddy.*

Like Donna Filomena, she's thinking about Eddy. She does nothing to hide her worry.

A cue for me to press on.

"I told you already, I'm not trying to get anywhere. I am not fighting him, but I am not giving him what he wants from me either. I can't."

Donna Filomena stares at me in silence for a moment, as I move around the kitchen slowly, like a ghost, bruised and broken like Alejandro wants me to be. Or like I want them to believe. Today I'm anything but broken, my hatred for them and my love for Eddy are keeping me alive. Barely, but I feel alive.

"Eddy talks at night," Donna Filomena says and I stop dead cold.

How does she know? I do of course, I sleep with him when Alejandro releases his hold on me, when he leaves to wander out. Alejandro is never home at night, always cruising the city, his territory, worrying about his 'business'.

I keep those thoughts to myself, instead I wonder in silence what she's heard Eddy say, but I keep my curiosity at bay.

"He screams sometimes," Donna Filomena goes on and I push my thin blonde hair back. It's growing, I'd let it go blonde again. Like it was, like Sebastian used to like it.

Sebastian, God I think of him every day, I mourn him in silence and hope to dream about him at night. That dream never comes, I keep seeing him everywhere during the day, sometimes it's like he whispers words in my ear and I find myself smiling, whispering back. I'm losing it, I'm losing my mind.

"There is no reason to hide now, Blondie," he'd say.

He is right, no reason to hide, but many reasons to show who I am and who I am not. I'm not Alejandro's. I am Blondie, I am Sebastian's Sad Eyes. Not a fugitive, not a whore.

Never.

"He has nightmares. He can feel something is wrong, he's not happy here. He was happy before Alejandro came for us," I speak softly and watch my words affect Donna Filomena's impassable stance for once.

Her shoulders curve in a little, her head seems to beckon for once.

Strike her, strike her now.

"He's afraid of his father. Don't you see, Donna Filomena? The damage, the hatred. He fears his father."

"Because you took him away from him, he doesn't know him," she tries to say, but her voice gives her away.

A bluff, she is desperately trying to protect a son like only a mother can, but she knows the truth. She knows what her son is like. She knows I am right.

"Eddy can see his true colours, Donna Filomena. Eddy is only six, but he remembers the blood, the gunshots, the violence. He sees it in his father's eyes every time he comes near him. He feels it every time Alejandro tries to spend some time with him, he fears his father because he can see the darkness inside him. And I know you can see it, too. I know you can, a mother knows her son better than anyone," I plant the seed of doubt and watch it grow in Donna Filomena's heart, as her chest moves faster.

"Alejandro loves his son," she spits the words out, her voice shaky.

Her cold façade is off, she's dropped it, after weeks, months of holding it up, Donna Filomena is falling to pieces, coming to terms with the truth.

"Maybe he thinks he does but you are a mother, like me Donna Filomena. I know you understand. There is nothing you wouldn't do to see your son happy. I did what I had to, to keep Eddy away from all this. Look at this," I raise my hands up, I point to the walls, that sumptuous, cold house, with golden, kitsch finishes that scream richness and power.

My golden prison.

"Eddy is his blood," Donna Filomena tries to say but I don't let her finish.

You have no idea whose blood runs in his veins, I bite my tongue like I've been doing for over six years.

He's the son of a brave, strong man. A fighter, a warrior that turned his life around to save others, to fight outlaws and bring some justice into this sad, sick world. He's Sebastian's son. His blood has nothing of the De la Crux.

The words pulse in my head, my only thought, as I take a step forward, I move closer to Donna Filomena and bury my secret as deep as I can.

I look into her eyes and lie, like only the heart of a mother knows.

"He's my blood too but I'd rather him far, far away from here, somewhere safe, where he can live without soldiers, without death and corruption all around him. I love him to the point I'd rather have him gone, far away from here. I love Eddy so much, I'd do anything to soothe his suffering, to make sure he grows up away from this hell we are living in."

Donna Filomena goes quiet, but her silence speaks to me, from my heart to her heart, I know she understands.

"I know I've asked you to take care of Eddy before, but I can feel I won't be here long," I press on, seeing a glimpse of humanity in her. "I know Alejandro will dispose of me soon and so I need you to promise me again," I register the surprise in her face but carry on, not giving her time to think. "If you love Eddy like you say you do, I need you to promise me you'll take him away from this place. Promise me, Donna Filomena you won't let him become a gangster, a killer. Promise me you'll save him. Promise me," I start to cry but I keep talking, I keep asking her to save my son.

She doesn't interrupt my plea, she doesn't tell me I'm crazy, that I am dishonouring the family like she'd said more than once at the beginning.

No, Donna Filomena just stands there and listens, her face straight, her lips set in a thin line.

"Before he kills me, I want you to take him away. Go with him, it doesn't matter where. Leave no trace, leave no sign of you anywhere. I will make sure Alejandro won't follow you, he won't know you are gone."

"You can't ask me to do this," she shakes her head but doesn't sound sure.

Hammer that doubt, deeper.

"You must. Eddy will be unhappy, he'll grow up angry and full of resentment like Alejandro," I watch her jump as I take her hand. "Maybe you had no choice with Alejandro, you couldn't do anything for him, but you can now, for Eddy. Please."

My lips tremble as my heart finally comes to terms with what my mind has been plotting from the very beginning.

I'm telling Donna Filomena to take my son away from me, away from this prison. I'm putting Eddy in the hands of a woman I barely know, but she's the only chance I have to save him from the devil. From the monster that is Alejandro De la Crux.

"Please Donna Filomena."

She doesn't say a word, but our secret agreement is somewhat sealed.

For days she doesn't approach me but when Eddy starts to cry one afternoon, telling me he hates that house, he hates his life and wants to go back to the island, sobbing his heart out for hours, Donna Filomena knocks on my door just as Alejandro's car disappears out the front gate.

"How? Tell me how you want to do it," she asks, lingering outside my door, her eyes rest on Eddy fast asleep in my bed, then back to me.

"There's only one way," I whisper, after letting her in. "The only way to make him stop looking for you."

Only one way, I tell myself like I've been doing for so long now, I convince my heart that there is no other way. The devil stops at nothing to get what he wants, nothing, but one thing.

"We'll make him believe I killed you."

CHAPTER 25
THE KID FROM THE TOWERS

SEBASTIAN

Every day I tell myself I need to stay calm but I'm losing it. Time isn't the only thing I am running out of, patience is at its minimum too.

I stay off the streets during the day and observe the life around me at night. From the little window of my old, dirty room- I've found one not too far from The Towers- I observe the life around me.

People seem to run from place to place, they look wary, more than usual. It must be the soldiers constantly patrolling the area, Alejandro's men are everywhere.

Something is happening in the neighbourhood, the air is heavy and people are scared.

A change of power, but not just that.

I can't put my finger on it, not until I meet Severino, not until his young eyes and mouth tell me the truth.

"He's cleaning up the neighbourhood, looking for Rats, for traitors. He's killing off all those that were affiliated or related to Sebastian Esposito."

He tells me this like he's talking about the weather, Severino doesn't even blink, his words hold no weight, no importance.

It's not the first time something this bad happens. He talks to me about death and revenge, like he knows what they are all about, like he's used to them. I listen without telling him he doesn't know how painful revenge can be. Sometimes it's so painful you wish you'd died instead.

Severino tells me about 'Lu Diavul', about Alejandro before I even tell him my name. He doesn't care, I've been nice enough to pay for his breakfast, that's all he needs. Food. He doesn't even flinch when I ask him questions.

I look at him, at his dirty, worn out hands, his chapped lips from standing out in the sun and rain all day, and I see myself, in that other life I told you about. When I was nobody, when I was a mistake.

Severino is like me, he has nothing, he's fresh meat for the mob. I keep him with me, sitting at that table as much as I can. I feed him and his pinched cheeks, before someone feeds him lies and promises of a happier life, handing him a gun.

Severino is only ten but he's not innocent, not like a child should be. He knows too much already, another child deprived of his childhood from the streets.

I met him one day, while I was sitting outside a café off the main street, off the main intersection; it's my favourite place to sit and watch the gangs walk around the area, I can easily spot them but they can't see me, unless they cross the street.

My eyes are always covered by sunglasses during the day, I sometimes have my hood on or a hat. My hair is long and tied back. I look like nobody, not like the Sebastian I once was, but Severino sees me that day and comes up to me to sell his stash of cigarettes.

Stolen Marlboro Lights, he gets a smile out of me, the last time I smiled must have been in some other life, when I still had my life- my Andrea, my Eddy.

"Uaglio'," *Kid,* I keep that smile on my lips. "Where did you steal these from?"

Severino doesn't even deny it, he knows I am street material like him. I know that the stash is stolen, he's selling it for half of what it's worth.

"It's my business," he gives me a frustrated glare. "You want or not?"

"How much?" I ask him for the price again and look away.

I can't keep my eyes off the road for too long, I'm too on edge, too nervous about the situation.

The soldiers are everywhere, I can see Alejandro's mansion up the Calliope hill from there and the gates are always closed, I'm losing hope. I can't find a way in, a way to get there without being spotted and killed.

"Come on, I'll give you a deal: twenty-five euros," Severino renegotiates the price.

Money, it's always about money. I wonder how deep he is in the business, if he'd stolen the stash by himself or someone is lurking around, waiting to collect his earnings. A pimp, like any other.

No, nobody is around and Severino has been wandering around the area for a while. All by himself. I buy the cigarettes and start to earn his trust.

"Yeah, I'll take them," I tell him and push the chair next to me towards him. "I want you to take a seat and have breakfast. You look like you could use some food."

I put the money on the table, so he sees I am not fooling around. Money talks. It 'sings' in The Towers.

Before he can say something, I tell the guy cleaning the tables we want juice and a croissant. Severino eyes me suspiciously but takes a seat, as I hold his stare.

"Why are you buying me food?"

"Because you look like you're going to faint. Did you have any food this morning?" I ask as he shakes his head.

"No, my mother went to work early. She left me a piece of bread and some fruit. I was saving it for lunch," Severino tells me.

His hands dive for the food, as soon as the waiter sets it on the table.

His fingers are dirty, but he doesn't even bother to wipe them. He eats it all, drinks up and I keep quiet, ordering some more juice for him.

"You are a cop, aren't you?" he's too smart to fool.

"No," I tell him. "I was like you. I was like you when I was a child. You know what I wanted the most when I was your age?"

He shakes his head, gulping down the juice.

"I'd have given anything to have someone feed me. I would have given everything to have someone care," I look at the road leading up the hill and spot a black car exiting the gate.

The hairs at the back of my neck stand on end, the only sound I can hear is my heart hammering in my chest.

Maybe Andrea and Eddy?

The gate closes immediately after and the car drives east. I lose it as it turns around the corner.

"Nobody does something for nothing. What is it that you want?" Severino asks me and then adds. "Who are you?"

I ignore his last question and tell Severino I do need something but first I want to know who he works with.

"I'm on my own, I'm not with those idiots on the scooters," his head turns to the side and I look that way, where a bunch of kids are laughing and chatting, in their designer jeans and shaved heads.

Street gang, too well dressed to be normal kids in The Towers, too arrogant to be nobodies. They are soldiers, fresh soldiers ready for the sacrifice.

Severino works alone, he tells me he does it to help his mom. She cleans houses all day to earn a living, since his father died of a heart attack.

"Do you have any brothers or sisters?" I ask him and he shakes his head, rubs his hair a bit.

"I had a brother but he was shot in the head when he was seventeen under our building. He was part of a gang, they'd had a fight with some guy the night before. They came and punished him. My father died soon after, my mom said she's alive because she needs to take care of me, but I can take care of myself," Severino's face hardens, he lifts up his chest and sits straight like a real man. "I can take care of us both."

I have no problem believing that, Severino looks like the kind of kid that doesn't cry, that fights back, doesn't let anyone walk all over him.

A young violent heart, another one that had to learn how to survive.

"I'm looking for a new set of eyes, a new set of ears, two fast legs and a smart mind," I tell Severino moments later. "I need someone to be me, when I can't."

My sunglasses lower a bit, I show him my eyes, like we do down there in Naples.

A man of honour looks at you in the eye, a man who isn't afraid, who isn't lying shows you his good intentions by looking straight at you. Like I am looking straight at Severino now.

He nods, as if reading my mind.

"I will pay you if you'll help me," I set all my cards on the table- he's too smart to be fooled, besides I don't want to fool him.

That's when I ask him about what's happening in the neighbourhood and Alejandro's name is mentioned. My name is mentioned, too.

"Listen to me Severino, I need you to find out more about Alejandro De la Crux and his family, his wife and son. I need you to follow them, I need you to be you and mingle in the crowd when they go out. I want you to tell me everything you can about them and their habits. Everything but in order for our agreement to work, I need you to keep it a secret. Don't tell anyone about this. Deal?"

"Deal," he runs his fingers over his mouth like he's closing a zipper and stretches out his hand.

I take it and shake it, like a real pact, a real business arrangement. Severino is a real man, even if a little one.

The next day he comes looking for me at the same time at the café with the first set of information.

"Alejandro is away from home most nights. His wife goes out only to take and collect their son from a private catholic school. And they go to church every Sunday morning."

Andrea, I imagine her holding Eddy's hand, dropping him at school.

Eddy, my breathing picks up thinking about my boy. I never told him the truth, I never told him I was his father.

I found them. They are alive and well.

I'm coming, I'm almost there.

CHAPTER 26
STRIKE ONE

SEBASTIAN

The more I see the more I know my chances are low. Very low. Alejandro has thought of everything, every little detail. He never leaves the house unattended, everything he does is thought out well. A car always leads the way before he goes out, before he takes his family out. Too many men around us, I wouldn't stand a chance.

I'd never underestimated Alejandro De la Crux, never. Not even the first time I'd seen him, the time I sat in his car when he'd handed me the money to protect his family, his ex-wife and son. I always knew what he was capable of and now I am seeing it with my eyes.

When you can't beat them, you have to start thinking like them, Salvatore taught me this during my first mission as an undercover officer.

I take a trip into Alejandro's mind, I study him like I guess he'd studied me close, before planning his revenge. I write down times, habits, notes everywhere.

The first night I follow one of his cars, the night after that I follow a few of his soldiers down to an old pier, using a scooter I bought in a second-hand shop.

His men are cautious, they make sure nobody is around and I keep at a safe distance like I'd learned to do in the forces a long time ago.

I watch them take a boat and disappear in the dark waters. It takes them twenty-three minutes to get back, I'm there waiting, and I get an idea watching them work fast.

Three heavy plastic barrels, they lift them off the boat and quickly into a van, they cover them with bread loafs and boxes, and the vehicles leave quickly for the main road.

Cocaine, it doesn't take me long to figure it out. It is Alejandro De la Crux's speciality, it always was. It's why he's so powerful down here in Naples.

Two nights later, I am there again but this time I am waiting on a little fishermen's boat I've stolen.

I need to see. I need to think like Alejandro to find a glitch.

They pass by not bothering to look at the boat twice, I keep near the rocks, just a small light on. Back and forth, I watch them make the trip three nights before I decide I am ready to play the game.

Break the balance, ruin his perfect plan, tear down his empire and force him to change his plans.

What the fuck do I have to lose?

I have nothing, nothing anyway. I am that kid again, I am Sebastian Esposito the nobody, the one that has nothing and is ready to gamble his fucking life to swim out of hell. I am drowning, I can't go on like this without Andrea and Eddy, knowing he's there with them every day, every night hurting them, hitting them a little deeper, a little stronger every time.

The fourth time I get to the barrels first. It's easy to spot them once you know what you are looking for. They are tied to yellow buoys in the middle of the sea, in the same spot I saw the soldiers stop each time. I can barely see them- dawn is still hours away- but when I do, I pull them up so fast, my body is soaked in water a second later and I don't give a damn. I have Alejandro's cocaine.

I am ready to fuck him, fuck him hard. I put the buoys back into the water and sail away fast, my heart is hammering hard, I let out a liberating yell just before tossing his stash in the water, all of it. His white shit disappears in the deepness of the sea and my face hardens.

He's lost money, he's lost business, I want him to doubt every single man that works with him. I want him to curse, to snap and lose control because that could be the only way to attack him, make him lose his focus. I need to give him something to worry about, something to fix, and take his mind off Andrea and Eddy.

He took them from me, I am taking a little something from him, to make him lose his balance, his confidence.

Eye for an eye.

Someone betrayed you, Alejandro, yes.

I want that doubt to haunt you at night.

Somebody knew about that cocaine, how you were getting it into the country and they sold the information to fuck you over. Somebody stole from you and now you have no drugs to sell, no power for the next couple of days.

Fuck you.

ALEJANDRO

"Shit, shit, goddam it!" I slam my hand hard on the table, looking at my soldiers, cussing and swearing their names under my breath.

I just lost fifty thousand euros worth of cocaine, goddam it. I scan each and every one of their worn out dark faces, in search of guilt, betrayal. Someone is to blame, I need to know who the fuck did this, who's trying to fuck me over.

"The ropes were cut," one of them informs me straight away.

The buoys were there floating, no containers under water. Someone had gotten there before them and stole my dope, they tell me in a haste, without breathing hoping to get out of it clean. They fucking wish.

Someone cut the ropes, someone that knows about my business. Someone that knows how I get my stuff into Naples. Someone, but who?

The Gipsy, all my bets are immediately on him.

He's the only one I can think of, the only man that wants me to fail, that wants me out of Naples.

If I can't give them the dope as promised, I can't be trusted.

That bastard, that son of a bitch.

I call for an emergency meeting, that same night. Just me, Gennaro and The Sentinel.

We meet up under a highway junction, under a dark bridge, each of us with a car of soldiers guarding our backs. We're not at war, at least not for now, but we all move around with security. We can never be too cautious, somebody might get the wrong idea, that they can kill us, that they can kill me.

Wrong. I always pull the trigger first, always. The Killer had been fucking lucky with me the first time around, I'd set things right with him and I'm going to set things right with these guys, too.

I tell them what happened and they just listen, shooting sideway glances at each other.

"You think it's The Gipsy?" Gennaro asks me and I nod, like it's fucking obvious.

I take his little disgusting kingdom from him and what does he do? Like I wouldn't figure it out. He takes my stash. He's fucked already, not matter what Gennaro and The Sentinel say. He's dead to me already.

"Shit," Gennaro mumbles under his breath and then says to The Sentinel "Did you see or hear anything?"

"No, not exactly," he says looking straight at me, like he's not sure he should say it or not.

What does he know?

I hold his look and cross my arms, ready to hear it.

"Do you know something? Speak up if you do, right now I'm thinking about cutting that asshole's throat."

"Alejandro," Gennaro grumbles my name and holds out a hand in front of him. "We need to act, yes. What's happened cannot be left unpunished, we need to work together, cooperation is the best thing for all of us. For your business too, yes?"

I nod even though I don't give a shit about business. I am not in Naples for business, I am in Naples for revenge, because I want to destroy everything about The Killer. I want to destroy The Towers and rip the place apart, but I don't tell him, I don't because I don't want them to see it's personal. Too much interest, never show you want something so bad. That's when others will want it, too.

"The last thing we want is a war between us," Gennaro says, pushing his black and grey hair back. "If you touch The Gipsy without a valid reason, others will come after you and The Sentinel and I will have to have your back. War is never good, we have a good balance of power. Business is good, let's not forget that."

I don't say a thing, I don't have anything to say. I know that The Gipsy is behind this already, I don't need to investigate. I want to punish him and get rid of him. My way.

"What do you know Sentinel, speak up, I know you know everything that goes on around in the city," I ask again, this time he decides to speak.

"I heard The Gipsy wants your head. I heard he wants you out of the city, he doesn't trust you. He's saying we should all keep our eyes open with you around."

"Well," I snarl and rub my lips, looking down at my shoes for a moment, a wicked smile slowly spreads across my face.

A smile fuelled by anger and resentment. Revenge.

"I say we know who's behind this already," I grunt and then look at Gennaro.

What more does he need? More proof? The Gipsy wants my head, he said so himself. He took my stash and wants to get rid of me.

Not if I get him first.

I head back home, we haven't decided anything, not the three of us. I have.

Gennaro tells me to wait, tells me to let him handle the situation. He'll have a word with The Gipsy, he wants to keep it peaceful. If he's guilty he'll pay for what he's done, he promises me.

Promises, promises. I have no use for them. They are not enough, not for me, El Diablo.

The way I see it, the Gipsy took from me, it's my time to take from him. My chance to take everything that is his. In a way he's done me a favour. I can stop keeping my head low, taking The Towers a little bit at a time. If it's a fight that he wants, he's going to get it.

As soon as I get home, I march down to the basement and I call three of my best men. I want them there in five minutes. I wait for nobody and they know that so well, all three of them are in front of me in four.

"We're going out again. Take me to where The Gipsy hangs out at night. Make sure two cars of soldiers are ready."

Everything is set, I know where to find him. I know every single thing about him. That's how I carry out my work, I want to know my enemy, know all their secrets, so I can choose how to end their lives.

Under the tunnel on his way home, that's where I'll take The Gipsy's life. It's perfect. One of my man's car is waiting for him on the other side, the other follows the Gipsy's entourage at a safe distance, so not to attract attention. I'm right behind that car. I want a front row seat on this one, I want to be there.

The streets are deserted, the stage is set.

The first car of soldiers I've sent ahead blocks their way, the second car blocks their way back. Trapped. Like a fucking rat in a cage, Gipsy…Gipsy… you tried to fuck the wrong guy.

I enter the tunnel and the shooting begins. By the time I reach the Gipsy's car, the fight is over, his men are sprawled on the street or slumped forward in their seats. I've lost two soldiers, I'll make sure to give them a decent burial. Now is not the time to think about that.

"Clear," one of my men shouts at me and I nod.

The Gipsy is on the ground, he's still alive like I asked. Broken nose, swollen eye, his face is covered in blood, but he's still alive. I want to look him in the face, one more time. One more time.

"You fucked the wrong guy," I snarl and take my gun out.

My soldiers tell me we don't have time, no time for this. We have to move; the police will be here in no time.

Right, I know. But first, first I need to look in the face the thief that has dared step over me.

"Look at me, figlio di puttana!" *Son of a bitch!* I shout at him.

The Gipsy turns to the side and spits on my shoes, murmuring something I can't make out.

"Stronzo," I kick him and point the gun to his head, twisting and turning it a bit, so he can feel the power of the barrel, playing against his temples. I have that power, I have him in my hands.

"You made a big mistake," I snarl and cock the gun.

"No, you are making a big mistake, Diavul," he spits out blood and then tells me one last thing before I pull the trigger. A threat, an omen. "There will be a war, a war because of this."

I fire. Then there's silence all around us.

I head back to the car fast, we drive through the tunnel in a haste, passing over corpses, uncaring of their mutilated bodies. I care about nothing, I don't care for The Gipsy's words to me. I put an end to those too. You see I am the master of puppets, nobody can rebel on me and my will. I tell people when to speak, when to walk and breathe.

The Gipsy's time on this earth has come to an end because I fucking said 'when'.

The next day I get a call, a visit and shouts from Gennaro. He said I went against his word, I tell him The Gipsy was selling the cocaine he stole from me. I couldn't let that happen. I lie, my speciality. I lie and I lie good, so good Gennaro's anger is tamed by my story.

He tells me we need to reconcile with the others, we need to make sure they know we won't hurt them, that their power and territories are safe.

"Sure," I agree, I'm not there to conquer Naples. I have what I want now. I have what I came for. The Towers.

CHAPTER 27
THE MADONNA OF NAPLES

SEBASTIAN

"I spoke to her," Severino tells me a week later, taking a seat next to me on a bench just outside the railway station.

We changed places that day, no café, no meeting in public. The streets are getting worse, I keep as low key as possible, but there seems to be a real revolution in the neighbourhood.

Two mornings ago, I almost thought I'd have to use my gun, when two soldiers entered the usual café and started to threaten the owner of the place.

Alejandro's soldiers were looking for information, they were after traitors.

I haven't been back to that place since.

My head turns immediately and I stare at Severino, his eyes seem softer today, like he's starting to feel my ache.

He spoke to her, to my Andrea.

"People call her La Madonna di Napoli," *The Madonna of Naples*, he tells me. Andrea is blonde, her skin is so fair and her eyes so blue, her looks can't go unnoticed. Her face is always solemn, she never smiles, he tells me she earned that name because she looks pure and ethereal, everyone stops to look at her when she walks by.

"This morning I saw her walk through the little streets in the Spanish Quarters. I followed the cars, she went to church with her son and Donna Filomena, Alejandro's mother," Severino eyes never leave mine as he says his name.

He tells me Andrea and Eddy are well, but they are hard to approach.

"I mingled with the crowd and followed them in the little streets, I asked for money, for food and a soldier pushed me to the side, I hit the wall. She stopped walking, your woman," Severino said, his stare seemed to soften a bit. "She said something to the soldier and pushed past him. Then asked me if I was okay and gave me this."

He pulls out some change and shows it to me, I just listen trying to quiet my heart.

"They seemed okay from what I could see."

I nod and pat his back, he's given me the best news anyone could ever give me, but they come with a price, the pain of knowing it was hard to go anywhere near them.

"She smiled at me, told me to buy something to eat and I thanked her."

I nod, taking in a breath before saying anything.

"Did you tell her what I told you?" I ask and Severino nods.

He has, my eyes flare with hope. I hide my face in my hands for a moment, trying to steady my pulse, trying to keep the tears in check.

They are still alive, they are well. I breathe out relief and Severino pats my back. My eyes are on him again as I imagine Andrea's face when she heard him say those words.

ANDREA

You are going crazy, I keep telling myself.

You are going to have a heart attack, I warn myself to stop, to just stop the nonsense.

My heartbeat hasn't slowed down since this morning. It's afternoon.

Calm down.

Eddy calls for my attention, he wants me to help him with a puzzle. I smile, only for him, only for my love and I get distracted by his soft giggles as I plant a kiss on his neck. My pulse is slowly going back to normal when I think about the words again.

"Grazie mille, Sad Eyes," and my heartrate escalates again.

That child, I can't stop thinking about him.

Sad Eyes, how could he know? He couldn't.

It must have been a mistake.

I must have heard wrong.

He wasn't talking to me.

He never truly said the words, maybe I'd just imagined it.

I imagined it, I try to convince myself that it's my imagination, my mind playing tricks on me.

The lack of food, low sugars, low pressure, my constant secret mourning for Sebastian's death. I'm keeping everything inside and my mind needs to let out. So, I imagine things, like I imagine hearing Sebastian's voice whisper words in my cars.

I look dead, I feel dead. Then this child walks to me and says two words, two words that don't mean anything to the world but mean the world to me.

Sad Eyes, no it couldn't be. Sebastian is... I can't even go there without risking a breakdown, my body is already shutting down slowly.

The puzzle pieces, I focus on Eddy again and help him put them together. He's very impatient, like me not like Sebastian. He was always the calmer one between us. Eddy wants to learn and learn fast, his attention on the next thing the moment he gets the hang of it. I don't have the patience that Sebastian had with him, to explain things and help him focus. I can't focus myself, I'm losing it.

"You are doing a great job with him, Sad Eyes," there it is again, his deep voice murmuring words in my ear.

I take a deep breath and imagine his fingers brush against my lips.

Stop, just stop.

Then I snap out of my haze, I feel a set of eyes on me. Eddy just asked me something and I didn't listen, I couldn't I was listening to Sebastian.

I've lost my mind, I know he's gone but I don't want to let him go.

SEBASTIAN

Severino isn't done talking. He wants me to know people like her, they talk about her as if she is an angel. She's always kind, never rude or arrogant. People pay their respects when she walks by, she's the wife of the new leader of The Towers, Alejandro has full control of the place.

La Madonna. That's what they call her. She seems like an angel, a fallen angel married to a devil, an evil man that's terrorizing the area.

"She'll be at a funeral later today," Severino tells me then, I feel my pulse pick up. "She'll be at the church, an important man died the other day, the former leader of The Towers, The Gipsy they used to call him."

I don't need Severino to tell me, I know what rumours are saying. Alejandro killed him, he took what he wanted, his territory and then killed the man off. He is going to the funeral, with his family to pay his respects. Like a real gangster would. There was no proof it had been him or his men and a gentleman, a man of honour like him, always pays his respects to the dead, to the family of the dead.

"You won't be able to get near her," Severino says and I nod.

"I know," I say and look ahead, at the sack in front of me, as I hit it punch after punch, listening to the train passing by.

My heart beats fast like that train, my mind is rushing, a part of me wants to find a way to see her, touch her but I know I can't. I won't be able to but for now I have to settle with just seeing her, seeing her and my son from a distance.

Calm down, I think leaning against the wall, in the small dark alleyway across from the church. Severino told me where they go every Sunday, I keep at a safe distance, dying to spot them, anxious to be spotted.

Don't be stupid, I can't risk being caught. I have one chance and one chance only to get them out of there and as much as it hurts I keep away, telling myself I will hold them again. If only for a second, no matter how short our last moments together, I will hold them and tell them they are my life.

I am losing any hope of seeing them, as the crowd disperses in the small bricked square that opens around the cathedral. Then I catch sight of a blonde woman, her hair is longer than I remember but it's been months. Almost three months, I feel the desperation wash over me as I squint to take a better look at her.

It's her, my heart knows it's her. It beats so fast, like it wants her to hear its cries.

Sono qui per te, Andrea. "I am here for you, Andrea".

My Sad Eyes is wearing a black coat and black dress to just below the knee, she walks down the white marble stairs like she doesn't want to, like she doesn't care what she's doing or where she is. Her eyes hide behind big black shades and my raging heart demands to know why.

Did that son of a bitch touch her? Is she hiding a bruise? My face hardens, I ball my hands into fists and mumble a threat under my breath.

Then I watch her turn around, her thin, weak arm reaches back and she takes Eddy's hand into hers. I hold my breath.

My son walks beside his mother to the car, serious solemn, while a hand slips around Andrea's shoulder, another one over Eddy's.

I begin to pant; my eyes are burning with rage. Alejandro walks behind them, pushing them to the car fast, with a sick, disgusting half grin on his face, as he gets them in the car first. I want to run to him and kill him with my bare hands, smash him to the ground, pull everything I can pull from him and break every bone in his body, until he begs me to kill him.

But I can't. I'd be shot in the head before I'd even touch him.

No Sebastian, no. I place a hand on the wall beside me and lean on it gently, covering my face, my eyes against my arm. The car has already disappeared down the city streets, when I manage to steady my breathing and regroup my thoughts.

I have to find a way to take them, maybe when Eddy goes to school or when something out of the ordinary happens. Their routine is too perfect, too under control, Alejandro keeps them close to him, well-guarded by his soldiers.

"Find out when something will happen, something different from usual, funerals, parties, communions, school plays. Be my ears Severino, don't talk too much to people and come back with news," I tell my little friend then, before heading back to my room.

"He's the devil you know," he warns me, his big brown eyes a little concerned. "Why are you after them? After his son and wife?"

I eye Severino and realize I haven't told him my name yet. He doesn't call me and so far that's made me rest better at night, but I can't keep asking him things without explaining. I don't want to use him, I don't want my silence around my identity and the reasons behind my actions to spark curiosity in Severino. Curiosity is as dangerous as ignorance, it can lead you straight to the grave in this fucked up place we live in.

"Because she's not his wife, she's my wife. Because he's kidnapped them both and took them away from me," Severino's eyes grow wide as I go on, my voice as low as a whisper. "Because I'm Sebastian Esposito and I'm here to save my family and kill Alejandro De la Crux."

The silence between us grows loud as Severino keeps staring at me, keeping still for once. He's the sort of kid that hates sitting around, just like my son.

"That's my son; his name is Eddy. He's just like you," I don't know why I tell him but it's not my brain, it's not my mouth letting out the words, it's my heart. My tired, heavy heart that needs to say it, needs to hear it.

"Like me? You mean old like me?" Severino asks and I shake my head.

"Good like you. Smart and good like you," I tell him and watch him smile a bit.

"I'm not good, I've done some pretty bad things," Severino stares at his hands as he says it, as if they are still marked of his sins.

"Sometimes good people do bad things because life takes them down a steep road. They trip, they fall, they do what they can to get back on their feet. That doesn't make you a bad kid, just a less fortunate one."

He puffs out a breath and then looks at me with that innocent stare only children can pull off and leave you stunned.

"Do you think I will be forgiven?" he asks me like I am his saviour, like I know what's going to happen next, in the afterlife.

I know nothing, I know what I must do but not what will become of me.

Still I'm not here to crush his hopes, his dreams of the future. I look at him in the eye and tell him what I know. I tell him what Salvatore taught me years back, the same words that had soothed my guilty soul.

"I don't know about the future Severino but I know about the present. You are helping a woman and child, you are helping a desperate man like me. I don't think you need forgiveness," I shake my head and press on. "I shall be forever grateful. I will take you away from here, I will. I promise."

CHAPTER 28

LIKE A PRAYER, LIKE A PLAYER

ANDREA

If mornings have a sound, they are Sebastian's humming while he works out on the terrace. It's some tune I've heard before but can't remember where or the words. I bet he doesn't remember them either. The thought makes me smile a little but it's such a lovely sound, light and soothing, it calms me down.

Mornings are for us, even Sundays. Eddy is in church, he'll be there for an hour. He told me he wants to sing and his friends are all there, so we take him every Sunday and keep that hour for us. We are bad people; we should be in church too probably. Good people normally do or so I was taught when I was a child. Now I know better, I know that good people are those that follow the rules of the heart, nothing else, nothing more. Hearts never lie.

"Are you trying to tell me something?" Sebastian's hands snake around my waist, I jump a little and let out a yelp.

I turn around and smile, my hair is up, it's messy and wild, just the way he likes it. Sebastian looks at it then down at me again, as my hands take hold of his strong forearms. They are bare, it's too hot outside to work with a shirt on and it's only nine a.m. in the morning.

Summer in Folegandros is boiling hot, I am not used to the heat, but he is.

Sebastian is from Naples, he's used to the warm weather, his skin is golden brown. I never turn that colour, not even if out in the sun all day, every day. I turn red and then bright pink *again after a few days. He calls me piggy, I call him 'Cioccolatino' Chocolate. He thinks he's funny, I think he's sexy as hell.*

Especially when he looks at me the way he's looking at me now. He wants to play, he's in a good mood as always.

"Tell you something? I'm not following you, Sebastian," I blink innocently, pretending I am not going about the house with nothing more than a t-shirt on.

Sebastian gives me a smile and runs his hands under the shirt, all over me, I shiver and close my eyes.

When his fingertips travel down to my waist and between my thighs, when they linger around the hem of my black underwear, I breathe in deep and lock eyes with him again.

"What is it that you want, island boy?" I raise a brow at him and bite my lips.

A rhetorical question, he's made it quite clear what his hands are after. What he is after. Me.

"Island boy?" he repeats, amused, staring down at me like I am a goddess. His eyes travel down to my lips, then up to my eyes again, until he decides he needs to touch my lips, to feel I am real.

His left hand cups my cheek, I tilt my head up towards him and we are so close, but it's never enough with him. More, more, I always want more of him.

"Look at you, always shirtless, so tanned. You seem to belong to the island in a way I never will," I bite my lips again as he rubs my soft lower lip. He plays with it, gently circles my mouth before moving down.

A shiver runs down my spine, my back arches as he presses his mouth to mine.

Warm, smooth and long. He kisses me like we have all the time in the world and I'm so desperate for more, I believe him. I tell myself that this is forever, that we'll always wake up beside each other.

"I don't belong anywhere, Pretty Eyes. I'm not part of the island, I don't belong to Naples or Rome or Italy. I belong here with you, wherever that is," *he tells me breaking the kiss, rubbing his thumb over my lip again.*

His body is pressed against mine, it holds me, steadies me, like Sebastian wants me to feel he's right there with me and never wants to leave.

I keep looking into his dark brown eyes, me the luckiest woman in the world.

"We should be in church," *I mumble and bite my lip, just as my hand slips down to the button of his pants.*

I know what game this is, our little game. When we explore each other like it's the first time, like we've forgotten all about what it's like to be together. When we do everything slowly, no rush, no eagerness to finish, we just want time to stop.

We get so lost into one another, we sometimes forget what's his and what's mine, we blend perfectly. We are perfect for one another in a way it makes no sense, we are so different.

Our love seems too perfect it scares me sometimes. What have I done to deserve something so beautiful, a man like Sebastian? What will I do if I lose him?

Once you feel that perfection with someone, you'll never feel it again, with someone else. Our love is the kind that makes you high and leaves you broken. After us, the world will eventually feel okay again, but never grand, never perfect again.

"We'll go to church later and confess our sins, the sins of the flesh," he smirks and touches me deep. I moan and take another breath. "Right now, I want to worship another temple, your body. I want to worship you, all of you. Now, slowly. You, I'm devoted to you and nothing else."

"Mommy, open your eyes," Eddy's voice wakes me up.

I had that dream again, the one about me and Sebastian playing around the house, our Sundays on the island. Those moments really happened, that perfection was once real. It feels so long ago, like it happened in another life, when we were two different people.

I stopped hearing his voice, my mind is slowly giving in to the idea he's not here anymore. The dreams, the one I was asking myself about, they finally came. Now I'm scared I'll lose them too, the dreams, the memories. I want to keep dreaming, I want to hold on to those moments we shared.

Sebastian is dead, I try to block all thoughts of him during the day, but my mind won't stop mourning him, it just won't shut down at night. It wants me to remember, it wants me to hold on to him a little longer.

I know the end is near and it won't be long till I finally see him again- that is my only consolation.

First save Eddy, then I can rest in peace. I am dead already, but I will never rest in peace until I know my son is far away from Alejandro.

Give me strength. Help me be brave, Sebastian, I think sitting up in bed.

"I'm awake, sweetie," I smile and Eddy smiles back.

I overslept, I am a bad mother. I overslept today of all days, my son's school is having a Christmas recital. I should be overjoyed, eager to watch my son perform. Today is the day, the perfect day for my plan.

It's time to say goodbye, I fight back the tears and kiss him instead.

No, no crying. I want him to remember me with a smile.

One day Eddy will find out about my sacrifice. He'll understand, remembering these last moments together, how much he means to me.

The world, my everything.

We have breakfast like any other day, no that's not true. I make the most of it. It will be our last, at least I know it will be. Eddy doesn't know, he knows nothing but the butterflies in his stomach for the big play. He's so excited, despite all the tension I feel inside, the ache and worry, I tease him about it.

"So at some point you are going to step forward and sing Hallelujah all by yourself," I say and he nearly spits out his cereals.

He can't stop giggling and it hurts, that sound I will miss it so much, but I don't want him to stop. His new life without me, I silently pray it will be full of laughter and joy.

"What are you talking about, mom?" he takes another spoonful and smirks.

"I'll raise my hand and say: Eddy has something to say to you all. That's going to be your cue," I tease him again and he lets out another giggle. And another one.

The pain, I try to control the ache I feel in my chest. I tell myself to keep that back straight and that smile on my face. He's a wonderful kid, despite what I've raised him in.

He'll be fine and therefore I will too.

Ten minutes later we are all cleaned up and dressed, ready to go, ready for the show. My show, Donna Filomena and mine.

She's ready too, dressed with casual but sophisticated clothes, her signature leopard scarf around her neck as usual but no heels. I told her, no heels.

"Ready?" I ask her, just as the soldiers walk into the room to escort us out.

"Yes, are you?" she gives Eddy a hug, but her eyes are on me.

I just nod, we talked about this already. It's the only way to do it, one chance and that's today. There would be no other occasion.

While I grab my clutch and Eddy's bag, Alejandro walks into the living room and his sudden appearance sends my heart racing, I lose the little colour I have on my cheeks but I keep my breathing normal, my face serious.

"Where are you going?" he asks Eddy or his mother, I am not sure.

Then his eyes dart to me and my body tenses, pain shoots up my stomach as I try to steady my heartbeat.

He wasn't supposed to be here, a voice whispers in my ear. *No, not today. He's never home in the mornings, why is he here?*

"To the school play," Eddy's sweet voice softens the air.

Alejandro pats his head and I feel like screaming.

I don't want him to touch my son, I don't want him anywhere near Eddy. The thought of those bloody hands on him, on Sebastian's son, gives me nightmares.

Murderer.

He dared to hold my child, after hitting me, after holding me down on the bed, abusing my body and ignoring my cries.

I sometimes imagine cutting them off, I hate the sight of his hands, the violence in their hold. I loathe him.

Keep quiet, stay calm. Remember why you are doing all this.

"Are you coming?" Donna Filomena asks and I know exactly why.

He must not suspect anything, he must not feel the tension.

"I can't. I'm going out, I have somewhere to be," he slowly pours himself some coffee, locking eyes with me.

I give him no smile, not even a blink. I am a wall of marble, I am cold as ice. He deserves to burn in the flames of hell, but I give him what I can. Ice cold emptiness and nothing more.

"Again?" Donna Filomena asks and he simply nods.

"We are going to be late," I say then and start to walk to the door but Alejandro grabs my hand, I jump.

He can smell something is off, he knows, he knows.

"I want you to come back immediately, as soon as it is over," he moves closer and grumbles in my ear, while I keep looking ahead, smiling at my son.

Everything's okay, everything is perfectly fine, I tell him with my eyes.

Eddy seems to buy it, but his smile doesn't reach his eyes. It never does, not anymore. Donna Filomena starts talking to him and he looks away from me.

"Yes," I glance his way, but never turning my head to fully face him.

"Yes, what?" he grumbles.

"Yes, I will," I say knowing very well he wants me to say 'sir', like he owns me.

He does, he owns me or so he thinks but I play stupid, I play innocent and I pay the price.

His hand squeezes mine so tight, I feel a small click in my knuckles. My mouth opens but I keep the sound from coming out.

"We need to go, mommy," Eddy calls out and Alejandro releases his hold on me.

I glare and walk past him, then my smile is back for Eddy.

"Yes, absolutely. We are going to be late for your hallelujah," I tease him again, I don't know where I find the strength, but I do, somewhere in that big heart that we mothers have.

We are out of there in no time, straight into one of the De la Crux's black cars, before Alejandro decides to send extra soldiers with us. My plan is going to work but with two soldiers. I can handle two.

"What do you need me to do?" Donna Filomena went straight to the point as soon as I mentioned to her the possibility of carrying out our plan on the day of the play.

"Nothing, besides take care of my son," I told her.

I really didn't need anything else, I could handle the rest.

"Just pretend you know nothing about what I am doing. Act shocked, surprised, play the part and protect Eddy while I do what I have to," I said and saw her shake a little.

"What if things don't go as planned?"

"They will, have faith but promise me you'll never come back. Promise me you'll never reach out to anyone. You are

dead; this life is over. Promise me Donna Filomena, let me rest in peace," I nearly sobbed the words out.

A glimpse of humanity, I saw it in her eyes then. She grabbed my hand and nodded.

"I promise, I will."

CHAPTER 29

THE SACRIFICE

SEBASTIAN

Time, place, action. I write down everything, everything I need to know about Alejandro and his daily routine. I scribble down my notes sitting in the car with Severino, we do this every day.

He helped me steal the car, we took it to one of his friends, friends of friends and we bought a fake plate number. Easy as that, you just can't sleep soundly in Naples. You close your eyes and you get your ass stolen. Just like that, poof, gone. Nobody's seen anything, no chance of getting it back.

I hadn't stolen anything in a long time – borrowed yes but stolen, I'd left that in the past. Guilt panged in my chest as we'd turned the car on and drove out of the parking lot but that was that.

I am at war, I use all the tools, the information, the weapons I can get and don't look back.

I'm searching for a flaw, something to work on, something that can get me closer to Andrea and Eddy, a moment of the day I can get close enough to Alejandro and kill him.

Some nights I manage to get some sleep and I picture it in my head, how I'm going to take his life. I want him to suffer, but I tell myself it doesn't matter. He needs to die, I want to destroy him, it doesn't matter how. I want Alejandro De la Crux off the face of the Earth. Every day that goes by, I feel my chest grow heavier, I feel restless and further from saving my family.

Make a mistake, leave something unattended, fucking let your guard down, I curse under my breath every single fucking day. But nothing, Alejandro is a motherfucking clock. He does the same things at the same time every day and when he changes his routine, he takes extra soldiers with him.

I can't get close enough to shoot him dead. I've punched the steering wheel so many times, Severino doesn't even flinch anymore.

Severino, he's been my eyes, ears and legs for days, weeks, months. He follows me like I'm his idol, like I'm the best person he's ever met, the best thing that could happen him. He respects me for my courage and determination, for wanting to save my family.

I don't have the guts to tell him I'm a worthless piece of shit, I'm responsible for all this. I am.

If I had shoot that son of a bitch that time I'd had the chance, if I hadn't let my guard down, we'd still be together, I'd still have my wife, my son.

Some days are harder than others, I find no comfort, not even in happy memories. They hurt so fucking much, sometimes I wish I'd forget and then regret the thought immediately.

I'm so fucked up, I rub my eyes, my face and try to calm my nerves. Something will happen, something will lead me to them. I just need to stay focused, keep my eyes open and wait.

Haste is my enemy, patience my strength.

My long-suffered patience is rewarded on a cold December morning.

Severino tells me about a Christmas recital going on at Eddy's school. It's my chance, my only shot.

"I told you they'd be going out," Severino says, eyeing the car, just as I start the engine and drive into the traffic.

It's bright and early, only one De la Crux car drives out of the mansion.

"It's them, I tell you," Severino urges me to keep a close watch, I try to follow without being noticed.

It's not easy in the daylight, I need to keep some distance, but my heart is aching to drive closer.

Don't lose them, it's them.

We go over the plan together one more time, as I keep my eyes on the black car ahead.

I'll drop Severino a few streets down from the school, he'll mingle with the other kids and walk inside, make his way backstage to talk to Eddy and try to get him out of there. He'll walk him out to the car, using the back doors. I'll think about Andrea.

"Then I want you to run away, I don't want you to stay back and help. Do you understand me, Severino?" I eye him and watch him nod. "You get your ass as far away from there as possible, as far away as you can from the fight. Wait for me in our usual meeting spot. Don't move from there, I'll come back for you. I'll take you with me, but if you don't see me coming…"

It means I failed, I don't need to finish the sentence, Severino is already nodding.

"Just take the money I left for you under that bench down the railway and keep away from the streets."

"I won't need to," the determination in his voice, makes my chest heavier. Severino touches my arm and smiles. "You won't fail. I believe in you."

ANDREA

The conversation with Alejandro made me nervous. I decide not to wait for the end of the play.

We are driving to school when the car slows down at a traffic light. I see the intersection in front of us, I eye Donna Filomena and watch her hold Eddy a little tighter.

My hands are so fast, my brain needs to catch up. I grab the kitchen knife I've been hiding in my boot and push the blade against the throat of the soldier behind the wheel. The other one turns our way immediately, his hand over the gun as on cue.

"Don't," I say through gritted teeth, the man eyes me, then his mate, his stare goes to the blade that's digging into the man's throat.

I keep my hand firm, the tone of my voice harsh, as Donna Filomena scoops Eddy in her arms and tells him not to listen, not to look.

"Drive," I snarl in the man's ear, seeing the traffic light go green again.

We move out of the intersection fast and just as we are about to take the speedway that will take us to Eddy's school, I tell the man sitting in the passengers' seat to drop all his belongings on the floor.

He blinks at me, his hands still up far away from the gun.

"Leave the gun, the phone, your wallet. Everything on the floor, now!"

Eddy is screaming, he's scared, but I can't say anything to him. I can't lose my focus, I can't.

The soldier eyes me then drops everything to the floor like I told him to. A second later his hands are back up in front of him where I can see them.

I press the blade a little further into the man's throat to make a point. To show them I am not joking. I am not. I have never been so serious in my life.

"Don't fucking make a move without me saying so," I warn them, my hand sliding in the front, to the driver's side, never losing eye contact with the other soldier. I know exactly what I am looking for and where to find it.

His gun, I slip it out and hold it tight in my right hand. It's in the other soldier's face within seconds.

"Open the door and jump," I tell him.

He looks at his mate, I feel the anger rise inside of me. He doesn't take me seriously, I push the gun against his head, cocking it, ready to fire.

"Did you fucking hear me? Do it now! Don't fucking test me," my eyes go wide.

I've lost my mind, I want them to see my desperation, just how far I'm willing to go. *I'm serious, so goddam serious about this.*

Eddy whimpers in the back and I'm so sorry, I want to say something but I can't look at him, I can't lose control now.

"Fucking jump or I'll blow your brains out. You decide, soldier. You decide," my eyes are wide open, I'm spitting out the words, my lips are pulled back like a ferocious animal.

I'm a tiger, nothing will stop me, nothing. I won't, not until my son is safe, until this hell of a life I'm living is over. I have nothing to lose, I won't be here to face the consequences and I'm not afraid to die.

"You are dead," the soldier laughs in my face and I push the gun a little harder against his head.

"I died a long time ago, soldier. You killed me. All of you and you are up next, if you don't JUMP," I shout in his face.

Don't push me, I glare at him.

If killing a soulless piece of shit is going to get me through with the plan, so be it.

Anything for Eddy.

Until my last breath, I'll fight for him, to save him, I think as I watch the man open the side door and jump out of the car.

"Close the door," I instruct Donna Filomena.

"Andrea," she says, holding Eddy tighter to her chest, playing the part.

"Now. Do it now," I shout and she moves quickly, leaning forward to close the door.

The car has slowed down a bit, I tell the soldier to take the next exit and stop.

He parks the car in front of an old rusty fence. We are out somewhere around the city, it's just land and old buildings. It's deserted.

With the gun to his head and knife at his throat, I tell him to leave the phone in the car and get out.

"Out!" I shout at him and he opens the door.

He hasn't said a word so far, the man turns to look at me as I step outside the car and tell him to walk.

I am right behind him, the gun on his nape the whole time, I'm so focused I almost forget to breathe.

Once we are far away enough from the car, I tell him to turn around.

The man's eyes are back on me, he doesn't seem worried, he doesn't look like someone ready to plead.

"What are you going to do? Shoot me?" he snickers, holding his hands up like it's a joke.

"You sure deserve it," I tell him, keeping the gun right in his face.

"You don't have the guts," he glares, holding my stare.

Wrong, I do. I have guts, what I don't have are doubts or second thoughts. Or mercy.

I aim low and fire, the bullet drives through his foot.

"Fuck!!!" he yells falling to the ground, holding his leg, screaming in pain.

Like a coward, I try to tighten the grip around the gun, I try to stop my arms, my legs from shaking.

I just shot a man, I didn't even know I could.

I just shot a man.

I just shot… I pant and swallow down hard.

No, he's not a man. He's a monster, like Alejandro, I wipe my conscience clean.

"You fucking bitch, you fucking whore," he screams.

"Shut up or the other one is going too," I bark, tears pooling in my eyes, as I cock the gun again and aim it at his other leg.

The soldier spits on the ground, mumbling something under his breath.

I shot a man, I try not to think, I try to block all the emotions.

Think about Eddy, this is for Eddy, I tell myself as I find my focus again.

"You still think I don't have the guts to kill you?" I snarl. "You are nothing, you are nobody. You have no name, no identity, no life, if not the life Alejandro tells you to have. You are a puppet," I take a good look at him, at the filth of a man cursing my name sprawled on the ground. "Do you have a family? A life, worth living, soldier? Cause this one's not worth living," I tell him and he shakes his head.

"You are just a whore, a fucking whore," he shouts to my face. "He'll find you and he'll kill you this time," he grunts shaking his head, like I'm crazy for thinking I can run away from Alejandro again.

Wrong, he doesn't know I'm not running, not this time.

"Good, I want to die," his glare falters, the man seems confused for a moment. I lower my gun to his chest and the tears start streaming down my cheeks.

Am I hesitating? No, I'm not. I'm having a moment. I'm not a criminal, not a killer. I am woman that values life and I'm about to take one. I have no other choice.

You let him live, he'll come after you, a voice in my head soothes my conscience.

Time is running out. I need to get Eddy away from here, so I forget about the tears, I forget who I am for a moment and I tell the soldier what is it to be.

"For your sins, for your crimes and for my freedom," I pull the trigger and this time I let the shot push me back, my shoulders slump down. This time I don't hold the gun tight in my hands, no. I let it drop to the floor in shock, like I wasn't expecting the sound, the horror. All that blood.

Breathe, Andrea. Breathe.

The man is sprawled on the ground, holding his stomach, his eyes rolled back, breathing in and out fast.

Finish him.

I'm not sure what to do, I've never shot anyone before, never killed anyone before but nobody has ever shown me mercy, nobody ever showed me understanding. Nobody tried to stop Alejandro and what he was doing to me and my battered body.

No mercy, I bend down to take the gun fast, I aim to his chest and shoot.

The moving stops, the gasps, the breathing. The world stops but me.

I run to the car without looking back, drying the tears with the back of my hand.

Don't hesitate, run.

When I open the car door, I turn to look at my son, his face is pressed against Donna Filomena's chest, her hands over his ears like I'd told her to.

She looks at me worried, I nod to reassure her. The plan is going to work.

Without saying a word, I drive us back on the speedway, heading south and out of Naples. I'm going out to the countryside, to a bridge, one bridge in particular. It's not far from a small train station, Donna Filomena looked it up for me. It's perfect, perfect for them to run away. What will happen to me on that bridge, I am still not sure. I have nothing planned. Once I get my son away from all this, I have no plan but one. The end.

"Perchè mamma, perché?" Eddy looks at me, his voice is broken by the sobs, his eyes are red from the crying.

Why mommy, why? Eddy doesn't see what I see, he doesn't know what I know and it's a relief. I can't explain it to him, I'll have to leave that to Donna Filomena. One day, one day.

All I can do now is hold him tight, breathe in his scent.

For the last time, the air is stuck in my throat, I can't take deep breaths, all I feel is pain. Everywhere.

I close my eyes and take in his scent one more time, just one. Everything smells, tastes, feels too good to let it go, but I have to, I have to let him go.

Mothers are not meant to say goodbye to their children, it's against nature. We shouldn't have to give up our blood, the very essence of our lives, a part of our hearts.

I take a good look in his big blue eyes, his amber cheeks and I move two curls out of his face.

Look at you, the best thing I've ever done, I smile and kiss every inch of his face.

Eddy hugs me tight and cries against my shoulder. I don't want to let him go, I don't want to give him up. I don't, but it's not about me and what I need. It's for him and what he deserves. A better life, one I can't give him.

"You have to go with Filomena, she will take care of you, Eddy. It's not safe for you to be here," I dry his tears and pull the hoodie over his head.

I help him out of the car and look into his eyes again as his small, soft lips move to speak again.

"I want you to come with us, I want you to be safe," he sniffs, I hold his hand tight and make him a promise.

"I promise you I'll be with you every step of the way, I will Eddy. I will think of you every day, every moment," my stare locks with Donna Filomena. It's almost time, I know, I know what she's trying to tell me but doesn't have the heart to say.

The heart of the mother knows what it's like to say goodbye, to give up a son.

I slip something into Eddy's hand. The blue pendant, the one Sebastian gave me on the island the last time I saw him.

That pendant is the only thing I have left of him, the only memory of us together. I have no picture, nothing else to remind me of what it was like to be happy, us three. Yet I remember every little detail of his face, how he looked at me, how he took care of Eddy.

That blue pendant holds our past, the love we shared. I give it to Eddy and tell him to keep it with him all the time. He holds it tight in his hand, sobbing quietly, and I press my lips on his knuckles, kissing every single one of them.

I tell him he holds me and Sebastian in his hand, we'll be by his side forever. That blue pendant is eternal and timeless.

"We'll always be together," I let the tears stream down my cheeks but I am back on my two feet, ready to tell Donna Filomena the last things she needs to know.

"Promise you'll never look for me, for Alejandro, anyone. Promise me you'll never be back, that you'll never speak to anyone about this," I search her face, my hands strong around her shoulders.

Donna Filomena holds my stare, her face solemn. I see determination and fear, but I know she's strong, a woman of another era. She will take good care of Eddy, I know she will.

"I promise," she says and I nod.

"As of now, you are dead. I'll tell Alejandro I shot you and pushed you in the river. You don't exist anymore."

Donna Filomena nods and my hands are back around Eddy's shoulders. I kiss him again and again, frantically, letting the tears flow.

He's so beautiful, my boy, we're still together, holding on to each other and I miss him already.

"Please go, take him away or I won't be able to …" I can't finish the sentence.

"Good luck," Donna Filomena tells me with little voice.

"Good luck," I tell her and then I squeeze her hand tight. "Grazie, Donna Filomena."

She nods and takes Eddy's hand in hers.

"And may God have mercy on our souls." Her last words to me are full of hope. I cling to them.

Have mercy, have mercy, my mind prays. *Let them reach their destination safely, let them live peacefully.*

My thoughts are jumbled, my emotions all over the place as they make their way to the small countryside train station.

Eddy sobs and turns to look at me, I can hear him mumble my name. I wave and smile, my mouth can lie but my eyes can't.

Alejandro has been torturing me, physically and emotionally for days, weeks, months and nothing. In the end my body didn't break, my mind didn't lose focus. I managed to stay in one piece despite all the cracks in my heart. Until now, it's breaking now, I can feel it giving in to the pain.

The rumble is sudden and loud like thunder, I touch my chest and I want to scream but I hold it back and focus on the breathing.

It's better this way. It's how it's meant to be, I tell myself again and again as I will myself to walk back to the car and wait in there for the train to come and go.

I watch them leave, I breathe in the gust of wind as the train departs again and takes my son away.

To a new life, one without me and his father. I can only hope I've taken the right decision but I'll never really know. I won't be around much longer; my time here is almost over. I need to finish what I've started.

My foot pushes down on the gas, I skid away, to the river, to the tall bridge. My time has come.

CHAPTER 30

LAST NIGHT ON EARTH

ANDREA

The sea is calm, a couple of waves every now and then. It's such a beautiful hot summer's day, it feels good to be in the water.

We swim to the first shallows and I can barely touch the sand with my toes. Sebastian however is standing, grinning at me, the water just below his shoulders.

I frown and place both feet on top of his, smirking at him, letting the little weight I have in the water be his burden. His hands find my waist instantly and he holds me close to him, I feel my stomach tighten.

Sebastian smiles down at me, as he tells me something I've heard before.

"Oi vita, oi vita mia," "Oh life, oh you're my life" he mumbles the words of a song from Naples and pauses to gently kiss my lips, I melt in his arms. "Oi core, e chisto core. Si stata lu prim ammore. Lu prim e l'ultimo sarai pe me." He slurs the words, his southern accent so melodic, my heart misses a beat. "Oh my heart, you're my heart. You were my first love and you'll be my last."

I smile and pull him down to me again, savouring the moment, loving those words and how they make me feel. My first, my last. I never felt like this before, no man has ever loved me in such a way. Sebastian holds me close and leaves me free to be.

Oh life, you are my life.

I pull at his lips a little, I don't want him to stop kissing me. Ever. It's like a thirst, my need for them. When we kiss, I know it's real, I know we are real.

"I love how you hold me," I whisper and tilt my head back, running my hands up to his neck.

The tattoo, I want to run my fingers all over it, I want to trace it with my tongue and taste the salt on his skin. His hands move down my back, around my waist.

"How am I holding you?" he asks, his voice is huskier as I glide towards him. I'm snaked around his body in an instant.

"Like I am yours and only yours to hold," I purr, closing my eyes a little.

Drops of water drip down my cheeks, but Sebastian catches them with his hand and then moves closer to kiss me again.

Hard, strong, deep. I gasp for air and I want none, I curse the air, I need another kiss from him, that is my air.

"I will hold you until you don't want me to," he says in between kisses.

"Forever then. I don't want you to let go," I whisper the words and then smile. "How much do you love me?"

He's told me, he's just told me using the words of a song, but I still want him to tell me.

"The greatness of the sea wouldn't be enough to compare," Sebastian answers and I smile biting my lip, letting that greatness comfort me. "Look at us now, where we are now. We made it all the way here, Pretty Eyes."

I nod and let the happy memories of us together be my light. We'd bought a house, made it our home. We are raising our son together, sharing our lives.

"What if I lose you? What if you lose me?" I mumble, drinking in the fierceness in his dark brown eyes.

"I'll find you, no matter where you are. Like a stone, no matter how strong the waves are, no matter how far the water pushes it from the shore, it will always go back to the shore eventually."

I kiss him again and moan as his strong arms flex around my back.

"I'll never stop looking for you, I'll never give up on us. I'll wait for you, no matter what. We are like that stone and that sea, Andrea. I'll find you or you'll find me."

One step closer to the bridge, then another. I walk slowly, I take my time. There's no rush, even though I know Alejandro's men are already looking for me.

We've been missing for an hour, the soldier that jumped out of the car has probably found a way to inform him. He'll be here soon, he'll come to collect what's his. Like he always does, but not this time. This time I won't let him take me.

I lean against the railing and throw Eddy's and Donna Filomena's belongings into the river. All of them. They are for the police to find.

A desperate woman kills her mother in law and her son, then kills herself.

A desperate woman. The description fits me perfectly.

I look down, at the impetuous water that runs through the valley. The bridge is high, I wonder how deep the water is, if it's cold, if it's muddy or clear. I can't see well from up here. And it doesn't matter.

I'll be long gone before I get to the water, a bullet will make everything easier. I pull the gun out and take a good look at it. It's shaky in my hands, I feel my nerves faltering, I force myself to keep it together.

"This is the end," I tell the wind, I tell the world.

I smile and push my hair back, I close my eyes and think of Sebastian, I think about that stone and that sea, I think about our promises.

"I'm coming for you, I'm coming," I cry and smile at the same time, as I point the gun to my head.

I can hear a car in the distance, it's skidding to a stop but I ignore it. Maybe a passer-by that wants to try and save me. Too late.

There's nothing left to save, I'd like to tell them, I'd like them to know why. I'm not crazy, it's not what it seems. I had a perfect life once but it must have been a dream, my life, my real life is a never ending nightmare. I don't want to live like that, anymore.

Enough.

I can't stop what I started, I won't risk going back to Alejandro. This is my only chance to escape.

I'll be free again, the gun is pressed against my head. I look up at the blue sky, I focus on the clouds and smile, letting the tears wash away the last doubts in my mind.

My last breathes are for Sebastian, I can only hope to see him again. Wherever I'm going, I hope it's with him. Then I think about Eddy and close my eyes tight. I'm ready, I'm ready for the end.

SEBASTIAN

"ANDREA!!!!!!!!!" I shout out her name with all the voice I have in me and she stops moving, letting the gun slide down a little.

She heard me, I'm out of the car in a second, running to the other side of the road when I shout for her again.

"ANDREA!!!!!"

This time she turns and when she sees me, her lips begin to tremble.

Yes, It's me, baby. I'm here.

Andrea shakes her head and lets out a cry. It comes out broken and voiceless but I hear it. Loud and clear.

My Sad Eyes, her face is wet from all the crying but all I can think of is my beautiful Andrea, my woman. I found her.

I don't understand why she's here, what she's doing standing on a bridge with a gun to her head.

And Eddy, where is Eddy?

All I know is that they were going to a play, I'd been following them at a safe distance, hoping to find the right moment to take them away. I'd make sure they were safe, before going back for Alejandro.

Only it didn't go as planned, nothing did.

A man jumped out of their car, before I lost them for a bit. When I figured the right speedway exit, it was too late, the car was moving again, into the countryside. Too many little roads, too many options.

"Let's try that way," Severino had pointed this way and I'd almost lost any hope of finding them when I'd recognized the car.

"ANDREA!!!" I shout again, I jump a railing and I'm on her side of the road, but before I make it to her, she drops the gun and starts running towards me.

"SEBASTIAN!!!" her yell is raspy and deep, like she's been hiding my name inside her for so long.

It has been too long, far too long.

I reach out for the woman I love and take her in my arms, hiding my face in her hair.

She is alive, it isn't too late. She's in my arms.

"You are here," she whimpers, shaking all over.

"You are alive," she cries, touching my hair, my lips. "You are alive. It can't be, I'm losing my mind. You are not here," Andrea is shaking her head confused.

I lift her up, holding her tight and bury a kiss against her neck.

I'm here, I'm really here, I don't want to let her go, not now, not ever.

I kiss her hair, her cheeks, my lips press against every inch of her face. Her nails dig into my jacket, as she sobs out words I don't understand.

Her cries run deep, they hold all the pain, all the suffering and the relief a woman can bear.

"I'm so sorry baby," I cup her cheeks and kiss her.

I can't stop telling her how sorry I am for everything. Once the words come out of my lips, I feel all the things I've been keeping inside, wanting to spring free.

I tell her I'm sorry I'd let her walk away from me that night, that I didn't realize what was happening, I'm sorry for not being fast enough, strong enough to save her.

But she's shaking her head, pressing her lips against mine, hushing me, telling me it's not my fault and I so want to believe her, my heart, my heavy chest wants to believe it's true but the guilt will always be part of me. I can't do anything to go back and change things. I wish I could, I so wish I could.

"He told me he'd killed you. I thought you'd died and … You are here, you came for us," Andrea cries again, this time she takes my face into her hands and looks at me, her ice cold blue eyes are full of life, the fire burns inside her again. I see it, I feel it.

"I'd die for you, Pretty Eyes," I tell her. "I'd bleed myself dry for you."

Then I kiss her hard, my chest grows heavy, I've waited so long to feel her again.

I don't want her to cry, not one single tear, not anymore. I want to take away all the pain and see her smile again.

Andrea pulls me to her but then breaks the kiss all of a sudden.

"Eddy," something flickers in her eyes, I don't understand what it means and I don't have time to ask.

"Sebastian!!" Severino calls out my name and I turn his way.

Two cars are coming up the road, black, tainted windows, Mercedes Benz.

"Fuck," I curse and grab her hand, lifting her up once, twice as we jump the railings and cross the road quick.

"Run," I shout, getting into the car and putting in the gear real quick.

The cars are too close already, I take one look at Andrea sliding down in her seat, putting her belt on, before I hear the first shot.

It breaks the silence and it hits the side of the car.

Andrea is screaming, pushing her hands over her ears.

My eyes are on the road, my hand on the gear, then on Severino, pushing him down in his seat.

"Down, stay down," I tell him and he nods, for the first time his eyes are wide and scared, like they should be.

Another shot, this time it misses the car. The road is bendy, I hardly use the breaks, I try to keep the speed up as much as I can.

Left, right, left, I follow the road and begin to panic as it gets narrower and narrower, it goes downhill in a steep twirl and I know, my heart knows before I see it where it will lead us. To a dead end. The road ends on the premises of an old abandoned factory.

"Shit," I curse and drive the car all the way down to a rusty gate.

The cars are behind us; I can't see them but I know they'll come down soon.

"Let's go," I pull the handbrake up and the doors bolt open.

We are out and running to the gate in a second. I let Severino through, then Andrea, then it's my turn to jump. That's when the cars stop next to mine and we run fast to the old building, never looking back.

Have you ever run not knowing if you'll ever make it to the end?

Moving targets, that is what we are and we don't know where the guns are aiming. Me? Andrea? Severino?

No, I don't stop to think, I can't get us killed. Instead I scan the building for a door, any door and when I see a big grey one, I kick the lock, slam my shoulder against it and push it open.

"Over there!" someone shouts, not too far from us.

They are getting closer, I assert as I reach for my gun and aim.

The first soldier turns the corner and I fire.

The sound echoes in the empty factory, as the man falls to his knees, screaming in pain.

Another one is right behind him, I aim at his stomach and fire.

Two men down, my jaw twitches, as I hear another shout coming from around the corner.

The third soldier is more cautious. He's one with the wall, moves slowly and takes a glimpse at me, just in time before I fire.

I miss.

Fuck!

My heart is in my throat, I hear Severino and Andrea panting and whimpering behind my back, but I don't turn around. My eyes never leave that wall, where the soldier is hiding.

How many soldiers? Two cars, I do the math; nine plus Alejandro. They are probably moving around the building, surrounding the entire facility and I need them in one place, where I can kill them.

S*hit,* I slam the door shut in haste and push whatever I can find in front of it.

Chairs, drawers, old pipes.

Andrea and Severino are next to me in a second, helping me as the screaming and shouting resumes outside.

"This way!" I hear another voice, just behind the door.

I need to find a window, I need to find an opening that I can use and shoot those motherfuckers, one by one. As many as I can, before they get through the door.

Andrea is looking at me, I can feel her worried eyes search mine.

"Run all the way up those stairs," I point to the old, metal staircase. "Take Severino with you. Look for a terrace, an emergency door, whatever will take you outside and back down again. I want you to get out and run up the road."

Andrea takes Severino's hand but doesn't move an inch. She stands there beside me, shaking, her eyes digging into mine.

She's hesitating.

"Go, Andrea," I urge her to move but she shakes her head.

"No, no. I've only just found you again."

I cup her face, leaning my forehead against hers.

We don't have time to discuss, no time to say anything, I let my eyes convince her it's the right thing to do. I nod and hold her stare, until she slips out of my hold, her eyes watery again, and takes Severino up the stairs.

Then, I find an opening, a crack in a window and aim my gun at another soldier's head. And I fire. I bring another one of those fuckers down, before I move up the stairs, just as the door slams open. I wait in the shadows, ready to take down some more.

CHAPTER 31

THE MONSTER

ANDREA

We've reached the top and I'm out of breath. All the running, the stairs, the horror of what is happening. Again, Alejandro is coming for me again.

I hear things flying downstairs, shouts, voices, so many voices I want to crawl behind something and disappear.

I want to disappear, I want to go back to the bridge, back to the moment I held the gun to my head and heard Sebastian call out my name. That moment there, I want it back.

When he touched me, when I felt his arms around me again, I want that back.

Instead, I am looking for a window, something we can crawl out of and maybe try to slip down. I don't know how many men, how many soldiers are with Alejandro.

I hear three shots, they seem close, I scream at the top of my lungs, my heart is tired. I can't do this anymore, I can't.

Severino stands there in the middle of the room as I run to the far back, looking for something, pressing my hands against every wall, every piece of furniture. The place is stuffy and bare, if not for a couple of desks and a filing cabinet against the brown stained wall.

I turn to look at him again, he's still standing there not moving, not saying a word as other shots are fired, things fall to the floor and people shout downstairs.

Fear, he's paralyzed, I realize as I run to him again and take his hand.

I don't know who he is, he looks homeless, he looks confused and scared. He's a child, just like my own, and I don't need anything else to know what's right.

"Don't be scared, I'm getting you out," I tell him and he nods, without looking at me. He keeps staring at the staircase. Any minute, any minute now…

"I won't let them touch you," I tell him, as I wrap an arm around him and open a small, dusty window behind a desk.

It's too narrow for me to slip through it, but not for a child like him.

It leads to a little balcony, to emergency stairs. I thank our good stars.

"Go down, Severino. Go and don't let them take you, stay away from the main gate. Do you understand? Find another way out, run up the road and call for help. Call for the police. Severino," I look into his frightened little eyes, his are so young and so innocent, I hate the world more and more. "Don't stop. Look for help."

He's out in a matter of seconds and I'm alone again, nowhere to hide, nowhere to go, no gun in hand.

I keep my eyes on Severino and thoughts of Eddy cross my mind. I wonder where he is now, if he's stopped crying. Wherever he is, he's far from this and I'm grateful. I let that comfort me.

I watch Severino slide under a half-open fence and run up the dirt road. He's made it, he's out of there and he's safe, no matter what.

I have no hope for help, none but at least someone will come looking, someone will come take mine and Sebastian's bodies, once Alejandro has had his way with us. At least we will rest in peace. Justice? There will never be.

The building goes quiet all at once. No more sounds from downstairs, I push my back against the wall and cringe.

"Andrea," it's my name, but this time it's not Sebastian's voice calling for me.

The devil, I shake my head and try to push back. Back where? There's no place for me to hide, no way out of this.

"Andrea," he comes up the stairs, the devil, he comes again. "Where are you, you little bitch?"

I wince, I'm shaking but my face is cold as a slate of marble. My eyes are squinting as he appears at the top of the stairs, his soldiers right behind him, gun in hand.

"You little bitch," he launches himself forward and grabs me by the hair.

I stifle a cry and look away from him, even if he tries to turn my face, I refuse to.

Don't listen to the monster, don't listen.

His hand pulls my hair harder and this time I can't hold back the cry.

"Non la toccare, figlio di puttana," *"Don't touch her, you son of a bitch"* I hear Sebastian's roar and I breathe out relieved.

He's alive, he's here. I look over Alejandro's shoulder and I see him being pulled up the stairs, two bruised and battered men holding him tight.

Sebastian's face is purple, his left eye covered in blood, he can hardly keep it open but it's on me, on Alejandro's hand pulling my hair.

"Don't fucking touch her," Sebastian sprints forward and manages to slip out of one of the soldier's hold but the other one pins him down and hits him in the head.

"Stop it!" I cry. "STOP!" I scream and Alejandro pulls my hair again, searching my face, I can smell his breath on me, pungent and bitter.

"It's never going to stop. You're never going to stop trying to fuck me over," his eyes try to dig a hole in my soul, but I block him out, I look back at him with the same harshness.

"Don't hurt him, please don't hurt him," I plea and watch Sebastian's head snap up.

"Don't beg him, Andrea. Don't give this motherfucker the satisfaction," he tells me before another fist slams into his face.

Blood drips out of his mouth, I watch in horror his head hang loose, unconscious.

Breathe, oh please breathe my love. Please, please.

Alejandro drops me then, I fall to my knees but hold my head up. My eyes are on him as he walks back to Sebastian, bends a little forward and grabs his hair.

He takes a good look at him, tilts his head to the side and snickers.

"I thought I'd killed you, I underestimated you."

Sebastian's eyes flicker, they look so glassy, drowsy. He's confused and maybe still unconscious, I cover my mouth and silence a cry.

My heart keeps breaking, I didn't know there still was something to break but here I am watching the man I love die because of me. I would do anything to save him.

"I would die for you," Sebastian's words echo in my mind and I want to tell him I would too, I would die for him. I don't want to live another day without him.

"I told you to stay away, not come back. You brought this all on yourself," Alejandro goes on, Sebastian eyes seem to focus a little now that he's holding his head up.

His lips part and he whispers something, Alejandro laughs. The sound is chilling, pure evil.

"What the fuck did you say?" he grunts in Sebastian's face and then I see it, the life, that fire in his eyes is back.

He's back.

"Fuck you," Sebastian growls and his head flies forward. Hard.

It hits Alejandro right in the face, blood starts rolling down his nose as he falls back with a loud thud, screaming and cursing Sebastian's name.

I don't know where he's found the strength but My Rock is on his feet again, shoving one of the soldiers to the floor, throwing the other one to the side, making his way to me fast.

Only he doesn't make it. Another soldier hits him from behind and Sebastian lands on the floor.

I scream with all I have in me and this time I shout Alejandro's name.

He turns to look at me, holding his nose with one hand, and I stand up. It takes me a few minutes to find something to say, something to stop what is happening because I know, I know he's about to kill Sebastian.

"If you kill him, I won't tell you what happened to Eddy. I swear to god, I'll take the secret to the grave with me."

I'm bluffing, I never would and I don't know where Eddy is.

I'll tell him I killed his mother and our son, before throwing them into the river. I want to watch him suffer, I want him to die knowing I killed the people he loved the most.

Eddy and my lies, the only weapons, the only hold I still have on this man, this monster.

"You'll take your secret to the grave with you," he considers it. "The secret about our son," I hate the edge in his voice but I nod, as Alejandro stares at me attentively.

"I will fight you, every day, until my last breath, Alejandro," I tell him to his face. "Until my last breath, I will try to run from you, to defy you. I will always try to escape from you, but if you let Sebastian go, I won't fight you, not anymore." I'm not even done talking and already Sebastian is saying no, shaking his head.

"It's too fucking late for that," Alejandro growls, he stands and walks back to me, his hand reaches out for my hair and I flinch disgusted, but he keeps touching me like he owns me and I hate it. I wish I could slap him hard, fight back.

I hate you.

"I wanted you by my side, despite everything you did, I still wanted you," he whispers in my ear. I close my eyes as his lips brush against my lobe, my stomach clenches.

He's delusional, absolutely mental.

"I wanted you to love me, to worship me. I wanted you on your fucking hands and knees for me, but you were always so fucking stubborn. What the fuck is it with you? I wanted to make you my queen but you preferred to be a whore, the whore of a dirty, fucking rat. And now you'll die like one."

"I'd rather die the whore of a rat than live like the wife of a worthless man like you," I say the words out loud, I want everyone in the room to hear me, the world to know how much I loathe this man.

"Oh, yeah?" Alejandro grabs my arm and squeezes it tight. "How good would that be, Andrea," he shakes his head from side to side, intimidating like a snake approaching its prey. "Not so fast. You die when I say so, when I'm over with you. I decide."

Then he turns to his men for a moment, looks at Sebastian being held down on his knees and his eyes are back on me.

"Tell me, Andrea. You still think you can keep me away from my son, you still think you can hide things from me."

He snaps his fingers and one of his soldiers runs down the stairs, only to come back up again a few minutes later with my son in his arms.

"No," I shake my head and cover my mouth.

Eddy looks at me then down at Sebastian, his eyes red from all the crying.

"Mamma," he cries and I move forward, as if to take him in my arms, but Alejandro holds me back, grabs my shoulder and squeezes it so tight, I cry out.

"Mamma," he cries again and then looks down at Sebastian.

"Your mom has been bad, really bad," Alejandro is the first one to speak, Eddy's stare speaks for himself.

He eyes the man he thinks is his father and glares at him, pure hatred. Alejandro takes a step back, not daring to touch Eddy, to try and comfort him.

Instead he turns to me and whispers in my ear.

"You really thought you could keep it from me, your little secret?"

The blood in my veins goes cold, I pant, my eyes roll back and my legs nearly give in.

He knows, he knows Eddy is not his son.

"I knew you were up to something, I can tell when you lie," he snarls, his lips brush against my cheek and I pull away, disgusted but he holds me still, I see Sebastian trying to spring loose again, shouting not to touch me.

Alejandro ignores him and grabs my face, squeezing my cheeks hard.

"I never really fucking trusted you."

Then he tells me about the bugs in the house, the cars with GPS. He's heard everything, all the conversations Donna Filomena and I had. He knew, what I was doing, he knew and he watched me carry out the plan knowing exactly how and when to stop me. Alejandro De la Crux, the master of puppets.

But the secret, the secret is safe, I finally manage to catch my breath.

I'm shaking my head, when I see Donna Filomena appear up the stairs, shivering, arms over her chest.

I can read her eyes now, they are not guarded as they've been for months. No, Donna Filomena looks back at me worried, her stare goes from me to Alejandro then to Eddy, who runs straight into her arms.

Hold him tight, tighter. For me. I pant relieved he's with her.

"How could you?" Alejandro glares at his mother, his voice hard, unforgiving.

"Alejandro," she says, not daring to step any further, keeping Eddy close to her body. "This isn't about you. It's not. It was for him, for Eddy."

"He's my son!" Alejandro shouts, releasing me and pointing a finger at her. "You listened to her, to this fucking bitch. You betrayed your own son."

"No," Donna Filomena shakes her head. "No, I never wanted to hurt you. It's not about you, it's not. It's for Eddy. He was in pain, I couldn't keep living with myself, seeing him hurting so much. He's just a child, I tried to tell you, I tried. You wouldn't listen. He wasn't happy, he was going to be sick, all the hatred, everything that was happening around him, he was going to grow up broken and resentful like…"

"Like me. Is that what you were going to say?" Alejandro takes a few steps forward, his cold piercing stare menacing. "I was living with a snake in my house and I didn't know."

"Leave her alone, she's got nothing to do with his," I shout at him but Alejandro doesn't even flinch, he turns to me again and this time goes for my neck.

I gasp as he presses his forehead against mine, pinning me to a wall, Sebastian is screaming in the background but I can't hear what he's saying. All I hear is the sound of my racing heart, pounding in my ears and in my throat.

Alejandro closes his eyes for a moment but when he opens them again, he looks at me different. Regret, sorrow, pity.

"You're right, it's all your fucking fault. I see it now, cunning bitch that you are. You still think you can hide from me, Andrea? You can't. I always know your next move, I always know what it's in your head. I am part of you, you can't run away from me. You can't and now you'll see what happens when you try," he shoves me to the ground and then walks slowly to Sebastian, who's grunting and swinging his arms around, trying to free himself from the soldiers.

"You'll see what happens when someone tries to fuck me over," he takes the gun out and I gasp. He points it to Sebastian, right in front of Eddy, and then kisses the pendant around his neck.

He's going to kill him, oh my god, he's going to kill him in front of Eddy.

"No, not in front of Eddy," I don't know what I'm saying, I'm crying, I'm begging but Alejandro isn't even listening, his eyes are on Sebastian.

"See you in hell," he says and grips the trigger.

Then Eddy's screams tear the room apart.

CHAPTER 32

THE HEAVY BURDEN

ALEJANDRO

"*A man who shoots to kill bears a burden over his heart,*" I think about my mother's words as I aim at The Killer's chest and pull the trigger.

A heavy burden, I've been carrying it with me for so long and now it looks as though I'm finally getting what I've been searching for all these years. My revenge.

The gunshot is still echoing in the room when the weapon slips from my hand and drops to the floor with a loud thud.

It's quiet for just a second and then I hear the loudest, most heart-wrenching scream I've ever heard in my life. The pain of a mother seeing his son on the floor covered in blood.

Eddy.

I shot Eddy.

He's lying there on the ground, his eyes are closed and he's not screaming anymore. I'd pay all the money in the world to hear his voice again. He's not moving.

I shot Eddy.

How? I stare down at him in horror, what I'm looking at doesn't make any sense. It's wrong, it can't be.

I shot my son.

He was with my mother; how did I not see him move? How did I not realize he'd jumped in front of Sebastian?

I shot him.

"No, no, no !!!" Andrea runs to him and falls to the ground. "Eddy."

Her hands are on his little body, she's pulling at her hair, then they are on Eddy again.

Blood, a red spot rolls on the floor beside my son.

My blood, I killed my own blood.

The soldiers stand around us motionless, they stare at me without saying a word, as Andrea touches Eddy's bloodied chest, then cover her face in despair. She's wailing and rocking, crying and screaming his name.

Everything seems to happen so slowly, but my breathing. I'm panting, I'm looking down at my son as I realize what I've done.

"He's not breathing," Sebastian says then, my eyes move to him.

I just gape and stare at him, on his knees beside Andrea, as I realize he's free to move, my soldiers released him after the gunshot.

I shot my son.

My mother is crying, on the floor next to them. I watch Sebastian check Eddy's pulse, try to breathe the life back into him and pump his heart, while Andrea holds Eddy's little hand, screaming his name, mumbling something in her language.

"Call an ambulance, someone, call for help," Sebastian shouts to no one in particular and to everyone there. Nobody moves.

"Call the ambulance, he's dying!" Andrea screams at the top of her lungs and I see two of my men run down the stairs- to the car to get their phones, I think. I am not sure.

"Oh, my God, oh my God. God, God, oh God," Andrea rocks back and forth crying her heart out, her eyes on Eddy.

His face seems to change colour, he looks different I can't put my finger on it. Like the blood stopped flowing, like the life is slowly fading.

"Eddy," Sebastian calls for him, touches his head, his cheeks.

I don't feel anything. I don't feel the rage anymore, I feel empty and dead, like I'm the silent, invisible witness of something. My own death, my doom.

Only I'm there, they can see me and I'm the monster that's done this.

I shot my son.

Andrea turns to look at me at some point, her eyes are red and swollen, she screams something at me and then pulls her hair a little more, while Sebastian doesn't give up. He's not giving up, he's still trying to pump Eddy's little heart, his hands now covered in blood.

His mouth blows air inside of him, his hands pump his chest, air, chest, air, chest. I look at my heavy burden, the one I was told I would bear. The death of my son with my own hands, my child.

I look in the eyes of every soldier around me and then bend down to collect my gun. My eyes scan it, I'd pulled that trigger so many times, not stopping to think, not even once about what I was doing. I'm the man with no heart, I take lives, I make people do what I want or dispose of them.

But my son, I'd taken my son's life.

My thirst for revenge finally caught up with me.

I can't wash that blood off my hands. No, not this time, I know I could never wash away the guilt of killing my own son. Never.

I shot my son.

I search the room again, my eyes drop down to Eddy one more time, to his lifeless tiny body. I look down at Sebastian, Andrea and my mother, before I stick the gun in my mouth.

"No!" Donna Filomena cries out and a soldier launches himself forward to catch my arm.

He can't. It's too late for me.

I close my eyes and pull the trigger and then everything happens so fast. My legs give in and I fall to the floor.

The last heartbeats are the loudest; I can hear them pang in my ears as I drift out of consciousness.

It's liberating, not to feel anymore. I don't feel anymore.

That heavy burden, it's gone. Just like me, I'm going. I know my mother's touching me but I don't feel it, she's screaming and I can't hear a thing. I don't deserve to, I'm the devil, I'm the man with no soul, no heart. I say when it's over. I'm over.

The end.

SEBASTIAN

I'm not giving up, my hands are still working on Eddy's chest, I want to hear his heartbeat, see his eyes open and look at me.

"Come on, come on," I keep repeating, a soft plea.

I don't look around, my attention is on Eddy, the only sound in my ears are my heavy breathes and Andrea's wailing.

She's on the floor, her hands over Eddy, she keeps holding his hand, touching his hair, crying out words, prayers.

Come on, come on, breathe.

"Don't leave me, don't leave me," Andrea starts crying again when we hear the sirens somewhere around us. Two, three, four… it's not just the ambulance, the police are on their way too.

Andrea is lying on the floor holding Eddy, I'm still trying to get him to breathe when the paramedics rush up the stairs and realize what happened, the horror we've just gone through. I want to tell them they have no idea, no idea.

They are quick, one runs to Eddy, pulls his shirt open and places the defibrillator on his chest.

"Do we need to call another ambulance?" he asks the other paramedic, who's checking for Alejandro's pulse.

The man shakes his head. No ambulance is needed.

Alejandro is gone, killed himself with his own filthy fucking hands.

Goddamn you, may he be damned. I have no time for him, my eyes are back on my son, lying in a pool of blood, pale and motionless.

"Ready? Clear," they are both working on Eddy now, I hear them talk, as our son's body arches back a little, the voltage running through his heart.

Andrea cries louder, I move to her side and pull her into my arms. We need to make space and let the men work, but it's so hard to step back, it's so hard to let him go.

I caress her hair knowing nothing I can say will make the pain go away, nothing I can do that I haven't already tried, to make things right.

I don't say anything, I keep her close to me, I just hold her without promising her things will be alright. We've been through too much to know that's a lie. Nothing will ever be the same again. Nothing, if our Eddy….

"Pulse. He's breathing," one paramedic says to another, as they ease Eddy onto a stretcher and alert the hospital with their phones, ready to take him away.

"He's breathing?" Andrea asks and they nod, as they tie his little shoulder with bandages to stop the bleeding.

He's so fragile, he's so small, he's too young to die.

Not like this, not now. God, I close my hand into a fist and dig my nails deep into my skin. I focus on the pain. I want to take the pain away from him, I want to take it all. Why didn't that bullet hit me? Why?

I can't break now, not now.

Don't let go, don't go anywhere, I touch his hand and hold it tight, until we are down to the main entrance and out of the building.

We are running, it's a run against time, desperation makes us push forward, I help the man ease the stretcher inside the ambulance.

"One person inside," I hear them say just before someone shouts my name and I turn.

An officer.

Police are everywhere, Alejandro's soldiers or what is left of them, are held against a wall, searched and handcuffed. One officer is behind me in a second, his hands take mine and wraps them around my back.

"Sebastian Esposito you are under arrest, you have the right to remain silent…"

I grit my teeth and try to take one step forward, one step closer to my son, my wife.

"Sebastian," Andrea cries out, she bends forward and our lips brush, a soft kiss before I'm pulled back again, the police officer is dragging me to one of the cars.

"Stay with Eddy, go," I tell her and she nods, covering her mouth, holding what's left of her together. She knows, she has to keep it together.

Sirens on, the ambulance is ready to leave and, just before the doors are shut close, I get a glimpse of my Andrea, my beautiful wife, holding the hand of our wonderful son, her face wet with tears.

I love you, but it's too late to tell her, to tell Eddy. *I was too late.*

I don't care what happens to me, I can rot in jail for all I care, if only I could buy my son a second chance, a new life.

My guts tell me it's probably the last time I'll see them.

The car door slams in my face and I finally let out my pain. I yell his name.

And I break.

CHAPTER 33

LIMBO

SEBASTIAN

Three weeks in prison feel like three years. I'm left to rot in my own thoughts, nightmares haunt me. I go from shouting my heart out to complete silence. I'm sometimes exhausted, to the point that I can't take living in this limbo any longer, feeling all this bubbled up anger inside of me, wanting to let lose but nothing I can do other than hit the stained walls in front of me. So I hit the walls, over and over again until I'm exhausted.

Every single day.

My life is made of little sounds that catch my attention. I'm alert, one guard walks by my door and I sit up. Doesn't matter if I'm sleeping or not, I never sleep anyway, I can't.

I think about Eddy and Andrea, every single breath I take.

Twenty days after my arrest and I still don't know anything about my son, no news. They threw me in jail, I've been in here before, as part of my mission. I'm in San Vittore, a prisoner of my own cover up identity and I'm far away from Andrea.

Eddy, memories of my son haunt my day and night.

Is his heart still beating? I don't want mine to beat anymore if his isn't.

I sit on my bed, wondering if his eyes are open and if he can see the world, if he's changed now that he's seen how horrible life can be, how evil a man can be.

Sometimes I think about his laugh, it starts slowly like a snicker and then grows louder and louder. It's contagious, I can't imagine how my life is going to be if I can't hear it again.

Nothing, I need nothing, I can live without everything, but not without Eddy. I need to know he's alive and well, then I shall rest in peace and rot in here in silence.

"Guard," I call them when I see one pace the corridor, but they don't stop or speak to me.

"My son, how is my son?" I ask them but hear nothing but threats, reprimands, punishments.

They are not allowed to talk to me, they don't care about my requests. I am a nobody.

Only one of them tells me they don't have any news of my son. He whispers the words to me and leaves without waiting for me to say something back.

Nothing I want to say really, nothing.

I'm paying for all my sins, damnation is going to be the end of me.

One morning I hear the door open and for once no orders are barked at me. Instead I sit up and watch the guard enter without the usual intimidatory look in his eyes. There's something else there.

"Sebastian Esposito, you are free to go," he almost hesitates, like the words cost him or something.

I blink at him, not sure what to say. Am I dreaming? Am I asleep?

I stand up and follow him out the door, into a locker room. All my things are given back to me- my wedding ring, my leather jacket, my shoes. Things. I don't want things. I ask again.

"My son, how's my son?" the guard takes a good look at me before answering.

"We have no news about your son, officer Esposito."

Officer Esposito, nobody's called me that since my last meeting with Salvatore, my sergeant. Then I became The Killer, I've been Sebastian Esposito the criminal ever since.

"We've been made aware of your real identity. You are now free to go, officer."

Officer, I haven't been one in a long time. I've taken lives, I've forgotten all about justice. I moved mountains to find my family, ready to make myself justice. I'm not an officer, not anymore.

The guard informs me a policeman is waiting for me outside, ready to escort me to Police Headquarters. A representative of the armed forces will be there with his deepest, most heartfelt apologies, ready to discharge me of my mission. No more undercover, no more missions. My covers have been blown.

Like a give a fuck.

Words, words. He tells me all this as if it should matter to me, as if I'd care.

I want to know about my son. Nothing else. I don't want to hear apologies for arresting me, keeping me in prison, no visits, no news from the outside but a lawyer, who doubted my truth, my own words.

Weeks in that dump, with criminals, real ones. Weeks of threats, of fighting back to stay up. Now they want me to accept their apologies. I have no time for this, no more time for them. I need to know about my family.

They tell me to change and wear my clothes, to take my belongings, that I'm free to go. I don't hang around to hear things twice, I'm out of there in a second.

As I wait in the small courtyard for the guard to open the main gate, I close my eyes and breathe the fresh morning air.

What time is it? Nine, ten? What day is it?

The day I start over, the day I set out on a search again, no idea what I'll find outside, what happened to my loved ones.

Again.

The gates open and I squint, the sun rays aimed straight at me, I need to shield my eyes with one hand.

Hope is the only thing I carry with me, I've got nothing else, my hands are empty, but my chest is heavy from all the worry.

It's so bright, I can't see it at the beginning. Or maybe I do, I just don't know what I'm looking at, it's too white, too shiny. Then my eyes adjust, and I see her.

A woman with light, blonde hair, she wears it down, it brushes her shoulders, over a white blazer.

She's looking straight at me, her head high, she keeps her face solemn until the gate opens completely, and I step out. Then she recognizes me, she sees me, really sees me and her face breaks.

Andrea, I cross the threshold and I stop walking.

She's there and she's not alone. She's holding someone's hand, I squint a little. A child, a child with bandages all over his arm and shoulder.

Eddy.

My eyes never leave hers, as she covers her mouth and runs to me, gently pulling Eddy along.

Eddy is alive, I finally breathe, my shoulders slump, I feel like collapsing to the ground.

But I stand there, I stand straight for them, for us. I can't move, I'm too busy admiring them, they're so beautiful, *la mia famiglia.*

I watch them amazed as they find their way back to me and I think about when we were on the island. That's what it feels like. Like I've just come back from a night out at sea and they are there waiting for me down at the docks.

It feels as though I've been through a rough storm all night and I'm going back home to them. Suddenly the worry, the hard work, the storm itself doesn't matter anymore. I'm home and they are there. They are well and we are together again.

"Sebastian," his little voice calls out for me and I can't take it any longer. I can't hold back, I don't want to.

"Oh Dio, grazie," *Oh God, thank you,* I mumble the words as I fall down on my knees, holding my head, tears rolling down my eyes.

His little arm, the one that's not broken, wraps around my neck and I drink in the sight of him.

Solemn blue eyes, beautiful cheeky smile, perfect little man. The best thing I've ever done.

"I've missed you so much," I can hardly speak, I choke out the words. "You have no idea, how long it took me to find you."

"But you found me," he says, smiling wide.

I did, I really did.

Andrea walks up to us then and I see her smile, a real one, spread across her face.

She drops to the floor with me and snuggles in my arms with Eddy.

I hold them tight, my family. We are a family again.

He's alive, my son is alive. I keep looking at him, I just can't believe he's here with me. With us. I never thought I'd see my kid alive again.

"They wouldn't let me in to see you," Andrea's raspy voice scratches my soul, deep down. I hold them a little tighter and then kiss her hard, once, twice on her full red lips.

"It doesn't matter, nothing else matters," I tell her as we lock eyes, my hand runs through her silky hair. "I knew I'd make my way back to you somehow, Pretty Eyes."

She nods, holding back the tears. She doesn't say anything, she's fighting hard not to cry. I don't want her to, we have time to talk, we have all the time in the world now.

I'm not sure how long we stay like that, on the pavement, out in the street in front of the prison of San Vittore, and I honestly don't care. We've been apart for so long, we've been to hell and we've been lucky enough to find our way back. Some don't, some never do.

When the darkness comes looking for you, it swallows you up, like a boot on the head, it smashes you down to the ground until you give up and let yourself go, until you let the darkness take you.

We are out in the light, out in the daylight and we are us. Free.

Andrea tells me everything that's happened, one deep breath at a time. She's told the police the whole story, she's told them about me, about what happened with Alejandro.

Most of all she tells me about Eddy, how the bullet missed his heart and hit his shoulder. I remember blood everywhere, but I wasn't thinking straight. It was my son's blood there on that floor, I'd lost my nerve.

"Eddy is doing well. We are okay," she nods and I cup her cheek, Eddy is still wrapped around my waist when he looks up to me and smiles.

"I missed you so much, so much," he keeps smiling, I can't help it either.

"I missed you more."

Then I turn to Andrea, she's leaning over my shoulder now, her beautiful blue eyes moving from me to Eddy, then back to me. I'm ready to pick us up, pick up back from where we've left off. We've waisted too much time already, I don't want to miss another moment of my life without them.

"Where to now?" Andrea asks as we head back to their car.

I wish I knew what to say, but I have no idea. I never thought about the after, never thought I'd survive the storm. I just smile and stare ahead, to where we are headed and say:

"Doesn't matter where. We're home already. I'm home with you."

EPILOGUE

ON AN ISLAND SOMEWHERE IN THE MEDITERRANEAN SEA

TWO YEARS LATER

ANDREA

The wind smells like the sea. I keep my eyes on the horizon and wait for Sebastian. He'll be here any minute, I've already spotted the boat approaching the harbour.

Eddy is playing along the docks, chasing little crabs that wonder along the shore and he's the happy child I know. He's himself again despite the storm, despite the wounds. They are healing but I worry about the scars, I wonder how deep they are, how much he remembers.

He has no recollection of what happened in that old factory, none. It's a blessing I know, but I know he will one day.

The past has a way of coming back, of haunting your present. One day I'll have to explain, I'll have to tell him my secrets and answer his questions. I'll be ready to tell him the truth about those scars. Just not today.

Today is all about us, no one else.

I wish I could lie and say everything is back the way it was. Nothing is and nothing ever will. I am not the woman I was years ago, before Alejandro came looking for us, nor is Eddy the child I brought into this world. He still has nightmares, but he's not scared as he once was. I'm teaching him how not to be afraid of the dark, there is no monster waiting, nobody will hurt him. He's gone.

Sebastian has changed too in his own way. He's still the man I married- kind, strong and attentive – but he never lets his guard down. He kept the gun even though nobody is after us, we're not hiding anymore. We are free now, free to be us.

"Don't look back."

Those were Donna Filomena's last words to me before we left Italy. She was still wearing black then, mourning her son, her face hard and contained as always, but I can see right through her now, right into that heart of hers.

The heart of a mother, I could tell she was relieved it was all over in a way, that her son's tormented soul had finally found some peace. That Alejandro wasn't out there ruining his life and the life of others.

Nobody is coming after us.

I'm still learning how to steady my heartbeat, but my panic attacks seem under control or so I like to think. I tell myself they are, under control, every day. Eventually, the crisis wears off and I feel like myself again. I am still standing. In the end I am still here, back where I belong, with Sebastian and Eddy.

We couldn't go back to Folegandros, it wouldn't have been the same.

All the mess we'd left behind, how we'd lied to everyone about who we were. I wish I could go there and explain, how sorry I am for everything, for betraying their trust. Maybe one day we will, right now we need to think about us, about finding our place in the world and try to live a normal life. As normal as we can.

We chose another island in another country, we're not telling anyone where we are but we're not lying about us, not anymore. We are not lying about where we've been. To hell and back.

Alejandro still comes to me sometimes, but I don't let him in. He's a presence at the back of my mind, always ready to hit me and push me down when I'm feeling low, but I'm learning how to quieten him.

Sometimes all it takes is a sound, a particular smell, just the fragment of a memory of what I've been through and all the pain comes back, it washes over me like a flood, ready to drown me in sorrow.

I keep my feet planted on the ground and let the feelings rush over me. I let those emotions take over, let the tears fall, there's no point in holding them back. I break, I cry and feel lost all over again. I'm not the only victim of abuse, I know, and what breaks me more is I won't be the last. But I have so much love in my life, I have Sebastian, my son to keep me from falling into the trap, that loop of depression and self-harm.

I stopped starving myself, even though I'm tempted to when the sadness hits.

I don't give in. I force a smile on my lips and tell that demon to go fuck himself, I'm not the woman I was, I'm so much more.

The boat is coming, I can see the fishermen searching the coast. The man of my life is coming home to me.

I smile and ignore the scars. They still ache at times, but I give them little importance.

I've learned that love is the only thing worth living for, the rest is noise, just noise.

Those scars tell me where I've been, what I've gone through and, no matter how deep the wounds, they didn't kill me. I'm still alive.

They are part of me, just as much as the pain, but I know this; it goes away, the ache, the desperation. It really does. I just wait for it all to stop and then pick myself up, clean up my mess and smile again.

There are too many reasons to smile, so many chances to be happy and not enough time to live. I survived, that alone comforts me. That suffering, I call it the past and I don't want it to be my future.

I don't think of the man that caused me pain, I don't think of the man that felt pleasure in cutting those wounds. My attention, my energies are all for the man that's helped me heal. I cured his, he cured mine and they don't hurt one bit when we are together.

I wave and smile at Sebastian, he's tying the ropes with Severino.

We've taken him and his mom with us, away from that hell of a place, The Towers. Sebastian said it was time for him to pay back, it was his turn to save a child from that sick, twisted fate. Just like he'd been saved many years before and I love him even more for that, I love the big heart that hides under his thick skin.

Sebastian is still working on the ropes but he's looking at me, I can feel those dark cheeky eyes on me.

He winks and mouths: "Ciao Bellissima" *Hey Beautiful*, and I smile again, I'm radiant.

I feel a couple of kicks then, my bump moves on one side. The baby is getting bigger, not long to wait now before we meet our little girl.

We are going to name her Luce, Light in Italian. She's our little miracle, another life lesson for us.

Our sun after the storm.

I watch Eddy run to his dad and jump into his arms. They talk all the way to where I'm standing, Sebastian promising to take him somewhere later.

Tell me, how can I not pick myself up? How can I not smile when I have so much to be thankful for, so much to look forward to?

"You are back," I whisper before he gently kisses my lips.

Salty, warm and smooth, Sebastian's strong tattooed arms wrap around me. Around us.

"You know I always come back, Pretty Eyes," he places a hand over the bump and the butterflies go wild, my cheeks flush.

This man, my Rock. We are stronger than before, we are a force of nature. I can't help but smile, how can I not?

Then Sebastian searches my eyes before leaning closer to whisper in my ear:

"No matter how big the storm, I always find my way home. I always find my way to you."

THE END

SCARS SOUNDTRACK

1) Enter Sandman- Metallica

2) Kill for me- Marylin Manson

3) My way- Limp Bizkit

4) Hysteria- Muse

5) Knights of Cydonia- Muse

6) Running up that hill- Placebo

7) No one knows- Queens of the Stone Age

8) Sunburn- Muse

9) Firestarter - Prodigy

10) Riders in the storm – The Doors

11) Sad Eyes- Bruce Springsteen

12) Like a Stone- Audioslave

13) Wishlist- Pearl Jam

14) Don't forget me- Red Hot Chili Peppers

15) I've been loving you too long – Otis Redding

16) Paranoid- Radiohead

17) Where is my mind- Pixies

18) Wish you were here- Pink Floyd

19) Comfortably Numb- Pink Floyd

20) Butterflies and Hurricanes- Muse

21) Rat in a cage- Smashing pumpkins

22) System of a Down – Chop Suey

23) Over and over- Jack White

24) The end- Kings of Leon

ACKNOWLEDGEMENTS

This is the hardest part to write. I'm scared I'll leave someone out.

Where do I start?

Big huge massive thank you to Gem Louise Evans for telling me to stop doubting- I know, I never listen. In the end I always doubt, I still do but knowing that you don't somehow makes it all better. Thank you, my wonderful friend.

Another huge, huge thank you to my bestie and PA Carolann Evans. You are my right hand, my left one too, always one step ahead of me. Brilliant and so supportive. How do you put up with me? My singing and mood swings? How? Love you, Pazzerella.

Thank you to my friend Stina Andersen, you always make me laugh or smile even when I don't feel like it. Thank you for beta reading Scars and telling me to breathe. I forget that sometimes :P tanti tanti baci.

Monja and Andrea, I don't know how to thank you for taking the time to run through the manuscript and help me with the edits. You are amazing and I can't say grazie enough.

Thank you to my friends Lori, Michele, Samantha, Sabrina, Vera, Louise- you ladies rock!!!! Can't wait to meet you in person.

Denise, grazie for everything that you do and for our little group chats and giggles. I'm so grateful to have you in my life.

Thank you to my fellow authors and friends Holly Webb, Leaonna Luxx, Kristina Beck, Toya Richardson, Claire Marta, Amali Rose, Whitney Cannavina, Kiera Jayne, T.k. Leigh,

Heather Lyn, Kelly Lowe, MEror, Lizzie James, Lily Mahoney for being wonderful and supportive. I got your backs, belle.

To Le Mie Belle Signore, my street team Denise, Carol, Susan, Shelly, Sharon, Lisa. I appreciate every single thing that you do. I'm forever grateful.

Thank you to all the lovely ladies in my readers group La Dolce Vita with Laura Rossi: Tre, Beverly, Elizabeth, Melissa, Lesley, Angela, Debbie, Bonnie, Erica, Ellen, Mary, Lisa Sabrina, Chasidy, Christine, Diane. From the bottom of my heart, dal profondo del mio cuore, thank you.

And of course Grazie Mille to all the Bloggers, for the constant love and support. Book Haven Book Blog, It's all about the happily ever after, I am a Book Hoarder, TDC reviews, The Redheads Reading Lounge, The Three Bookateers, Escape Reality book blog, Hopelessly Addicted to Romance, SJ Book Blog, The Laundry Librarian, A Bibliophile World to Share, In Between the Pages Book Blog, Bursting Bookshelf, 3 Degrees of Fiction Book Blog, Six Feet Under book Blog, Jenz Book Jewels, Jewel Book Lover and so many more. Please don't be offended if you don't see your blog here, I really appreciate every single one of you.

Last but not least, thank you to my wonderful family for all the love and support; Luca, Carlo, mamma, papà, Alessandro and Veronica. You are my world.

You can find me here:

Author Page https://www.facebook.com/laurarossiauthor

Author Group https://www.facebook.com/groups/1652427688131420/

Instagram https://www.instagram.com/laurarossiauthor

Amazon https://www.amazon.com/…/B01M7O…/ref=dp_byline_cont_ebooks_1

Goodreads https://www.goodreads.com/author/show/2381552.Laura_Rossi

Website https://laurarossiauthor.wordpress.com/

Ciao Belli !!! ☐ Until next time <3

Printed in Great Britain
by Amazon